A LAZARUS RISING STORY

LIE CLOSE
TO ME

New York Times and USA Today Bestselling Author

CYNTHIA EDEN

Published by Hocus Pocus Publishing, Inc.

Proof-reading by: J. R. T. Editing

PROLOGUE

"Termination."

The word drifted to Luna, a low whisper that she knew the doctor hadn't expected her to hear. But then, he'd never understood just how strong her senses truly were.

"The test subject isn't like the others. Her experiment was a failure. If we hope for the others to continue as planned, then the only option is her termination."

Luna wrapped her arms around her stomach. Slid down the wall. Curled her body near the floor. They were talking about her. She knew it. They were going to terminate her. *They're going to kill me.*

And this time, she wouldn't be coming back from death. There would be no waking up, as she'd done before. There would just be the end.

Would heaven be waiting for her? Or would it be hell? Funny, she'd actually thought that she was already in hell.

Her breath slid in and out of her lungs. And the fear just grew worse.

"What's wrong?" The voice wasn't out loud. The warm, rough, masculine voice was only in her head. Not because she was crazy. She wasn't. Well, at least Luna wasn't completely crazy. She was part of a government experiment. An experiment that should have created stronger, better soldiers. Super soldiers. An experiment that had brought the dead back to life — and given the test subjects enhanced senses, greater strength...and psychic bonuses.

Project Lazarus. The test subjects rose from the dead.

But she wouldn't rise again. Not after her termination.

"Talk to me." Again, his voice rolled through her mind.

He was another test subject, and they'd discovered — early on — that they could communicate with each other telepathically. Their link had just snapped into place. She'd woken on an exam table, her body completely nude, terror clawing at her, and he'd been there from the first instant. Telling her to breathe. Telling her that everything was going to be okay.

But nothing was going to be okay ever again.

"You're afraid."

He'd always been so good at reading her emotions. Emotions were supposed to be dangerous for their kind. Rage and fear were felt too powerfully by the test subjects. Most of the other subjects were good at controlling their emotions.

She…wasn't.

Was that why she was being terminated?

"Luna…"

She swallowed as she sat huddled on the floor. She sent out a fast, sad psychic message to him. *"Good-bye."*

"Good-bye? Where the hell are you going? Are they sending you out on a mission?" Now anger hummed in his words. Odd. He never let emotion slip through. She often thought he was just like ice. She was fire, always raging, always getting out of line, but he'd pull her back. He'd keep her in check.

"I'm the team leader. No one who belongs to me goes out alone."

She didn't belong to him, though. She didn't fit in with the others. Something had gone wrong with her experiment. Maybe the preservation process hadn't been handled properly. Maybe she hadn't received enough of the Lazarus serum. Whatever had happened… *"They're going to terminate me."*

Silence. Cold. *Ice.*

Luna swallowed. Luna — that was her name. She knew because they'd told her. They — the doctors in the white lab coats. She'd actually awoken with no memories at all. They'd said she volunteered to be part of Project Lazarus. That she'd once been an Air Force pilot. That—

"No." His voice seemed to slam through her whole body. "You aren't being terminated. I won't fucking let them do that to you."

For once, he wasn't controlled. She could feel his fury. And it wasn't cold.

"It won't happen." Again, his rage blasted at her.

But she could hear footsteps coming toward her. The doctors. She knew what they'd do. They'd tranq her so that she couldn't fight them. The tranq would put her to sleep, and she'd just never wake up again. A painless way to go, she supposed.

They'd killed her before. As part of the experiment. To make sure that she could come back from death like the other test subjects did. And she *did* rise. But...

Each time she died, she lost all of her memories again. The other test subjects didn't remember their lives before they'd come to Lazarus, but they could recall everything *since* they'd been given the Lazarus serum. They remembered their government missions, their life at the Lazarus facility. They could die, and come back, and they'd still remember everything that had happened to them after they'd woken as Lazarus subjects.

Each time she died, she lost it all.

And her emotions raged out of control.

Was it any wonder she'd been put up for termination? But… *"I don't want to die."* Luna knew her pain would transmit in her psychic message.

"I won't let them do this to you!" It was like he was roaring in her head. And for just a moment, she actually had a fast impression of him in his room. She could do that, sometimes, *see* through his eyes. Usually when she was stressed and scared as all hell. He was slamming his powerful fists into his door. Knocking in the metal that should have been even stronger than he was. Only…She didn't think anything was stronger than Maddox.

My Maddox.

If only. Another life.

Blood spilled from his fists and that door flew inward. She had the fast impression of guards, running toward him. Shock was on their faces. And their hands — they had tranq guns in their hands. As far as she knew, they'd never used those tranqs on Maddox before. He was the leader. He was ice. He was —

The guards fired. He roared and took two of them down. They just seemed to fall before him.

More shots were fired, and suddenly, the world that she saw through Maddox's eyes went dark.

And she could only see her own room. Her own cell. So small. She was still on the floor. Still had her arms locked around her knees. Maddox had been fighting to reach her. He'd been fighting *for* her.

"I don't want to die," Luna whispered.

Her door opened. She expected to see guards. Instead, it was two doctors. Doctors in their lab coats with their fake smiles. A woman with red hair. A man with brown hair.

The woman inclined her head toward Luna. "We need you to come with us."

Maddox had fought.

So would she.

Luna rose to her feet. Her hands fisted at her sides. "I don't want to hurt you."

The fake smiles froze.

Luna squared her shoulders. "But you aren't going to terminate me."

The redheaded doctor shouted for the guards. Too late. Luna was fast. So fast. Faster than she'd ever shown them. She rushed forward and shoved the woman and the male out of her way. They flew back, collided with the walls, and then Luna was in the corridor. She could hear the footsteps of guards rushing toward her, but she didn't slow down. She just pushed herself faster, harder. Her bare feet hit against the tiled floor. She hurried forward, wanting to get to the stairs. If she could get to the upper level of the facility, she could break through a window or door and get outside. Once outside, she could run. She'd never stop running.

Something hit her in the shoulder. A fast burn. A tranq. She stumbled a little, but managed to grab the stair railing and haul herself up. *Up, up, up…*

A blond guard was at the top of the stairs. He had his gun aimed right at her. He shouted, "Stand down!"

Luna could have sworn there was sympathy in his eyes. Maybe he wouldn't fire at her.

But then she heard the thud of footsteps coming close—more guards, piling up behind him. And they didn't have sympathy in their eyes.

Only grim determination.

She stilled on the stairs, half-way up. "I don't want to die," Luna said again.

"It's just a tranq," the sympathetic guard said. "Just a tranq."

He didn't understand.

Luna gathered her strength. Then, with a guttural cry, she launched herself forward. She took out one guard, two, a third—

The third guard fired at her.

Another hard burn pierced her body. But this time, her legs went numb. She fell, tumbling back, unable to control her movements. She hit the stairs, slamming into them again and again as she tumbled down. Her arm broke. The snap filled her ears. Her ribs fractured, she could feel the pain cutting through her, and then her head — her neck —

Darkness.

***

Maddox Kane stood in the middle of the cell, his shoulders tense, his hands fisted, and his gaze locked straight ahead. He was chained up, they'd *never* chained him before, and he wondered how much effort it would take to snap through the chains.

Footsteps were coming toward him. Soft, hesitant. Scared.

He waited.

The door swung open. A doctor was there, a guy in a white lab coat. Sweating. His Adam's apple bobbing. The fellow opened his mouth to talk —

"Luna," Maddox growled her name. He'd tried to reach her as soon as he woke up. Tried to connect with her, but he'd only gotten darkness. Darkness, when normally, Luna shone with light.

The doctor backed up a step. His brown eyes darted down to the chains that held Maddox in place. "I apologize for the restraints. Until we can determine what caused you to attack —"

"Luna."

More sweat. And the guy's heartbeat was racing so fast that Maddox was surprised it didn't burst out of his chest.

The doctor's hand rose. He pulled at his collar, as if it were choking him. "We…we have a problem."

They sure as hell did. If Luna had been hurt…if she'd been terminated…

Maddox lunged forward. The chains snapped. He locked his hand around the doctor's throat. "What problem?"

The guy's eyes were about to bulge out of his head. "Sh-she…"

"*Stand down, Kane.*" A hard voice blasted from the intercom. He knew that voice. The voice of the man who liked to pull the strings at the facility. Dr. Henry Danwith. "Stand down, and wait for orders."

He wasn't in the mood to stand down.

"You have a mission waiting," Henry announced.

How long had he been unconscious? He'd assumed it had only been a matter of minutes, but now, he began to wonder.

"A retrieval mission," Henry continued. "We've lost a valuable asset, and your job is to hunt her down."

Her?

"She has a head start on you. But I have faith in your hunting abilities. No one can escape from you."

Maddox let go of the useless doctor. Whirled to stare at the video camera that was positioned in the top right corner of the room. "Who is my prey?"

But in his gut, Maddox knew, he *knew*…

"Luna Ashton escaped the facility. You have to bring her back."

CHAPTER ONE

She…hurt.

The pain came to her first, dragging her from the darkness of sleep. Every single inch of her body ached. A sharp cry slid from her mouth, and the sound jarred her into full wakefulness.

Her eyes opened. She stared up, catching the bright path of sunlight that came through—a window?

Her head turned. A broken window waited a few feet away. A broken window…and…

Where am I?

Her hands flew around the floor—the dirty, dust-covered floor. It felt grimy beneath her as she shoved herself upright. She gazed down at her body and realized she was wearing a green hospital gown. And—

Her hand lifted. She even had one of those white bracelets around her wrist. The kind the staff always gave to patients when they entered a hospital.

Her hand dropped. She stared around once more. *This* wasn't a hospital. Or, at least, it wasn't one that had been in operation any time recently. There was no furniture in the room. No bed. Nothing. A door waited a few feet away, but it was closed.

There were no sounds that reached her. Nothing at all.

Her heart beat faster.

How did I get here?

She rose. Her knees felt a little weak, but they held her up. The paper gown brushed over her legs. She felt a draft near her ass, and, automatically, her hand slid behind her as she tried to pull the gown closed.

Her bare feet shuffled forward. She reached for the door. Opened it and found herself staring at a hospital corridor. Or, at least, that was what it looked like. A long hallway, one that had dozens of doors branching off from it. There was what appeared to be a nurse's station up ahead, only that station was empty.

No computers. No office supplies.

No nurses.

The whole place was eerily silent, and it smelled old. Stale. As if it had been shut down for a very long time.

What in the hell was happening?

"Hello?" Her voice seemed to echo back to her. "Is anyone else here? I-I need help."

Nothing. She hurried forward, shoving open the doors and finding room after room to be empty.

Deserted.

Her breath heaved out of her as she moved faster and faster. This whole set-up was wrong. How had she gotten to this place? Why was she in a hospital gown? And—

She stilled.

Who in the hell am I?

The last question had her heart constricting in her chest. Her gaze flew frantically around. She knew she was in some kind of abandoned hospital. She could recognize what a hospital *was.* Just as she knew what doors were and that she was wearing a hospital gown. She could see things and recognize them, but…

She had no idea who she was.

Her gaze jerked down, going to her right wrist. Going to the plastic, white band that circled her wrist. She held it up to her eyes, staring at the small letters that had been neatly typed there.

Luna Ashton.

If anything, the constriction in her chest got worse. There was nothing else written on the bracelet, just that name. No date of birth, no blood type, nothing else.

What was happening? It felt as if she were trapped in some kind of nightmare. She pinched herself, hard, wanting to wake up, right the hell now.

A faint sound had her tensing. The soft pad of a shoe?

The sound had come from behind her, back down that long corridor that she'd desperately searched. She whipped around, her hand flying to her chest, and a scream getting stuck in her throat because — suddenly — she wasn't alone any longer.

He was there.

A man with black hair, cut short and close. A guy with broad shoulders and a built, powerful physique that stretched the battered coat and black t-shirt he wore. Jeans covered his long legs and black boots were on his feet. He stared at her, watching her with an intense, almost *burning* green gaze. A faint line of stubble covered his hard jaw, and his hands were clenched at his sides.

Uh, oh. Every instinct she had screamed a wild warning. This guy wasn't the cavalry. He was trouble. Danger with a big, giant D.

"Luna…" His voice was deep, growling.

She backed up a step. He knew her. Well, he knew the name on her bracelet. Goosebumps rose on her arms.

He advanced.

"Stop!" The yell emerged from her throat, sounding raw and desperate. She felt raw and desperate, so the sound made sense.

And he...stopped. Froze at her command.

"Stay away from me." Again, desperation sharpened her words, making them high and shrill.

He shook his dark head. "Not possible."

What? He'd better *make* it possible.

"I came here for you," he continued in the deep voice that made her goosebumps worse. "Followed your trail." His gaze swept over her. "Even when you cut out the tracker."

She didn't know what he was talking about.

"Enough games, Luna. You know you can count on me." He lifted his hand toward her.

But she—*Luna, I'm Luna*—shook her head. "I don't know you at all. Why would I ever count on you?"

He blinked. His bright green gaze immediately became shuttered.

And a new, terrible thought occurred to her. "Did you...do this to me?"

He just stared at her.

He *must* have done this. No one else was there. Just the two of them. The guy was in the creepy hospital with her. So he had to be responsible for her insane situation. "Did you roofie me or something?"

I know what a roofie is, but I don't know who I am! Maybe that was a side effect of whatever drug she'd been given? Maybe everything would come back to her the longer she stayed conscious?

"I didn't roofie you." His voice…there was something about his voice that she…*liked.* And how weird was that? The guy was scary, dangerous, and she should not find anything about him sexy. She was in the middle of a breakdown, and she shouldn't be noticing that his voice was way too deep and rumbling.

"Why don't I know my name?" She took another step back.

His shoulders tensed. His heart was beating so fast and hard and—

Luna gasped. "How can I hear your heart beating?" That wasn't normal. She was sure it wasn't normal.

"You have enhanced senses. You can hear far better than an average human. Just like you see better." He exhaled on a long sigh and then—

Then he charged at her. Only he moved way, way too fast. Luna let out a quick scream, and she turned to run. But it was too late. She'd reacted too slowly. He grabbed her, his hard, too-big hands locking around her body, and they both crashed to the floor.

Except he turned his body, moving so that he cushioned her, and he took the brunt of the impact when they hit the tile.

"You're faster, too," he grunted, "normally. You're not moving at top speed right now." His eyes narrowed. "Why the hell not?"

Wait, he was asking *her?* And had he really just flown down that long corridor in barely a second's time? Maybe two seconds, or three, max, but—

"How did you get here, Luna?" His hands were around her waist, trapping her there. Her legs were between his, and the hospital gown had definitely ridden up. She was pretty sure her ass was totally exposed.

She felt heat blast her cheeks. "Let me go."

If anything, his hold tightened. "Why would I do that? I spent the last week tracking you."

He had?

Her hands were pressed to his chest. The guy was *huge* and crazy fast, and he *knew* her. He'd been tracking her.

A shiver slid over her body.

"You're cold. Fuck."

In a blink, he had her on her feet once more. She started to run—seemed like a good plan—but he snagged her wrist. His fingers curled all the way around it, and Luna felt manacled to him as he bit off a single word, "*Don't.*"

She stared up at him. She had to tip back her head to meet his gaze. He was way too big, and he scared the ever-loving hell out of her.

Then he shrugged out of his battered coat. He let her wrist go long enough for him to shove her arms into the coat's sleeves. The coat absolutely swallowed her, but it was warm. She'd just realized that she was ice cold. Now the warmth from his coat—his warmth—was pressing against her. The coat smelled of him. A rich, masculine scent that she found oddly appealing.

She inhaled, savoring that scent a little, and then Luna looked up. His face had gone rock hard, and he stared at her with a fixed intensity.

"How did you get here, Luna? Who helped you get out of the Lazarus facility?"

Her lips parted, but she didn't know what to say.

His gaze swept down her body. A furrow appeared between his brows. "No shoes. And is that just a paper gown? I mean, shit, we don't react to the cold the way most people do, but it's fifteen degrees outside. And this place has been shut down for years. The windows have more holes than glass in them. You've got to be shivering that sweet ass off."

She was shivering, but it was mostly from fear. "You...know me."

"Hell, yes, I know you."

"I'm...Luna." The more she said her name, the more — oddly — right it felt.

His stare hardened even more. "You don't remember."

No, she didn't, so Luna shook her head.

He swore. Long and viciously.

She started to back up —

He snagged her wrist once more. "Oh, hell, no. You won't be running from me again."

Yes, oh, hell, yes, she would. Luna knew she just had to wait for the right moment. This wasn't that moment. She could tell.

"You died." If anything, his face became even harder. Even more intense. "Sonofabitch, *you died.*"

Okay, now, she was worrying that he might be straight up crazy. She'd been willing to buy the super senses thing he'd talked about before — um, she *could* hear his heart beating when she focused and that was weird — but she was obviously not dead.

He yanked her closer to him. Glared down at her. "You're not like the others. Everything goes away when you die, dammit. You forget *me.*"

Her hand lifted. Her fingers were shaking. Those shaking fingers slid over the dark stubble on his jaw, moving up his cheek, trailing over his skin.

His body hardened against her. "Luna, what are you doing?'

He felt real. Not like some figment of her imagination. Not part of a nightmare, but—

She pinched him.

He just blinked at her. Didn't cry out in pain. Didn't change his expression. "Luna?"

"You're real."

He nodded.

"Who…are you?"

"Maddox."

The name didn't mean anything to her. He stared at her, waiting, as if she was supposed to have some sort of reaction to his name. She didn't.

He growled. The sound rumbled from deep in his chest. "Maddox Kane. I'm the leader of our team."

She was still touching his cheek. Still wearing his coat. Still trying to figure out how to get away from him.

His nostrils flared. He had a nice nose. Long, straight.

"Blood," he bit out. "*Your* blood."

She wasn't bleeding. She'd notice if she were, right?

He whirled and bounded down the hall, moving scarily fast again and dragging her with him. Her feet stumbled at first, but then, amazingly, she was actually able to keep up with him. They moved so fast that the rooms passed in a blur. He rushed through an open doorway that led into a stairwell, and then they were barreling down those stairs. It was dark all around them, but she found she could see perfectly. His hold on her wrist was unbreakable as they burst out of the stairwell and onto another floor of the abandoned hospital.

And as they entered that new floor, a coppery scent hit her. Blood.

She stopped.

So did he.

Luna swiped her tongue over her lower lip. "You smelled the blood…upstairs?"

His gaze raked her. "My sense of smell has always been stronger than yours."

How about stronger than even Superman's must be? Her eyes squeezed shut. "I know Superman. I mean, I know who he is." The words tumbled from her. "But I don't know who I am. How I got to be in this place, wearing a paper gown and a hospital bracelet."

His fingers slid under her chin. Tipped her head back.

She didn't open her eyes. If anything, she squeezed them shut tighter.

"It's only the personal memories that you lose." His voice was soft. Almost tender. "You keep all of your procedural memories—the skills, the memories of how to do things like riding a bike, tying shoes, or firing a gun."

Now her eyes popped open. "Do I fire a lot of guns?"

He nodded. "You keep your instincts. Our primal instincts are the strongest motivators for Lazarus subjects."

It sounded like he was talking in some kind of code to her.

"Our lives before Lazarus are gone. That's a side effect of the serum we're given. We keep facts — general fucking trivia — but we lose who we were." His jaw hardened. "Small price to pay for cheating death, right?"

She didn't understand him. Or anything that the guy was saying to her. What in the world was Lazarus?

But he'd already turned away. He was pulling her with him, toward the scent of blood. There were two swinging doors up ahead, and an old sign above them read OPERATING ROOM. He shoved open the doors to the OR.

When she went inside, fear slid through her, coiling like a snake in her gut. There was an exam table in the middle of the room, and it…

He let her go.

She stared at the exam table, transfixed. Broken straps hung from the table. She counted six straps. They appeared to have been torn in half. Blood soaked the table. Blood dripped on the floor. It smeared across the old tile, heading toward the door.

But there had been no blood in the hallway. Or on the stairs. All of the blood was in this one room.

"It's your fucking blood." Anger hardened Maddox's words.

Luna flinched. "H-how can you tell?" She didn't have any cuts on her body. She didn't feel hurt anywhere.

"The smell." He advanced toward the table.

Um, okay.

Maddox stopped near an instrument tray, one that had been upended and tossed onto the floor. A bloody scalpel was on the tile, along with tweezers, a long syringe, and a few items that Luna really didn't want to know *what* they were.

Her legs were rooted to the spot. Had she really been strapped to that table? "I'm not bleeding."

"No." He'd crouched near the discarded tray. Maddox picked up the syringe, sniffed it. "Tranq." A low snarl. "At least they had you knocked out so you didn't feel the pain." He dropped the syringe. "Doesn't make me want to fucking destroy them any less." Maddox surged back to his feet.

She hurried toward him. "I'm not bleeding," Luna said again. "There is no blood on me. I couldn't have been in this room." *I don't want to be in this room any longer. I need to get out. I'm having a hard time breathing.* "You're wrong."

He stared at her. "You heal faster than any Lazarus subject I've ever seen. One of your gifts. Whoever had you in this room—they hurt you. But you healed. You got away from them. You ran—" He pointed to the trail of blood on the floor. "You got upstairs. You were trying to get out, but—"

"There's no blood on me," Luna repeated.

"Because someone must have cleaned you up. Put you in that gown."

And what? Just left her, unconscious? "I woke up in one of the rooms upstairs." His coat was the only thing keeping her warm. She felt absolutely ice cold. "And *you* are the only person in this building with me."

So if she'd been hurt, it didn't take a genius to put together the puzzle pieces in order to figure out who'd been the one making her life a living hell.

His shoulders straightened. "Luna, no."

She backed up a step. "You scare me."

A furrow appeared between his dark brows.

"I don't know who I am. How I got here. But I took one look at you, and I was afraid. You know what that tells me? Some part of me recognizes you. Some part of me knows you're a threat to me."

His lips thinned. "You don't understand."

No, she didn't. And that was part of the problem.

"I'm taking you back, Luna," Maddox told her. "You need to be examined. We have to find out what happened here."

Her heart was racing again. She needed some kind of weapon to fight him, but there was nothing in the room to help her because she was *not* picking up a bloody scalpel. And being in that place was making her chest feel too tight. "Where," she managed, "is 'back' exactly?"

He stalked toward her. "I'm not picking up any other scents here. Maybe your blood is just too strong, and it's messing up my head."

That made no sense to her.

He kept advancing. "But we're getting out of here. I'll come back with the rest of the team, and we'll tear this place apart."

He still hadn't told her where 'back' was. But since she was only too happy to get out of that particular room, Luna didn't argue as they hurried up the stairs. He led the way, keeping a hand curled around her wrist. She wished like hell that she could find a weapon, but there was nothing in the stairwell or the hallway. And the guy was *big*.

He took her out via a broken window, making sure that she didn't cut her skin on the jagged glass. When she eased away from the shadows of the building, the sunlight was almost blinding. Too bright. Bright, but it was still cold out there. A small puff of fog formed near her mouth.

Luna glanced back at the building. Dead vines slid up the sides of the hospital. It looked like an old, forgotten grave. Sagging into the ground, falling back into the woods. And the woods were everywhere—thick trees surrounded the place. She didn't see any other nearby buildings. Maddox led her down an overgrown path, and she found herself in the remains of a broken parking lot. A gleaming motorcycle—a big, beast of a bike—waited there.

She shivered.

He pulled her closer. "Should have brought the SUV," he muttered. "But I thought this place was another dead end so I scouted out with the bike."

His body felt like a furnace to her.

"Luna."

She looked up at him. His eyes were bright again. So focused on her. And once more, she thought... *You scare me.*

But there was something else happening, too. An awareness was sliding beneath her skin. When he looked at her that way, when he held her so close...

Desire.

A desire as dangerous as the fear she felt for him.

"First order of business is getting the hell out of here." He lifted her up, moving as if she weighed nothing, and he put her on the motorcycle's seat. Her bare legs sprawled on either side of the beast, and another shiver slid over her because the paper gown had seriously hiked up again.

His gaze locked on her legs. Lingered.

Uh, oh.

His face hardened. Sharpened. He licked his lips.

Then his gaze slid to her face.

He wants me.

Could she use that? Maybe. It was the only weapon she had. So…Luna lifted her hand. Put her palm on his chest, right over his heart. It was racing so fast and hard beneath her touch. And as her hand lingered against him, the beat became even faster. "Are we lovers?" Luna asked.

His pupils widened, the darkness swallowing the green of his gaze.

Before he could answer, she pushed, voice husky, "Do you want to be my lover?"

He moved even closer to her. She was still straddling the bike, and he was pretty much dominating her with his massive size.

She caught his hand, brought it to her thigh. His hold immediately tightened.

"*Luna.*"

"Will you kiss me?"

His stare was on her mouth. "What in the hell is happening? This isn't you."

It wasn't? She had no clue. But a desperate woman had to use whatever weapons she had. "Maybe I can remember, if you kiss me." She eased out a quick breath. "I know you. I feel it inside."

His hand was burning her thigh.

"Kiss me," she said again because she needed him closer. Just a little closer.

He moved closer. Her hand slid over his chest. Down to his side.

"I couldn't find you." His words were a rough rasp. "*You were gone.*" Then his mouth crashed down on hers. He kissed her with a wild need. A frantic desire that caught her off guard — and one that stirred a matching need inside of her.

Desire erupted, stunning her with its force. Her nipples ached, tightening into peaks, and she leaned toward him, opening her mouth more, wanting his kiss, loving his taste, wanting so much —

Keys. You want the keys.

Her fingers closed around them. She'd slid her hand into the front right pocket of his jeans, and Luna snatched the keys out in a blink. But she was still kissing him when she should have been pulling away. When she should have been figuring out a way to distract him so she could haul ass away on that bike.

How do I want him so much? From one kiss?

She wasn't cold any longer. She was absolutely burning hot.

"No!" He jerked back from her. Stared at her with a possessive lust. Then he spun on his heel. Stalked away. He seemed to want distance between them. "I just found you. I don't know what in the hell is happening, but I won't screw this up!"

She cranked the motorcycle. Revved the engine.

Maddox whirled back to her. "Luna?"

He was only a few feet away. The guy moved *fast*. But she moved fast, too. So did the bike. She shot that baby forward.

"Luna!"

She didn't stop. The wind bit into her face. Her hands clamped around the handle bars like talons, and she drove the motorcycle with a single-minded intensity.

Escape. She had to get away from Maddox Kane.

He terrified her. He was dangerous. He was scary strong.

And he was way too sexy.

She didn't trust him, not for a moment, and there was no way she'd let that man get close to her again.

No way in hell.

***

"Sonofabitch," Maddox Kane muttered as he watched the motorcycle race away.

She'd tricked him. Kissed him, turned him the fuck on, and then fled the instant he'd turned his back. Of course, turning his back had been an amateur move. Especially with a woman like Luna. But he'd had to step away —

Or he would have been lost.

The motorcycle turned, hitting the main road and leaving the abandoned hospital behind. He could have stopped her. He *was* that fast. He could have launched his body at the motorcycle and tackled her.

If he'd done that, though, Luna would have been hurt. He didn't want her hurt. That had never been his goal.

Maddox pulled out his phone. Swiped his finger over the screen and placed his call. "Found her," he announced. "But she's running. Heading for town. If you see her before I get there, *don't* move in, do you understand? Keep a visual on her. Make sure that no one hurts her."

Laughter was his answer. "Shouldn't I be worried she'll hurt the humans?"

He didn't answer. Maddox shoved his phone back into his pocket. He started walking fast, and then…running. He wouldn't get winded, wouldn't get tired. But he *would* get to the small town that waited up ahead. Bitter, Colorado. A place that the ski lovers never bothered to visit. Too quiet. Too far off the beaten path. So far off that the town's only hospital had closed long ago.

Who the hell brought Luna to this place? He'd find out. It was just a matter of time.

Soon, he'd have Luna. And when he did, he'd make sure she never escaped again. Even if he had to damn well handcuff her to his side.

CHAPTER TWO

She stopped at the gas station, mostly because the motorcycle was about to run out of gas. The gas station sat on the edge of a small town, a sleepy little place that had just appeared, seemingly from nowhere. She braked the bike near a pump and then realized...

No money.

Her hands shoved into the coat pockets that Luna still wore. *His* coat. And then she almost sobbed in relief because her fingers came out grasping a wad of cash. She hurried toward the little service store, shoving open the front door. A bell jingled above her head, and an elderly man behind the counter turned toward her with a smile.

The smile froze on his face. "Miss, are you okay?"

She was barefoot, her hair had to be sticking out like she'd just been in a wind tunnel, and she was wearing a hospital gown. Oh, crap. Luna stumbled forward. She dropped the cash on the counter. "Gas." Her voice was too sharp.

"And…clothes?" The last was more of a desperate question.

His brown eyes were wide as he looked at the money, then her. "Got some t-shirts and jogging pants in the back over there. No shoes, though. Sorry."

A shirt and jogging pants would help enormously. She headed toward the items he'd indicated.

The guy cleared his throat. "Miss, do you need help?"

She could use some help, yes. Luna paused. Nibbling on her lower lip, she considered things. "The cops." A person went to the cops for help, right? Luna glanced over her shoulder and caught the man's gaze. "I-I think I need you to contact the cops."

"Yeah." He gave a quick nod. "That might be a good idea."

Without waiting to see if he made the call, Luna scurried toward the t-shirts. She found one that seemed roughly the right size—it had a picture of a mountain range across the front. She snagged the smallest jogging pants she could find and rushed into the bathroom with her prizes. The store manager called out to her, but she didn't stop. She slammed the bathroom door shut and sucked in some desperate, ragged gulps of air.

The bathroom was small, more like a closet than anything else, and a big mirror hung right over the sink. She turned her head, gazing into the mirror, feeling absolutely like she was looking at a stranger.

The woman before her had wild, dark brown hair. Definitely hair that was sticking up in every direction. She tried to smooth it down, but her efforts didn't help much. Her hair was a heavy, tangled mass that tumbled over her shoulders. Shadows lined her eyes—dark eyes. A rich brown color that didn't seem familiar at all to her.

She dropped the stolen coat. Yanked off the hospital gown and tossed it into the garbage can. Her naked reflection loomed back at her in the mirror.

He said it was my blood. All of the blood in that terrible hospital—Maddox had said it was hers.

Outside, she heard the jingle of the gas station's front bell. She ignored the sound as she leaned closer to the mirror. There were no cuts on her body. No bruises. There was no way that had been her blood.

She jerked on the jogging pants, pausing only long enough to rip off the tag on them. Luna put the tag on the edge of the sink. The pants were soft against her skin, and sure, they were too long, but she just rolled them up. Then she pulled on the t-shirt, again just tugging off the tag and putting it on the sink. Because the gas station hadn't been selling a bra, her nipples shoved right against the front of the shirt. She fixed that problem, though, by putting back on *his* coat.

And she could have sworn the thing still held his heat.

Her fingers slid over the sink, grabbing the tags, right before she bounded out of the bathroom. "I have the tags!" Luna called out as she hurried down the aisle. She turned the corner, the cash register coming into view. "You can take them and ring me —"

Luna stopped.

The elderly man at the cash register wasn't alone. She'd heard the jingle of the front bell, but she'd been so intent on dressing that she hadn't stopped to think…

The sound meant a new customer had entered the store. Only she wasn't looking at just any customer.

He's here. Already. He'd found her already.

Maddox Kane stood near the check-out counter. His hands were on his hips. His jaw was locked, and his green eyes gleamed.

Oh, shit. Her toes curled against the floor. "Did you call the cops?" Luna asked the attendant, voice hopeful.

"He *is* the cops," the gas station attendant told her.

What? No, that wasn't possible —

Maddox reached into his back pocket and pulled out his wallet. He flashed it at her. "FBI."

Her temples pounded.

"I'll take care of her," Maddox murmured, nodding to the attendant who watched them with an avid stare. "Sorry for the trouble. She's been off her meds, and her family is mighty worried about her."

Off her —

Luna surged forward, but Maddox moved faster. He grabbed her arm and then he locked something cold and hard around her wrist.

A handcuff. He'd just *handcuffed* her.

The attendant whistled. "Man, you sure are fast."

Maddox's body pressed against Luna's. His gaze didn't leave her face. "You have no idea." Then he locked the other handcuff around his own wrist. "You're not going to get away again, Luna."

She yanked at the cuff, twisting her wrist, fighting the hold with desperate rage.

"It's Lazarus-proof, Luna." Now his voice was low, barely a breath, for her ears alone. "You won't break loose."

Lazarus-proof. Was that supposed to mean something to her?

"Time to go." Now he was being loud again. He nodded to the attendant. "Appreciate the help. Always good to count on a responsible citizen."

This wasn't happening. Her frantic gaze flew to the older man. "Don't let him take me!" she begged. She wasn't above begging. "I don't know what's happening. Just call the local cops. Real cops and—"

"Stop it, Luna. Don't say another word. I don't want to have to hurt him."

It was Maddox's voice. Clear and strong. And…

In her head?

Her knees trembled. She almost fell, but he was there, of course. Maddox led her toward the door, their hands cuffed together. He shoved open the door, and the bell jingled. A happy, ridiculous sound that didn't fit with her current circumstances.

Her gaze flew toward the motorcycle, only it wasn't there. "What—"

"I hid the bike. I'll have it picked up later. We're in the SUV."

A big, black SUV waited to the right. A solidly built guy—wearing all black, with perfectly straight, black hair and coal eyes—stood by the driver's side. His stare was focused on her.

Or rather, on her toes.

"Why doesn't she have on shoes?" The guy wanted to know as Maddox dragged her closer to the SUV. He opened the back door for them.

Maddox went in first, pulling her after him. The handcuff tugged on her wrist. The cuff was right above the hospital bracelet that she still wore. A hospital bracelet…from an abandoned hospital. What was going on?

"At least she's wearing clothes," Maddox tossed back to the new fellow. "When I first saw her, Luna's ass was bare."

Red stained her cheeks. So the hospital gown had gaped. Hardly her fault.

The other guy didn't respond. He slammed the door shut after her, then jumped in the front seat a few moments later. He cranked the vehicle, and a blast of hot air slid out of the vents as the vehicle hurried away from the station.

She shuddered when the air hit her.

Maddox immediately hauled her closer to him. "You always feel the cold worse than the rest of us."

He'd tracked her. Cuffed her. Tears stung her eyes. "You aren't FBI."

"No." He didn't even pretend to lie.

Her head turned toward him. "Why are you doing this to me?"

His eyes widened. "You're crying?'

A tear slipped down her cheek.

"Stop it!" Maddox demanded.

"You shouldn't have cuffed her," came the mumble from the front seat. "It sent her over the edge, don't you see that?"

She wanted the cuffs off. If he took the handcuff off, then she could just jump out of the vehicle while it was moving. Sure, the impact might hurt, but she'd take being hurt to being this guy's prisoner any day.

Maddox's gaze hardened. "If the cuffs come off, she's going to jump out of the car."

Her lips parted. "Did you just read my mind?"

His stare held hers.

"You were in my head when we were in that gas station." Her voice was shaking and husky. "I *heard* you talking to me, even though your lips didn't move."

Maddox didn't speak.

The man in the front seat cleared his throat. "That's just a Lazarus thing, baby."

Had he called her baby?

Maddox growled. "*Don't.* Just shut the hell up for now, Jett."

"I don't want to be here!" Luna yelled as her control seem to shatter. The scenery was passing too fast. They'd left the little town. These two men were taking her somewhere. Where? Why? "You're kidnapping me!" She yanked on the handcuff. Nothing happened. "Let me go!" Her voice grew even louder. Wilder.

"I am not going to hurt you." Maddox's voice stayed low. Soothing? "I swear it."

"I'm supposed to believe you?" Luna shrieked back. "You have a handcuff around my wrist! You just lied to that man back there about being a cop!" She moved as far away from him as she could get—which wasn't very far because he was so freaking big, and they were *handcuffed*. "I think you're the one who put me in that freaky hospital!"

He shook his head. "I didn't. I was *hunting* you."

That didn't sound better. "I don't believe you. I don't *know* you."

"Oh, shit," the one he'd called Jett exclaimed. "Her memory is gone again? Did she die?"

This was madness. She had to get away. She—

Maddox touched her cheek. "I'm sorry."

For cuffing her? For terrifying her? For—

"Go to sleep, Luna."

The hell she would.

His jaw tightened. *"Go to sleep."* And this time, his words were out loud *and* in her head. They seemed to sink through her very bones, and she didn't want to sleep. She wanted to run. She wanted to escape, but...

Her body slumped against the seat.

And she slept.

***

The SUV slammed to a halt. "You just knocked out Luna!"

Maddox cradled Luna in his arms. If he hadn't been holding her, the sudden stop would have sent her flying into the front seat. She hadn't put on a seatbelt.

"You knocked out *our* Luna," Jett groused. "What in the hell, man?" He'd turned around in the seat, and he glared at Maddox. "She's one of us. We don't use our powers against one of our own. You don't turn on the team."

Maddox met Jett's glare. "She doesn't remember us. I found her in that old hospital, wearing a paper gown, absolutely terrified. There was an exam room in the basement. Her blood was everywhere."

Jett's face went hard and mean. "What in the hell?"

"Someone had been working on Luna. One of our tranqs was down there." A very special tranq because it took one hell of a lot to knock out Lazarus subjects.

And that was what they all were. Test subjects. Government experiments. Super fucking soldiers.

He was the team leader. Jett was his right-hand man. And Luna…

Luna is the one who went missing.

"She was about to try jumping out of the car." Even still cuffed to him. She'd been that desperate to escape.

"You were in her head." Again, anger hummed in Jett's voice. "You aren't supposed to go in without permission."

Maddox locked his jaw. "I did what had to be done."

Jett's stare didn't leave his face. "Yeah, you keep telling yourself that shit."

"Get the vehicle moving," Maddox snapped at him. "I could only pick up Luna's scent at the hospital. No one else's. Those bastards who took her could be close by. I don't want an ambush, not until I can get her someplace more secure." Getting her to safety was priority one. Once she was safe, then he could explain things to her.

As he'd explained to her before…over and over. Because this wasn't the first time Luna had woken with no memory.

But it *was* the first time she'd woken without him at her side. They'd been paired together by the Lazarus doctors. He'd been given the job of her anchor once they all realized how different she was.

I wasn't there this time.

Jett resumed driving. But his angry gaze cut to the rear-view mirror. "We need to call this in. Let the lab coats know we've got her."

Maddox eased Luna back against the seat. He fastened the seat belt around her. Her hair had fallen forward, and he tucked a heavy lock behind her ear. "That would be one option."

Silence.

He looked up. Jett was still watching him in the rear-view mirror. "You should keep your eyes on the road," Maddox advised.

"No one else is freaking here." Jett's voice had turned rough. "What other option do we have?"

Maddox tried to figure out how much he could trust Jett.

"It's *me*," Jett snapped at him. "How many times have we saved each other?"

Because the three of them were a team. Maddox, Jett, and Luna. They'd been brought into the Lazarus program together. They'd all woken up in the lab together for the first time. And none of them had known jackshit about what was happening.

"They were going to terminate her." Maddox glanced down at his knuckles. He'd broken them to hell and back when he'd busted out of his room at the facility. He'd been so desperate to get to her. "But then the facility was breached. She vanished. No one knew where the hell she'd gone..." His words trailed away. He'd tried to reach Luna on the mental link they'd shared, but he'd only touched darkness.

For a while there, he'd feared she might be dead.

For a while there, I went fucking insane.

Only one thing had brought him back.

Luna. The doctors — their "handlers" had told him she still lived. That he had to find her. Hunt her.

He'd agreed. Acted like the good soldier he'd once been. He'd nodded. He'd even let them put a tracker under his skin so they could keep tabs on him during the hunt.

He'd cut that tracker out two days before. He'd made sure Jett had done the same. The guy had agreed, not even questioning him.

Jett had questions now. "They were going to kill Luna? I mean, *permanently?* Are you sure?"

"Yes."

"So…if we follow orders and take her back…"

"They want her back so that they can terminate her. When she was loose, when she was somewhere out in the world, she was a threat to them." Them…the federal government. The doctors in their lab coats weren't the bosses of the operation. The bosses were the pricks in suits who came in to observe and to whisper their instructions. Didn't the dumbasses get it? Lazarus subjects could hear whispers from a mile away, if they just focused hard enough.

Maddox focused plenty hard.

"You always follow orders." Jett wasn't looking at him in the mirror any longer. His gaze was focused straight ahead.

Maddox found himself looking at Luna again. "They don't know we have her. Not yet."

"So…what is it that you want me to do?"

A weary sigh escaped Maddox. "Keep driving." Because they were pretty much in the middle of nowhere. "Just get us to the safe house, okay? Then we'll make plans."

Jett drove.

And Maddox found himself sliding closer to Luna. *Take her back so that the docs could kill her?* So that she'd never rise and open those deep, chocolate eyes of hers? Never stare at him as a slow smile curved her lips?

Hell, the fuck, no. He'd destroy everyone in that lab before he'd let them kill her. Dr. Henry Danwith's worst mistake had been sending Maddox after Luna.

Because now that he had her back, Maddox was never going to let her go.

CHAPTER THREE

"Come back to me."

Luna's eyes opened as awareness flooded back to her in a quick rush. She let out a quick gasp when she realized she was in a bed, and she sat up, jerking the covers with her—

"It's okay." Maddox stood at the foot of the bed. His hands were held up in front of him. "You're safe."

The hell she was. "What did you do to me?" Anger seethed in her voice. "Did you *drug* me?"

Maddox winced. "No, not exactly."

She jumped from the bed, but Luna didn't go toward him. She just glared at him. "What, *exactly*, did you do then?" The cuffs were gone. Thank goodness. No handcuff circled her wrist, and the hospital ID tag had been removed, too.

Nothing else was gone, though. She was very relieved to note that she still wore her jogging pants and her t-shirt. Maddox's coat had been tossed over a nearby chair.

"It's part of my power, okay?" He lowered his hands. "All of the Lazarus subjects have psychic, well, bonuses, I guess you could say."

He was making her temples throb again.

"My gift is that I'm a one-man knock out team. If I can get close enough to touch my prey, I can put them under. Very handy technique when you're trying to infiltrate an enemy camp." He gave a little shrug. "If I focus hard enough, I can put people out *without* touching them. But that drains my energy faster, and the crash afterwards is a real bitch."

"Impossible."

"No, it's a bitch. I can barely walk after—"

"You're messing with me. Telling me incredible stories when the truth is that you *kidnapped* me! You cuffed me, you drugged me, and you took me to—to—*where in the hell am I?*" Her frantic gaze flew around what looked like a bedroom. Wooden walls. King size bed. Four-poster. Big windows that looked out at a snow-capped mountain range in the distance. The sun was setting, casting long shadows over the mountains.

"You're in a safe house. Only Jett and I know you're here."

That meant no one was going to come and help her. Fine, she'd help herself. Luna braced her body, preparing to launch at him.

"Don't." Maddox shook his head. "Give me a chance to prove what I'm saying is true before you go for the tackle."

Her breath was coming too fast.

"We've been in this situation before." His lips twisted. "You wake up. You don't know where you are. Who you are. And you think I'm the threat." He shook his head. "I'm not. I'd never be a threat to you."

She wanted to believe him. That was the crazy thing. Inside, a big part of her was desperate to believe him. But..."So says the man who cuffed me."

He looked vaguely uncomfortable. "You stole my motorcycle, hauled ass away, and you were going to get the local cops involved. No way could we afford that kind of exposure. I would have needed to knock them all out and did you really want that on your conscience?"

"On *my* conscience?" Her voice rose a few octaves.

Maddox crossed his arms over his chest. His broad chest. Why was she noticing that?

"Luna."

Now she frowned at him. "Why did you say my name that way?"

His brows shot up. "What way?"

Tenderly. Like it was some kind of caress or something. But she bit back those words.

When she didn't answer, he rolled his shoulders. "Luna." Not as tender. More firm. "You're part of an experimental government program. Project Lazarus. You were once an incredible Air Force pilot, but you volunteered to enroll in Lazarus." He cleared his throat. "We all volunteered."

"How do I know that? How do I know I volunteered? You could just be saying this crap to me. Telling me—"

"There are videos back at the Lazarus facility. Videos showing us all willingly volunteering to be test subjects." He paused. "The government wanted the best for this program, and that's what they got. We were given the serum, and when we woke up, we were stronger, faster."

Yes, he'd said this before—

"And we could come back from the dead."

She swallowed the *very* big lump in her throat. "Are you crazy?"

He gave a negative shake of his head. "Neither are you."

She hadn't thought she was the crazy one.

"There were side effects, though. Things we weren't told about." Now his gaze turned to emerald chips of ice. "The biggest side effect is that we lost all of our memories. Our lives before Lazarus vanished."

Her breath hitched. Okay, now this story might be going someplace. "Is that why...I don't remember?"

"You're different." He hadn't moved from his position at the foot of the bed. "Other Lazarus subjects can die—our missions are incredibly dangerous—and when we rise again, we remember...well, we remember everything that has happened *since* we received the Lazarus serum. But you—you're different. With each death, it's like your mind gets wiped clean. You become a blank slate again. All memories are gone."

Luna realized she was biting her lower lip way too hard. "So you're saying...I *died* recently?"

"Judging by all the blood in that hospital, yes, Luna, you died."

And her memory had been wiped. *If* she believed this crazy story.

If she believed Maddox.

The man who'd cuffed her. The man who'd kissed her.

The man who'd knocked her out with—a touch?

"I can prove it all to you," Maddox said.

That was actually what she feared. "I-I saw you in the hospital. You were fast."

His lips quirked. "I can be faster." He headed toward the window. Opened it up and let a blast of cold air inside. "Why don't you watch?"

They were on the second — no, looked like the third floor of a cabin. What did he want her to watch, exactly?

He jumped through the window. Literally just launched outside. Luna screamed and ran to grab the window frame. The window was massive, so big and wide, and he'd just shot outside as if it were nothing.

She looked below.

He was standing there, hands on his hips, gazing up at her. "You'll want to step back now," Maddox called.

She — what?

But he was barreling *back* through the window. He'd jumped up — jumped up three stories — and he was shooting through the window. She stumbled back, but Luna moved too slowly. Their bodies collided, her feet tangled with his, and they twisted, turning, and Luna found herself falling onto the bed.

With Maddox on top of her.

Oh, *um.*

He braced his hands on either side of her head, making sure that his weight didn't crush her. His legs were between hers, his body warm and hard, and his eyes seemed to shine at her. "Believe me now?"

What he'd just done was amazing.
Impossible.

"Believe me?" This time, his voice was in her head. Only in her head. Because she'd been staring at his mouth, and his lips had *not* moved.

"G-get out of my head," Luna whispered.

His mouth tightened, but she could have sworn she actually felt him leaving her mind. She suddenly felt colder.

Even though he was still pressed against her.

"Get off me," Luna ordered.

He slid back. Offered her his hand so she could rise, too.

She was perfectly capable of rising on her own, but she took his hand. His fingers curled around hers. Held her tight. And then she was standing right next to him. She tipped back her head and stared up at him. "You said that I'd awoken before, and I didn't know you." They'd done this routine before. Her stomach knotted. "How many times?"

He glanced away.

Her hand touched his chest. "How many times?"

Sorrow flashed on his face when he peered at her again. "More than you want to know."

Oh, shit. Tears stung her cheeks. "So, what's the protocol? You talk me down, over and over again?"

"Something like that."

She couldn't deny what he'd showed her. Couldn't keep pretending that this madness wasn't happening. Instead, she needed knowledge. She needed to figure out just what was happening so she could go forward. Her shoulders squared.

"There it is," he murmured.

She didn't understand.

His fingers skimmed over her shoulder. Down her arm. "You square up. You get determined. You stop thinking I'm feeding you bullshit, and you march forward."

Luna swallowed the lump in her throat. Or rather, she choked it down. "You know me really well, don't you?"

Maddox shrugged. "I tend to know what you will do. That's why I was sent to find you when you went missing. Because the lab coats feared you might wake up and need some talking down."

His words didn't reassure her.

His gaze slid over her face. "A few things are different this time, though." And his hand fell away from her shoulder. "You've never tried the seduction technique on me before." He turned, giving her his broad back, as he marched toward the closed bedroom door.

"Really?" Luna considered that. "Why the hell not?"

He stilled. "What?" His voice sounded a bit strangled.

"I'm attracted to you." Was she supposed to pretend she wasn't?

He whirled back toward her.

"I think you're sexy, hard to miss that." She waved vaguely toward him. "But I am also scared of you. There is something about you…" Again, she wasn't going to lie. "Something that absolutely terrifies me."

She saw him swallow.

"Want to tell me why that is?" Luna pressed.

"You shouldn't be afraid of me. I would *never* hurt you."

Easy words to give.

He laughed. "Are you trying to see if I'm lying, Luna? Are you focusing? Can you hear my heartbeat?"

And — when she focused, when she drew in a deep breath, released it, and listened — she could. Steady. Strong.

"The lab coats think Lazarus subjects are human lie detectors. We can detect changes in breathing, can smell sweat, can hear the pounding of a liar's heartbeat." He cocked his head. "So am I lying? Or do I mean it when I say I'd never hurt you?"

She thought he meant it. Fair enough. Time to turn the tables on him. Her hands rose to her hips. "Am I lying when I say that you terrify me?"

His lips thinned.

"Am I lying," Luna continued quietly, "when I say that I want you?"

Now his lips parted.

Right. Just so they were clear. "I don't understand—if you're the guy who is always there for me when I wake up and I don't know who the hell I am…if you're the guy always taking care of me—why haven't we kissed before?"

"I didn't say we'd never kissed." His voice was a growl. "I said you hadn't tried the seduction routine before. You're not the teasing type." And, once more, he headed for the door.

She felt her eyes widen. "Are we lovers?" Luna blurted.

He opened the door. Maddox left the room, and he didn't answer her question, damn him.

A blast of cold air blew through the still open window. Luna headed for the window, preparing to close it, but…

I could run right now. She could try jumping from the window. If she truly believed his story, then she had to buy that she could survive the jump, too, just as he had.

But…

But if she truly believed his story, did she want to run from the one man who held all the answers that she needed?

Luna closed the window. Then she hurried out of the bedroom. She rushed down the stairs, her feet pounding on the wood. She barely noticed the cabin around her, vaguely aware it was super nice. Fancy in a touristy style. Lots of exposed wood. White furniture. White rugs.

Maddox was in the den, standing in front of a massive fireplace. He raked a hand through his hair as he stood there.

"You can't leave me hanging!" Luna called to him as she bounded away from the landing. "Are we lovers?"

The front door opened. The other guy was there—Jett? He'd obviously caught what she'd said and a broad grin split his face as he walked inside, pounding his boots on the rug. "Answer the lady, Maddox," Jett practically challenged. "I am dying to hear this one."

Maddox spared him a withering glance. "Screw off, Jett."

Jett lifted the bags he held and kept advancing. "Even though I come bearing gifts?" He turned his head toward Luna. "Gifts for you, lovely lady. Gifts of clothing that you *didn't* steal from a gas station."

She'd *paid* for those clothes! Granted, with money she'd stolen from Maddox but—

"Sweaters, jeans, boots." He brought the bags toward her and sat them at her feet. "Socks. And, of course, the all-important...*underwear*. Panties, bras—"

"*Stop* talking, Jett," Maddox snarled at him.

Luna was flushing.

Jett shrugged. "But Luna likes pretty underwear. You know that. It's her thing—"

"OhmyGod." Luna stared at him in horror. At him, then Maddox. Then Jett again. "Am I sleeping with you, too?"

Jett burst out laughing. "I wish." He winked. "Though if you're offering—"

Maddox shoved him, hard enough to send Jett flying across the room. "Keep your damn hands *off* her."

The humor vanished from Jett's face.

"She doesn't remember jackshit, got it?" Maddox's expression was absolutely lethal. "You don't screw around with her." He looked back at Luna. "No, you are *not* sleeping with him."

She scooped up the bags.

"If you were," Jett called out with a wry smile, "I'm pretty sure Mad Maddox would have killed me by now." He winked. "He's the jealous type."

Did that mean she and Maddox were involved?

Maddox moved to stand protectively in front of her. "Get changed, Luna." His gaze had dropped to the front of her shirt. And his gaze *burned.* "Use the underwear," he added, rasping. "Or I'll have to kick Jett's ass."

The underwear? She flushed, hard and hot, as she realized that her nipples were shoving quite clearly against the front of the too-thin shirt she'd gotten at the gas station. And Maddox's gaze was on the great view she was offering him.

His gaze whipped back up to her face. "Maybe I'll kick his ass for fun."

"Those primitive instincts," Jett remarked with an aggrieved sigh. "Always such bitches for us to handle, huh? Rage, lust, jealousy — they're like kryptonite to us."

He was just saying more things that didn't make sense to her.

But Maddox cleared his throat. "That's important to remember, Luna. Very important."

She'd pulled the bags up to cover her shirt. And her nipples. Nipples she was sure were hard just because of Maddox. What was up with her reaction to him?

"Lazarus subjects experience primitive emotions differently from normal humans. We feel them far too strongly. When we rage, we're lethal."

Jett stalked closer. He gave a grim nod, all traces of humor suddenly gone from his face. "The darker emotions can wreck us."

"Dark emotions?" Luna parroted.

"Jealousy is killer." Jett winced as he cast a quick glance at Maddox. "Sorry, man."

Maddox was still staring at her. "Lust can get beyond our control. We can want things too badly."

It felt like he was warning her.

Maybe because he was?

"And when you want something long enough, when you want something badly enough…eventually, nothing will stop you from having what you want."

He wanted her. She knew it with absolute certainty. Luna licked lips that had gone too dry. Still clutching the bags, she said, "We aren't lovers."

Jett gave a low whistle.

Maddox just watched her. "No."

She turned toward the stairs. "I'm going to change."

"We're not lovers," Maddox added, his voice following her. "Not yet."

***

Maddox stood on the cabin's back deck, staring out at the night. The door opened behind him, but he didn't glance over his shoulder.

"I don't think we were followed from Bitter," Jett announced. His steps padded closer. "And when I picked up Luna's supplies, I made sure no tails were on me."

Maddox nodded.

"You think she's going to try running?" Jett put his elbows on the deck's wooden railing. "Is it wise to just trust Luna on her own?"

"She believes what I told her." He shrugged. "If she tries to run, she'll be on her own again. Someone hurt her. Someone *took* her. We're the best protection she has, and I think she realizes that now."

"Luna isn't exactly defenseless. Maybe she'd prefer to be on her own."

Maddox glanced at him.

Jett cleared his throat. "Right. Not like she can get away now." He swiped a hand over the back of his neck. "So what are we doing? Going totally off-grid for her? Because, look, yes, it's obvious you've been hot for Luna a very, very long time, but if we cut ties with our handlers, then we'll be next on the termination list."

He already knew that. "You think they've been telling us the truth?"

"What?" Real surprise flashed on Jett's face. "Why wouldn't they tell us the truth?"

Why indeed?

"We're the good guys here, Maddox. We've been going on missions that help people. Making rescues that no one else could handle because it was too dangerous. We've shut down domestic

terrorism operations that would have *killed*
normal soldiers. We've saved lives, how can you
question that?"

He knew they'd helped. He also knew…
"Luna is one of us. And the lab coats were ready
to kill her."

"She *is* a weak link," Jett muttered.

Maddox stepped toward him.

"Easy!" Jett threw up his hands. "Swear to
God, man, you have got to get this shit under
control. Ever since her escape, you've been on
edge. Cage the Mad Maddox part, got it? Get
your control back. You have her. Things should
have fallen into line again for you."

"I'm not sure she escaped." That was the
story they'd been given. That Luna had escaped
the facility. And he'd been told to bring her back.

Jett blinked. "If she didn't escape, what the
hell happened?"

"She was strapped to an exam table in that
old hospital." He'd been so fucking furious when
he saw the blood-covered operating room. He'd
wanted to tear apart the whole building. "I think
she was taken."

"Why would someone take her? That doesn't
make any sense. You want a hostage, you don't
take a super soldier." Then he seemed to catch
himself. "Oh, shit. You think they knew about her
weakness."

He hated that word. "Luna *isn't* weak." He glanced back at the cabin. The light in her bedroom was on, shining bright. Was she listening to them? Maybe. Better to be safe... "Run with me."

"Uh, we're just going to leave her? What if she makes a break for it?"

"Luna isn't leaving." He pitched his voice higher, in case she was listening. "Not if she wants to find out how she wound up in that hospital. Because I swear, I will figure out what happened to her."

Then he grabbed Jett's shoulder. In a flash, they were far away from the cabin. No other houses were nearby. He'd picked the place specifically for its isolation. His gaze went back to the upstairs bedroom. To the light that shone there.

Luna wouldn't leave. But, if she did, he'd see her fleeing. He'd catch her. "Now we can talk."

Jett huffed out a hard breath, fog immediately appearing before his face. "You think she was taken because of her memory loss."

"If someone had tried to take you or me, then we'd have woken up and known exactly who was on our side and who we needed to destroy." Maddox pushed back his fury. "But when Luna wakes up after a death, she's defenseless. The bastards who took her could have fed Luna any story, and then, bam, if she believed them, they would suddenly have one powerful super soldier on their hands."

"Fuck."

Yes. "She's vulnerable. She doesn't remember who took her from our facility, she doesn't remember who hurt her at the hospital. The SOBs could walk right up to her, and she wouldn't know what they'd done to her."

Jett's head lowered. "That's why she was up for termination. She can be dangerous to the team. We can't trust that she won't turn on us if she wakes up and doesn't know—"

Maddox grabbed him, fisting his hands in Jett's shirtfront. "She *won't* be terminated."

"Easy." Jett didn't fight back. But his body had stiffened. "You know I like Luna. She's saved my ass plenty of times."

Maddox didn't let him go.

"But don't you get it, man? The only people who can help Luna are the people at *our* lab."

The people who wanted to terminate her.

"Maybe they can fix her," Jett added. "Did you think of that? How the hell do you even know they were going to terminate her? Who told you that shit?"

"Luna. She told me. Right before she went missing." His hands let go of Jett.

Jett paced a few feet away. "Are you sure she was telling the truth?"

"What?"

"Maybe she thought…if she told you that before she vanished…maybe she thought you'd believe she *had* been terminated. That she was dead. If that was the case, then you wouldn't look for her. We both know that you're the best hunter Lazarus has. Without you, she might still be free."

"She wasn't free." His hands fisted. "She was fucking tortured in some hospital. Luna *didn't* lie to me." Her fear had been too real.

"I'm just saying…hell, how well do you really know her? We woke up with her in the lab after we were all given the serum. But we don't know a damn thing about what she was like before Lazarus."

"I don't know a damn thing about what *you* were like, either," Maddox threw back at him.

"Right. And I don't know who you were. All of that was lost to us. Everything was lost."

And Maddox would be lying if he didn't admit he fucking hated that fact. Who the hell *had* he been? What about his family? His parents? The test subjects had all been assured that they hadn't left any spouses behind, but surely he'd had other relationships? A lover? Close friends? "I'm not turning her over to the lab coats at Lazarus, not yet." *Not when they could be waiting to kill her.* "I want to learn more."

Jett gave a grim nod. "Seems like the best way to do that is by going back to the hospital where you found her. There has to be *something* left behind that can help us."

"So you're on board?"

A ragged sigh escaped him. "I *like* the woman, you know that. And the things she can do…" He shook his head. "I'll never forget how she saved that kid in Panama."

A kid who'd run straight into the crossfire during a battle. The bullets had torn into his small chest. Jett had roared when he'd seen the boy fall. He'd broken cover and raced into the street, desperate to help the child.

But Jett hadn't been able to stop the blood.

Luckily, Luna had.

"Does she know about *that* yet?" Jett asked. "Her psychic bonus?"

"Not yet. Hell, man, I just got her to believe I wasn't the bad guy."

"But…aren't you?"

Maddox glared at him.

Jett just laughed. "I'll go back to the hospital. If there's evidence in the place, I'll find it, okay? I'll also take care of the motorcycle we left hidden in Bitter." He pointed to the house. "You keep her safe until we can figure out what the hell to do."

He planned on staying very close to Luna.

Jett took a few steps away from him, then stopped. "If we find out that she did turn on Lazarus, that she ran away and turned on us all, what then?"

Maddox made sure his thoughts were secured. He'd always had the strongest psychic safeguards. No one got in his head, not unless he wanted the person inside. "I'll deal with her."

"I was afraid you'd say that." Jett shuffled forward. "I always liked her…"

Maddox had always liked her, too. Hell, *like* was far too tame of a description for what he felt for Luna. He hurried back to the cabin, making sure he scanned the perimeter. The SUV's engine started with a growl and then he heard Jett driving away.

And it was back to just being him and Luna.

When he went inside, he'd make sure he kept his damn hands *off* her. That would be his step one. Then he'd get around to interrogating her.

He threw open the cabin's door and strode inside. Her scent hit him right away. A sweet, seductive scent that was pure Luna. She didn't wear lotion, never had, but she carried a light, flowery scent that had always appealed to him. He followed that scent and found her in the den. Her back was to him as she stood in front of the fire. Her dark hair trailed over her shoulders, falling onto the green sweater she wore. Tight jeans clung to her legs, and black boots rose to her knees.

"We're alone now." She spoke without looking at him. Obviously, she'd heard Jett leave.

Maddox raked a hand over his face. He should go upstairs and get showered.

"That's good." Luna turned toward him. She advanced with slow but certain steps. "With him gone, I'll have the chance to find out…" Her words trailed away as she kept advancing.

She only stopped when she was directly in front of him.

"Find out what?" Maddox asked as his brows climbed.

She put her hands on his shoulders. Rose onto her toes. Pulled him toward her. "To find out if we were lovers." Then she put her mouth against his.

CHAPTER FOUR

She shouldn't have kissed him. Before Luna actually put her mouth against his, the plan had seemed sound enough. She'd wanted to see if her reaction to the dark and dangerous Maddox would be as strong as it had been before. Maybe when she'd kissed him at the creepy hospital, the adrenaline and general terror she'd been feeling had screwed with her head. Maybe she'd only *thought* that kissing him had ignited her body into a crazy maelstrom of need and lust that made her want to rip the man's clothes off.

So she'd needed to test things. Needed to see what her reaction would be to him under different circumstances. And if Lazarus subjects were really all about primitive responses, well, what was more primitive than lust? Surely she'd be able to tell if they *had* been lovers. Right? Maybe?

But when her lips pressed to his, when her tongue snaked along his lower lip and he gave a deep, guttural growl, her plan went straight to hell.

Maddox wasn't some passive participant in her little experiment. His hands—those warm, strong, bear-like hands of his—closed around her hips. He lifted her up, moving so that her chest was pressed flush to his. Her legs got a mind of their own, and they wrapped around his hips.

Bad, bad move...

But it felt so good.

His lips opened beneath hers. He took over the kiss, tasting her, savoring her, and the wild avalanche of need? It came back. Even stronger than before. Her nipples tightened against him, they ached, and she found herself arching her hips toward him, moving almost desperately. He was just kissing her, and she was frantic. Wanting him so badly. *Wild.* From his mouth.

She was in so much trouble.

Luna tore her mouth from his. "We're lovers." Her breath heaved out. Her legs were still wrapped around his hips. His hands were tight around her waist. "You lied to me!" Anger mixed with her lust. He thought that because her memory was gone, he could take advantage of her. The bastard—

He sucked in a deep breath. Then another.

Her legs slid away from his hips as he lowered her—very slowly—to the floor.

"Told you," and his voice was *deep,* "we're not lovers. Not...yet."

He had to be lying. Didn't he? "It's not normal." His hands lingered on her hips. "Even I know this. You don't kiss someone and ignite."

His lips curled. "That what happened? You kissed me and you ignited?"

Her cheeks burned. "Don't act like you don't feel the same way." She'd *felt* his physical response, and it was as big as the rest of him.

"Oh, I feel it. I want you like hell burning."

Was that good? Or bad? Both?

"But I haven't had you yet, and that's the truth. Though if I'd realized our reactions to each other would be quite so…intense…then I damn well would have gotten you in bed sooner." His gaze clouded. "And fuck the rule the lab coats have about the subjects mixing together."

Now that was interesting. "Lazarus subjects aren't supposed to have sex with each other?"

"The lab coats say we're too dangerous for that. Sex is too primitive. Too wild."

With him, she had absolutely no doubt that things would get wild. She felt singed where he was still touching her. Like he was branding her with his fingers.

She also wanted his mouth on her again.

But if that happened, she was pretty sure her new clothes would be hitting the floor.

I don't know anything about my sex life. What if I have a lover somewhere? The thought shot through her head, and she gave a gasp. "If we're not together, then am I sleeping with someone else?"

His pupils expanded. Maddox growled.

"Is that a yes?" Luna demanded.

"It's a hell fucking *no.* Not like I'd miss you having a lover in the Lazarus facility. No one goes into a cell without others knowing about it."

"Cell?" That one word chilled her. "Am I kept in some kind of prison?"

He didn't answer.

Oh, jeez. "Are we all kept locked up?"

"The lab coats are testing us. Soon enough, we'll be able to integrate with everyone else again."

And that was it—she could actually hear the difference in his words, and she'd noticed the slight hitch in his breathing. "Is this what it's like when you lie?"

Maddox's gaze narrowed.

"Because you *don't* believe they'll let us integrate with everyone else."

He let her go.

"What *do* you think they'll do?" Luna pushed him for the truth.

His jaw hardened. She didn't think he was going to reply until he finally spit out, "Use us up until nothing is left."

"Maddox—"

But even as she called his name, his head whipped to the left. He frowned, then he swore.

"What's wrong?" Luna asked but then she heard the faint sound, too. Engines, tires rolling over gravel…coming closer.

"That's *not* Jett," he snapped. He rushed across the room. Yanked open a drawer and pulled out a gun. He tossed it to her, and she caught it automatically. The gun felt comfortable in her hand. Familiar. She automatically checked it, making sure it was loaded and ready to go. When she looked up, he'd taken out another Glock.

"Multiple vehicles." His head was tilted as he listened for the sounds. "Coming in fast."

She swallowed. "And I'm guessing these *aren't* people on your team?"

"For this mission, the team was only me and Jett. And, no, the people coming aren't mine." He advanced toward her with an angry stride. "They're coming for you."

Her hold on the weapon tightened.

"Don't worry, Luna. They're not getting you. They'll have to fucking go through me first."

She believed him. "How many are coming?"

"Four vehicles. If they're smart, they have at least four men in each one. But it will take more than that to stop us."

The vehicles were getting closer. Way too close.

"What's the plan?" She was sweating, and her heart was racing. "Do we go out with guns blazing?"

"No." A smile flashed on his face. A smile that did not make Maddox look reassuring or friendly. In fact, she was pretty sure sharks had smiles like he did. "I'm going to talk with the bastards. We need to know who they are. And why they took *you*."

Talk? But—

"Stay inside. And if the bullets start flying, remember, no hits to your head." His fingers rose and pressed to her cheek. "Even we can't come back from a bullet to the brain."

What? And he was just going to prance outside like it was nothing? What if he took a bullet to the brain?

"Don't look so worried. I've got a secret weapon."

Was that secret weapon the fact that bullets could bounce off him?

But his hand slid down her cheek. He leaned closer. Pressed a kiss to her lips. "It was so easy to get addicted."

"Addicted?" She stared at him, completely lost.

"To you. A taste was all I needed." For an instant, he almost looked tender. Then a hard mask slid over his face. "Stay inside. If I need you, you'll know."

"Maddox—"

But he was already gone. Not rushing out the front door and heading for the approaching vehicles, but moving soundlessly out via the rear of the cabin. And she was left standing there, holding a gun.

She glanced around the room. "I don't think this works for me." Not one bit. She wasn't the stay in place type. Luna bounded up the stairs. Found a room on the second floor that was covered by darkness. She used that darkness to hide herself as she crept toward the window, then she peered down at the scene below.

She had a good vantage point from this position. And she'd be able to make one hell of a shot.

"I'll watch your six, Maddox." She tried to find the mental link he'd used with her before. Wasn't sure if she'd succeeded or not. *"And don't you dare take a bullet to the brain."*

***

Four vehicles. He'd been right about the number. Maddox watched from the shadows as they roared in. They weren't trying to be silent. Probably because they knew there was *no* way they could sneak up on super soldiers. Their vehicles screeched to a stop, and then men jumped out as fast as they could — men wearing bullet proof vests.

At least they were *attempting* to stay alive.

"We want her, not him," one of the men barked. "Get her, *now.*"

Oh, the hell, no. Maddox let out a high whistle.

Immediately, the men spun toward his position in the dark. One fool even let a shot loose. It missed, of course, by like three feet.

But the shot did piss Maddox off.

He moved fast, snaking through the trees and then coming out next to the last SUV. The men had their backs turned to him as they searched the darkness, and it was easy enough to run right up to them.

He didn't kill them. No point in that. Not yet. He wanted them alive.

But they didn't all have to be conscious.

One touch, and one man went down in absolute silence. Maddox flew toward another. Grabbed the guy from behind, pumped his psychic energy at the bastard. The fellow went down, too. Maddox took out several more of the SOBs that way before the others even got smart enough to turn in his direction.

And when they did, he stilled. "About time." Maddox smiled at them. "Which one of you dumbasses is the leader?"

Instead of answering, they opened fire.

***

"Maddox!" Luna screamed when the bullets flew at him. "No!" She'd opened the window, and she took aim, firing to take out those men. She hit their arms, sending guns dropping from their hands as they howled in pain. They were wearing bullet proof vests, so their arms were vulnerable, and those spots were also the best way to make them too weak to hold a gun. One, two—

They fired back at her.

She ducked, making sure her head was safe. She'd lost sight of Maddox right before she'd had to take cover, but he was alive. She'd seen him running. She'd seen—

"Luna!" A man's voice. One she didn't recognize. "We're here to save you!"

What?

"The man who took you—he's *not* FBI."

FBI? Oh, yeah, that was the story Maddox had given to that elderly gas station attendant. How did those guys know that? Had they talked to the attendant?

"*We're* the FBI. He's a dangerous criminal!"

More gunfire. A fast *bang-bang-bang*.

Luna clutched her weapon to her chest.

"We believe he's been drugging you. He abducted you some time ago, and we were just able to track you down, thanks to the help of a concerned citizen in a nearby town."

Silence. No gunfire at all. Just rapidly racing heartbeats.

"Come down here, Luna! We're here to take you home!"

Her breath sawed in and out of her lungs.

"Don't even think of moving, Luna." Maddox's voice. Blasting in her mind. *"The bastard is lying. He's sending two men toward the house. They're about to break in the front door."*

She craned her head, trying to see below without making herself a target. At the same moment, she heard the crack of wood from downstairs. She knew the front door had just been smashed in.

She wasn't going to sit there while the men cornered her. She'd go face them. Luna slipped away from the window.

"Fuck!" Maddox's curse was strong and furious. *"They're taking something in. Get out, Luna, get –"*

But his words were cut off as more gunfire rang out. She had the fast impression of pain. Maddox's pain.

Then she heard a loud boom—one that came from downstairs. The whole cabin seemed to shake even as the scent of smoke and fire reached her. Eyes widening in horror, she ran from the bedroom and peered below. The lower level of the house was burning as flames spread far too rapidly.

The fire totally blocked the stairs. She was trapped on the second level. To get out, she'd have to go through one of the upstairs windows. Going out the front windows wasn't an option—that was where all of the "FBI guys" were. So she rushed to a rear bedroom. She shoved open the nearest window and jumped through it, clutching her gun tight on the way down.

"Got her!" A high, cracking voice.

Her knees didn't buckle when she landed. She whirled toward the man's voice. Saw the guy pointing his weapon right at her. "No, I've got you." And she fired before he could, a lightning fast move that had the bullet tearing through his arm. He scrambled back, howling in pain, automatically clutching his wound…and also dropping his weapon.

As she stared at him, another bullet blasted. This one came from behind her. Luna whirled, expecting to feel a bullet slamming into her body, but Maddox was there. He jumped in front of her. Maddox gave a rough grunt, then he was firing.

She could hear more vehicles approaching in the distance, and the blaze was raging out of control, burning through the cabin like wildfire.

"Fuck this…" Maddox sucked in a sharp breath. He whirled around, glared at the men in black vests who were closing in on him and Luna. *"Drop."*

She didn't understand. Did he think they were just going to drop their weapons? Or—

They dropped. The men literally dropped to the ground. She saw four fall, as if they'd just been knocked unconscious. And, of course, they had. *Maddox's power.* He'd told her he could do that. He'd said he usually liked to touch his prey because it was easier to knock them out that way. When he attacked without touching, he'd warned her that he used too much energy. What had he said? Something about the crash after?

"The crash afterwards is a real bitch."

Beside her, Maddox swayed. Her arm immediately wrapped around him, and when it did, she felt the wetness on his back. Blood.

Oh, God. "Maddox?"

His head turned. She could see him perfectly. She'd been able to see all of their attackers perfectly, even though darkness reigned outside. Was night vision another super soldier perk?

"Get...SUV," he rasped. "Not much...time."

Okay, there were lots of SUVs to choose from. Luna got them to the nearest SUV. The keys were even still inside because someone had been especially accommodating.

"Drive..." Maddox whispered.

She'd been able to figure out how to drive a motorcycle, she'd automatically been able to aim and fire a gun, so she could handle this ride, too, no problem. Had to be one of those procedural memory things he'd told her about.

Maddox slumped into the passenger seat. "Get us…out of here."

His heartbeat sounded funny. The beat wasn't fast and strong like it usually was. She cranked the vehicle, but didn't rush away from the scene. Her hand reached out and touched his cheek. "Maddox?"

"It will…only be for a little while…" He swallowed. "Don't worry, I'll…come back."

The scent of his blood was strong. Too strong. "Is the bullet still in you?"

He didn't speak.

"Maddox?"

Nothing. His heart was still beating, but it was so slow. Way too slow. She was afraid that he was dying.

Footsteps rushed toward her. Her head whipped to the right. She saw a man there, tall, muscled, with tousled red hair. He had a gun pointed at her. She'd been so intent on Maddox that she'd forgotten everything else.

I thought all of the guys were unconscious. Why isn't he on the ground, too?

Then the redhead fired his gun. She ducked, fast, and glass rained down on her. No way did she want a bullet to the brain. She threw the vehicle into reverse and slammed on the gas. The

SUV immediately lurched back, then rammed into the vehicle that had been parked behind it. Dammit!

"Luna!"

That roar had come from the jerk who'd fired at her. She shifted gears and whipped the steering wheel around. Her foot shoved the gas pedal into the floorboard.

The redhead saw her coming toward him, and the guy cursed. "I fucking saved you! You *owe* me!"

He had to leap out of her way. And the guy could leap really, really well. Too well. Like super soldier well. But she didn't stop to ask the man just where he'd gotten his super soldier bonuses. Instead, she kept the gas pedal pinned to the floorboard, and the SUV's engine roared as she hurried away from the cabin. When she got to the main road, she could hear other vehicles coming from the left. The drivers weren't close enough to see her, not yet, but they were coming in fast. Luna whipped the steering wheel toward the right.

She flew down the road. She kept the SUV's lights turned off, not wanting to alert anyone to her presence, and she hauled ass. Minutes ticked by in silence. The darkness stretched around her. Soon the only sounds she could hear were her racing heartbeat and her own ragged breathing.

No one was following her. They'd gotten away clean.

Finally, her shoulders sagged. "That was close." She gave a little laugh. "You know what? I think I was kind of kick-ass." She'd been like an action hero the way she'd jumped out of that window. She was...

Her head turned toward Maddox. A very still and silent Maddox. Luna realized that she didn't hear any sound at all coming from him. Not a whisper of a breath. Not the stutter of his heartbeat.

She slammed on the brake pedal. "Maddox?" Her hand flew toward him.

Then she screamed because Luna realized he was dead.

***

Sonofabitch. Luna had been right there. Right the fuck there. And she'd gotten away.

He holstered his weapon. Kicked one of the unconscious bodies of the absolutely useless guards who'd come with him to the cabin. Humans. Mercs that he'd hired to help out on his mission, and they couldn't do jack. Maddox had blasted them with a psychic hit, and they'd all gone down like toy soldiers falling in battle.

He'd even staggered. But, luckily, he'd been hiding in the woods, hanging back and watching the action from a safe distance. Maddox hadn't even known he was there, so the prick hadn't been able to focus his considerable power on the threat he hadn't seen. Even though he'd been warned by his partner about what Maddox could do, seeing the guy up-close in action had been a whole new level of screwed-up.

More vehicles were approaching. Back-up that would be useless. Sure, they could track the GPS in the SUV that Luna had stolen, but Maddox would have her ditching that ride at the first opportunity. The guy was smart and too damn strong by far.

Of course, Maddox hadn't been the target for tonight's attack. Luna was. Luna was everything.

If the others found out just what she could do, every super soldier out there would want a piece of her. They'd literally be fighting each other in order to get her.

Too bad. I got to her first.

But they didn't know all of Luna's secrets. Not yet. He did, though. *I can track you, Luna.*

And that was why he had the advantage.

CHAPTER FIVE

"Don't stay dead. Don't stay dead." Her voice reached him, soft and desperate. Then he felt her fingers, sliding over his forehead. "Everything you told me has to be real. You can come back. Your brain is fine." A ragged breath blew lightly over his face. "Don't stay dead. Oh, please, God, don't let him stay dead."

Hearing always came back first for him. Weird, but that was the way it was. Then he could feel things. Like her hand on his face. Such soft, silken fingers. And...

His heart lurched in his chest. A hard surge and then his heart was racing.

"I hear it!" Luna's voice had gone high. "Your heart is beating again! You're back!" Her body smashed against his. She was on top of him, hugging him fiercely, and he was...in a bed?

Maddox opened his eyes. Luna's face was inches from his. Her tousled hair tumbled over her shoulders. A wide grin curled her full lips, and her dark eyes gleamed.

"I'm so happy," she said. "I could just kiss you."

If that was what she wanted…

His hands rose and sank into the thickness of her hair as he pulled her toward him. She was still smiling when his mouth pressed to hers. She was straddling him, her sex right over his rapidly swelling cock. When a guy woke up and found a damn goddess on top of him, he tended to react one very definite way.

Arousal flooded through him. Wild, fierce hunger. Lust—dark need for her. His tongue swept into Luna's mouth. He tasted her. He had her moaning. His chest was bare, and he wanted her shirt, gone, too. He wanted her naked. Wanted *in* her.

He'd fucking wanted Luna for far too long.

His hands went to the bottom of her shirt as he prepared to rip the thing out of his way.

"Wait!" Luna jerked back. She sat up, and that movement had her sex automatically shoving down harder against his cock. A low growl escaped him.

Her eyes widened. "You were just dead."

"Not any longer." Definitely alive and ready.

Her tongue swiped over her lower lip. She had one sexy little pink tongue. There were all kinds of things he'd like to do with her tongue.

"I dug the bullet out." Another swipe of her tongue. Was she trying to drive him crazy? "Then nothing happened. I-I got you into a motel room."

Ah, so they were in a motel? He spared a quick glance around him. A queen size bed — too small for him. A desk. Two chairs. An old TV. Some paintings of flowers hung on the walls.

"I had to leave you while I ditched the SUV." She exhaled on a long sigh. Her hands had flattened against his bare chest. "You feel really warm," she murmured.

She had no idea. But he was trying to hold back the lust, for the moment. "What did you do with the SUV?" Because he knew the vehicle probably had a tracker on it. If it was close by, then the jerks he'd left at the cabin could follow the signal and find them.

"There was, an, um...guy. He was about five blocks from the motel, hitchhiking. I gave him the keys to the SUV and told him to drive fast."

Maddox blinked.

"He was super happy to get the car." Her fingers were sliding over his skin in a small caress. "I figured if the vehicle was still moving, then anyone following it would keep moving too." Now she caught her lower lip between her teeth.

Did she have any idea how much *he* wanted to bite right then? He'd used so much of his energy back at the cabin when he knocked out those assholes. Then he'd gotten shot. And coming back from a death was never easy. His control was at his weakest when he first rose. "Luna…"

"They won't hurt him, will they? I mean, the people who are after me…they won't care about him."

"They aren't interested in him," Maddox muttered. But they'd question the guy. And they'd circle back to this area with the information he gave them. Especially if he'd just been five blocks away from the motel. So Maddox and Luna would have to get moving again. But first…

He closed his eyes.

"Uh, Maddox?" She leaned down toward him. He felt her hair slide over his chest.

His cock shoved so hard against the front of his jeans that Maddox figured the zipper was leaving an impression on him.

"Is everything okay?" Luna asked. The scent of flowers surrounded him.

Things were *not* okay. "You need to get off me."

She didn't move.

His eyes opened. "Unless you want to get fucked right now."

He expected her to fly off him. She didn't. Instead, Luna tilted her head to the side. She studied him as if she were seriously considering the matter.

Oh, hell. She didn't get the danger she was in. "My control...it's weak when I rise." And having his favorite temptation right in front of him was not helping matters. "So you need to move. Right now."

Her lashes lowered. "I was scared."

Why was the woman not moving? She had to feel his dick shoving against her.

"You were gone for a long time. And I didn't know what I'd do if you didn't wake up."

He should say something reassuring. That was obviously what she needed right then. She —

"I think I want to fuck you."

His hands flew up. Locked around her waist. "*Luna.*"

"I want you. I felt the attraction the first time I saw you, even if I was terrified." Now her long, thick lashes lifted, and she met his stare directly. "I don't know who is after me or what will happen if those people *get* me. But I know I do want you. And I want to know what it's like to be with you."

Did he look like he had to be told twice? "Luna." Okay, he was still trying to warn her, though, because this first time... "My control...it's *shot.* I won't be slow or soft or —"

She gave a light, nervous laugh. "I don't have a point of comparison right now. So how about we just see what happens? Maybe I don't like slow or soft."

Sweet hell. "I don't have a point of comparison, either." His voice had gone guttural.

Her eyes widened.

"Ever since I woke up in the Lazarus lab, *you* are the only woman I've wanted. No one else would fucking do."

Her lips curled once more. "That's really sweet."

It was obsessed. But if she wanted to call it sweet, who was he to argue?

She let out a slow breath, then her hands went to the hem of her sweater. She pulled it over her head and tossed it to floor.

He didn't breathe at all. His gaze was on her breasts. She wore a black bra that cradled her full breasts, and she slid her hands behind her, unhooking the bra, and tossing it aside, too, as—

Maddox moved fast. He surged up, rolled their bodies, and pinned her beneath him on the bed. Then his mouth was on her breast. Tasting her sweet nipple. Laving it with his tongue. Licking. Sucking.

She moaned and arched toward him. Her hands curled around his shoulders as she pulled him closer. "That feels good." Her voice was a breathy temptation.

If she thought that felt good…*wait, baby. Just wait.*

His right hand slid between their bodies. He unhooked her jeans, slid down the zipper. He worked his hand between her legs, moving his fingers under the edge of silk that was her panties. He stroked her sex. Strummed her clit. Felt her get wet for him.

Hell, *yes.*

He heaved back. Yanked off her jeans and threw them. She wasn't wearing shoes or socks. Luna was left just in the scrap of black silk that hid her sex.

For a moment, he just stared at her. Luna's nipples were tight. Dusky. The curve of her hips was sexy as all hell. Her legs were silken and perfect, and he wanted them wrapped around his hips. Or thrown over his shoulders. He wanted her moaning. He wanted her coming.

He'd have all of that.

The bed was too fucking small so he stood, moving to the side.

Worry flashed on her face. "You're stopping? But—"

He caught her ankles. Kept his hold gentle with a fucking effort. Then he pulled her toward the edge of the bed. He pushed her legs apart. Let his fingers trail over the crotch of her panties. She arched toward him.

"I like that," Luna gasped.

Good. He wanted to learn every single thing that she enjoyed. And then he wanted to do those things to her over and over again.

He knelt near the bed.

"Maddox?"

He tugged on the panties. Too hard. They tore. But he forgot them instantly because he was staring at her sex. Looking wasn't enough, though. Time to taste.

His mouth went to her. On her. She nearly came off the bed. He licked her. He stroked her with his fingers. He worked her clit until her moans were high and her hips were arching toward him in a frantic rhythm.

She came against his mouth. Luna cried out his name, pleasure ringing in her voice, and that was just what Maddox had been waiting for. He surged to his feet. Yanked open his jeans. His heavy cock shoved toward her even as her body trembled with aftershocks of release. He drove into her. His fingers clamped around her hips as he lifted her up to meet him. Her sex was fucking tight and hot. He nearly went out of his damn mind.

Her legs wrapped around his hips. Her nipples were tight and waiting, so he bent, licking her. He withdrew from her, thrust deep. Skin to skin. He was skin to skin with her. She was marking him, every single inch of him. Did Luna realize that?

"Maddox!"

Pleasure was hitting her again. Or maybe it had never stopped. Her cheeks flushed. Her gaze seemed to go blind, and it wasn't enough for him.

In that moment, he wanted to absolutely *own* her. He yanked her up, pulling her against his body. He held her in his arms, kissed her deep and hard even as he turned and pinned her body against the nearest wall. He plunged into her again and again, and her nails raked over his back. He loved the bite of pain. Loved every fucking thing.

He had Luna. He'd wanted her for too long.

Sometimes, it seemed as if he'd always wanted her.

Withdraw, thrust. Withdraw.

Her mouth was on his neck. Licking. And she *bit* him. Marked him.

He exploded within her. The pleasure rolled through every cell of his body, and he held her, too tight, too hard—he held her as the climax nearly freaking destroyed him.

He didn't remember his lovers before Lazarus, but Maddox didn't think sex had *ever* been this good. No way. No damn way.

His heart thundered in his chest. His breath heaved in and out. His head lifted, and he stared down at Luna.

He'd tried to warn her that his control would break. That he'd get too wild. Now, though, he wondered if he'd scared her. Maybe he'd read her reactions wrong. What if—

"We started with a perfectly good bed," Luna said, her voice husky and a little twinkle coming to her eyes. "Want to tell me why we ended up against the wall?"

He had to kiss her. A quick, claiming kiss. "Bed wasn't big enough for all I wanted to do." He was pretty sure if they'd stayed in that bed, he would have broken the thing. It wasn't made for someone like him.

"I liked what you did." Her lips curled. Her hand pressed to his chest. Right over his heart. "A lot."

She was going to wreck him.

Her hand rose, moving to cup his cheek. Then her silken touch slid even higher, caressing his temple. Stroking him so tenderly.

The heat of her hand seemed to burn right through him, breaking past the skin and going—

"I'm going to marry Luna."

Maddox froze at that announcement. He'd been staring out at the beach, enjoying the sound of the waves crashing into the shore. He damn well loved the beach, always had. He'd been one lucky asshole to grow up in Gulf Shores. But at his buddy's words, he whirled around. "What?"

The guy nodded, his blue eyes hard and determined. "I'm going to marry her. So I'm telling you right now, she's mine. Keep your hands—"

"Maddox!"

The beach faded. The blond-haired man with the blue eyes vanished. Maddox's heart pounded frantically in his chest, and dizziness had him shaking his head.

Luna's hands pressed to his cheeks. "Are you okay? I just…I swear, I lost you there for a moment."

He carried her to the bed. He was fucking still *in* her.

"Maddox?" Worry whispered in her voice.

"You're mine." His own voice was guttural. He didn't know what the fuck had just happened. Some kind of hallucination? Whatever the hell it had been…rage and jealousy were left in the vision's wake. He lowered her to the bed. *So what if we wreck it?*

"What happened?" Luna asked.

She was beneath him on the bed. He'd risen onto his elbows, wanting to make sure that he didn't crush her. Her eyes were locked on him.

His cock was heavy and full, as if he hadn't just emptied out inside of her. But that was the thing…he *always* wanted Luna. He'd been able to keep his lust in check before, but now that he'd had her, there was no going back. "The past doesn't matter." He wasn't sure why he said those words.

Maybe because he realized other bastards had been lucky enough to have her before him.

He withdrew, only to drive deep into her again. She was slick from her release, from his, and he knew she was sensitive when she let out a shuddering breath.

"Is it always this good?" Luna tipped back her head.

He licked her breast. "No." He didn't need memories of other lovers to tell him that.

Withdraw. Thrust. Not as frantic as before. Slower. Almost tender. *Almost.* He could do that with her. For her.

I'm going to marry Luna. The words whispered through his head once more. He caught her hands with his, threaded his fingers through hers, and pinned them to the bed. The bed frame was creaking beneath his thrusts, and he was just getting started. Now that he knew what she enjoyed, what she liked, he'd make sure he gave her everything she needed.

His cock slid over her clit as he drove into her once more. She moaned his name. "I think…" Her breath panted out. "I like wild and hard…*and* slow and deep."

He stilled. Her voice—so sexy.

He gave her slow and deep. Gave it to her until her nails were raking down his back. And then…

Then he gave her wild and hard. Slamming into her, driving her hard toward her release, making her cry out for him over and over again. Her legs were spread wide, she was completely open to him, and he took her. Took her until she started to yell with her release, but his mouth slipped over hers, catching the sound. Her sex clamped greedily around him, and the contractions of her climax sent Maddox over the edge.

"You're mine." The words tore from him. From the possessive darkness that clouded so much of his soul. *"Mine."*

CHAPTER SIX

"We've got a problem."

Maddox pressed his phone closer to his ear when Jett made that grim announcement. Luna sat on the motel bed, the covers pulled up to her chest, and her dark eyes were on him. The phone had rung moments before, and he'd hunted the damn thing down—

"Are you listening to me?" Jett barked. "The old hospital was torched. There isn't going to be anything for me to find in that place because it's been blown to hell and back."

Dammit. "Yeah, the same shit happened to the cabin."

"What?" Jett's voice cracked.

"After you left, a team found us."

Jett swore.

"They used explosives on the cabin. Came in armed, and their goal was to take Luna."

"And what did you do to them?" Jett fired right back.

"Took them out, but not before one of the assholes managed to get a shot at me."

Silence. Then… "Shit, you died, didn't you?"

Luna's hold tightened on the covers. Maddox knew she could hear every word of the conversation. "I'm back in the land of the living now. But since I wasn't exactly helping the cause, Luna had to get us the hell away from those guys. I didn't learn a damn thing from them."

Luna gave a hard, negative shake of her head.

He frowned.

"Where are you?" Jett demanded. "We need to regroup."

Yeah, they did, but… "This location isn't secure enough. Luna and I are leaving. We'll meet up at the safe house just outside of Aspen." Jett would know the place. "Make absolutely sure you're not followed."

"Yeah, man, I will. But watch your own ass, got me?" Jett's sigh carried over the phone. "And make sure you watch her sweet ass, too."

Maddox ended the call and tossed the phone onto the desk. He'd yanked on his jeans right before he'd grabbed the phone—mostly because the phone had been *in* the pocket of his jeans.

"There's something you need to know." She clutched the covers to her breasts, and for some reason, he thought her shoulders were incredibly sexy. Who was he kidding? Everything about Luna was sexy. "You were…um, I think you might have already been dead, or at least really out of it, so you didn't see the last guy who attacked…"

He stalked closer to her. "What guy?" He'd been sure he knocked out all the assholes who'd been left. His priority had been to make the scene safe for her.

"He fired when we were in the SUV."

His chest seemed to burn. "Some asshole shot at you while I was out?"

"Don't worry." A smile came and went on her face. "I nearly ran him down with the SUV." Her lashes flickered. "It's the *nearly* part that I think you need to know about. The guy jumped out of the way. Like, *jumped.* Leaped kinda like Superman, and I don't think that was a move that a normal human could ever make."

His shoulders stiffened. "You're saying a super soldier was there?"

"I think that's what he was." Her lips pressed together. "He, um, he yelled that he'd saved me. That I owed him." A weak laugh escaped her. "Since he was shooting at me, I figured he had to be lying. He was trying to kill me right then, not save me. So I just hauled ass and didn't look back."

A super soldier. "Describe him."

She slid from the bed. Luna pulled the covers with her and kept them wrapped around her body. "Tall. Your height. Wide shoulders—like you. Red hair. I, uh, he had light colored eyes. He was trying to hurt me. There's no way he saved me from anything." She paused. "Right?"

"Right." Tension had knotted his muscles.

"He's...do you know him?"

Not based on the description she'd just given him. But... "Luna, there are...rogue super soldiers out there, too. I heard the lab coats talking about them. Our Lazarus facility isn't the only one in existence, and at some of the other places, the subjects broke loose." And he'd learned that dark secret right *after* Luna had gone missing.

She tensed. "Maybe they don't like being locked away. Being kept in cells like animals." Her gaze seemed to have gone cold. Distant. "If you take me back, will I be locked away?"

"I'm not taking you back." The words just erupted from him. But, fuck it, that had been his plan all along. Screw what he'd told Dr. Henry Danwith. Taking her back to possible termination had never been an option for him.

Luna took a quick step toward him, then stopped. "You're...not?"

"No."

Her cheeks flushed. A very, very dark red. "I didn't have sex with you as some kind of bribe."

Now his eyes widened.

"If that's what you're thinking." Her chin shot up into the air. "That's not what happened. I

wasn't trying to buy freedom or something like —
"

He closed the distance between them and curled his hands around her shoulders. "I know that."

"Good. You should know it."

His lips wanted to curl, but he didn't let them.

"So what happens now? We go on the run together? We just disappear?"

"Our first step is meeting up with Jett again. You heard what I told him — there's a safe place waiting for us just outside of Aspen. We get there, we regroup with him, then we figure out our next move." He thought Canada might be a good option. Just keep heading north until they were free and clear.

Her hand rose and pressed to his heart. "You're helping me."

He looked down at her hand. So small. Delicate. How could such a light touch burn straight to his soul?

"Thank you," Luna whispered. "God, I feel so silly right now. When I first saw you, I was actually afraid of you."

His temples pounded. His breath came faster. The room around him seemed to grow dim.

"Can you imagine? You're the hero. No way should I fear you."

He couldn't see Luna. Instead...he was suddenly somewhere else. Between one blink and another, he was—

"You think Luna is going to love you?" The blond glared at him. "Hell, no. She'll see you for the monster you are."

Maddox lifted the knife in his hand. A knife that...dripped blood.

The blond staggered to his knees. His hands came up, going for his stomach, as he tried to stop the blood that poured from him.

A door opened behind Maddox. A woman's sharp gasp filled his ears. He whirled around.

Luna. Luna was there. Standing in the doorway. Staring at him in absolute horror.

"What did you do?" she cried.

"Luna—"

Boom! A bullet tore through his back. He felt it burn through flesh and muscle, and then he saw the pain on Luna's face. Her lips parted. Her eyes went wide...

And blood bloomed on her side.

Even as he reached for her, more gunshots were blasting. The knife fell from his fingers as he grabbed her, holding her tight, but her body had gone slack against his.

"Maddox!" Luna's fingers were on his cheek.

He pulled her closer and shoved the covers away from her body.

"You zoned out on me," she told him, shaking her head, a furrow appearing between her brows.

His hands slid down her side, searching for—

She had a scar on her side. In the exact fucking spot where he'd just seen a bullet tear into her. His fingers pressed to the scar.

"Maddox?"

He touched his own body. The rough ridges of a scar were about three inches from his belly button. His hand slid to his back. Touched another scar. Both scars were in the exact spots where he'd just seen himself get shot.

Fucking hell. What is happening?

Her hand started to fall away from his cheek.

He grabbed her fingers, holding tight. "Did you see it?"

"See what?" She gave a little shiver.

"I—" But he broke off. *Did you see me…killing that blond bastard who said he was going to marry you? See me…getting shot? Only you got shot, too, baby. One of the bullets went into your body. You fell into my arms.* But he couldn't tell her that.

"Maddox, what's happening?"

He forced air into his lungs as he let her go. "We need to shower." He gave a decisive nod. "Then get the hell out of here. It's not safe to linger too long." He had to think. Had to figure out what the hell was happening. "You go into the shower first. I'll be right behind you."

"Is...everything okay?"

No, things were far from okay. Because he thought he'd just had a flash of his past. Of *their* past. And the flash had been brutal.

Worry turned her eyes even darker. "Your heart is racing really fast."

Yes, it was. And his temples were throbbing, and he was sweating, and he could *see* her bleeding in front of him. Echoes of gunshots seemed to fill his ears.

"Maddox?"

He swallowed. His body felt strange. Too tense. Too hot. And his temples were pounding too hard.

"Why do you look like you've just seen a ghost?"

Because he had.

***

The shower water poured down on Luna. Maddox had gone from being a hot, wild lover to...

A distant stranger. His eyes had turned arctic on her, and he'd practically pushed her toward the bathroom before jerking the door shut. Sure, her after-sex etiquette was definitely on the rusty side, but was a guy supposed to shove a lover into the shower? She didn't think so.

She shivered even though the water was steaming hot. Her fingers trailed up her body, lingering for a moment on the scar near her right side. He'd touched that scar, and his eyes had flared wide with an expression pretty close to horror.

Her own eyes closed as she pushed her head under the shower. The sex had been phenomenal. Amazing. She didn't need to remember her other lovers to know that no way had sex always been that good. A woman recognized something special.

But, apparently, a guy didn't. Dumbass.

She heard the door open behind her. She turned, and, through the fogged glass, she could just make out Maddox's large form. He stood in the doorway a moment, and then he stalked forward. She sucked in a quick breath, right before he yanked open the shower's glass door. Tendrils of steam immediately escaped.

Maybe he'd decided to join her. A little sexy time in —

"You're taking too long, Luna. We've got to haul ass before the enemy team circles back." His jaw hardened as his gaze shot down her body. "If they've put a tracker in you, we're screwed."

She blinked. "Did you just say...*in* me?"

A curt nod. And his fingers went to the waistband of his jeans. He shoved them down, and, yep, the guy was aroused. Very aroused. But acting like he wasn't. He stepped into the shower with her, and she immediately backed up.

"Um, I thought you were telling me to get out—"

His hands went to her waist. No—up, his slightly callused fingertips moved to the scar on her side, and for an instant, she could have sworn torment flashed on his face. But then the expression was gone. He was big, strong, naked, *aroused,* and suddenly staring at her with cold eyes.

What in the hell?

"The tracker is a trick that the Lazarus lab coats like to use. They put the trackers under the skin, in scars you already have. They're easier to hide that way."

The water didn't feel quite so warm any longer.

"You originally had a Lazarus tracker in you, but then either you cut it out, or someone else did. That's why the lab coats needed me to find you. They couldn't locate you on their own." His eyes held her captive. "But that doesn't mean the dicks who had you in that godforsaken hospital didn't tag you, too. You could have one of their trackers beneath your skin."

"It...makes me sound like an animal."

His lips thinned. "A tracker would explain how they found us at the cabin. And if they've got one on you, *in* you, then they'll be busting in here at any moment. If we run and you're tagged, they'll find you, wherever you go."

Their bodies were almost touching. The shower was small, and he was way too big. Her nipples were tight and thrusting toward him, and the water snaked down her body. "How do we find out if I'm tagged? I mean, if I've got one of those trackers in me?"

His fingers were sliding over her scar. "We need to scan your body. If it's there, we have to cut it out."

Wonderful. "How do I get scanned?"

"Usually, we'd need something like an X-ray machine."

Not like there was one of those just stashed in the motel room closet. "If I do have this tracker in me, I'll be leading the bad guys right to me, wherever we go."

"Yes."

He wasn't pulling punches. "So I need to go to a hospital? Won't the doctors get suspicious if they see a-a tracker inside of me?"

His shoulders rolled. "No other option. If you've got a tracker in you, we have to get it out."

The guys who'd kidnapped her could be bursting in the door any moment, and she didn't exactly relish the idea of going to a hospital—like, *ever* again. Luna cleared her throat. "You're blocking my way." He was a wall of pure muscle standing between her and the shower's exit.

His breath heaved out. The water glistened on his chest. Rolled down his rock-hard abs, down, down to the heavy length of his cock that thrust right toward her.

Oh, damn.

He angled his body a bit to the side, making room for her to exit. He was turned on, turned on very, uh, hard. So why wasn't he saying something?

She brushed by him, but stopped. "I don't get you." Anger hummed through her. "Are you the one-and-done kind or something—"

Luna didn't get to finish. In a flash, he'd pinned her to the tile wall of that shower. "Never done." His eyes weren't cold now. They *burned.* "Not with you. And I don't give a fuck about any bastard from your past."

Wait, *what?*

His hands tightened on her. "You're *mine*, and I'm not going back." His mouth crashed down on hers. The kiss was fierce, hot, and absolutely consuming.

She sank her fingers into his hair. Held tight. Yearned. And wanted—

His mouth tore from hers. *"We don't have time. Fucking hell."*

She was panting. So was he.

"I want you, Luna. Never doubt that. But your safety comes first." He backed away, as much as the shower would allow. "So get that gorgeous ass out of here. Get dressed. We'll steal a ride and find another safe place to land." His eyes gleamed. "Then I will have you again."

She didn't understand him. Desire was heavy within her. Her breasts ached, and all she wanted was to jump the guy but…

Danger. Tracker. Evil guys closing in.

She slipped from the shower. Wrapped a towel around her body. She could feel his gaze on her with every movement that she made. Her shoulders hunched a bit as she hurried from the bathroom. Luna was sure that she was leaving a trail of water in her wake. Steam spilled into the motel room with her. Her gaze cut to the left, then to the right. His phone was on the table there, his phone and…

Right. A knife. Because, of course, the guy would have been armed with a knife. He'd probably had it strapped to the inside of his ankle or hidden in his boot. She hadn't exactly noticed him removing a knife when they'd been all hot and heavy earlier. Hell, maybe he'd even kept his boots on while they were having sex. She'd been a wee bit too involved to focus on details like that, but now she hurried toward the weapon.

Luna picked it up, holding the knife carefully. After drawing in a deep, bracing breath, her fingers slid down to her side, to the scar that marred her body. The only scar she'd found on herself. If trackers were hidden in scars, this was the most likely place for one on her. Her fingers slid over the small ridges, searching for any spot that felt rougher, thicker. Her eyes narrowed. That one spot...right *there*.

Was a tracker under her skin?

One way to find out.

Luna clenched her back teeth, and she let the blade sink into her skin.

CHAPTER SEVEN

Blood. Luna's blood. The coppery scent hit Maddox's nose, and he let out an enraged bellow. He leapt from the shower and raced into the motel room, his fists clenched and death in his heart. He would destroy—

"I-I think I got it." Blood dripped down her hip. She held a knife—his knife—in her right hand, and her left was pushing against her side. "It was in the scar, just like you said. No need for the…hospital now."

Fucking hell. She'd just carved herself open. He bounded to her. Took the knife. Threw the damn thing. "Luna."

She gave him a smile. A *smile.* And his chest burned. "It's okay." She seemed to be attempting to reassure him. "Just a scratch."

No, it fucking wasn't okay. And it wasn't a scratch.

"I…can you help me? I-I feel something in there."

His gaze dropped to her wound. Her blood-covered fingertips were sliding over her skin. His body trembled for a moment. Fury and fear clawed through him.

She shouldn't hurt.

"Get it out," Luna whispered. "Please."

He hadn't wanted to do this. He should have kept his mouth shut in the shower. He'd planned to check her near Aspen, then if she'd had a tracker, he would have put her under while it was removed. But...

Shit. "Yeah, baby," he fought to keep his voice gentle, "I'll get it out." His fingers slid over hers. He pushed against the slice she'd made on her skin. The trackers were never hidden too deep. He pressed down, and she sucked in a fast breath. Then...

The tracker slipped into his hand. It was half the size of Luna's pinky fingernail. He dropped the blood-covered tracker and smashed it beneath his bare foot.

"They know where I am." Her eyes were wide. "I thought I was being so smart by ditching the SUV. But they know..."

Someone knew. At this point, he wasn't sure who all they were dealing with. Just how many people were out there gunning for Luna?

"We need to go," Luna said as another long, fat drop of blood slid down her side.

He looked at his fingers. Luna's blood was on his hands. "Yes," Maddox bit out. "We do." But first he was going to clean her up. Get rid of the blood. Luna healed fast, faster than any super soldier he knew, so the wound would close on its own.

"You're angry with me."

It wasn't anger. "Baby, I fucking hate when you hurt."

Her eyes widened.

He pressed a kiss to her cheek. "If I had my way, you'd never know pain again."

***

They came upon the police car an hour after they'd left the motel. Maddox had stolen a pick-up truck. One with good tires and four-wheel drive. He'd taken the liberty of switching tags with another vehicle, a tactic to buy him a little more time.

They'd ridden in silence as the dark miles had passed by. Luna hadn't spoken, and he hadn't known what in the hell to say to her.

Then he saw the police lights up ahead. Maddox stiffened as the swirling blue lights lit up the road. "Shit."

Luna leaned forward. "I think there's been an accident."

At first, he'd worried they might have stumbled right into a road block, but he could see the patrol car was positioned on the side of the road. Another vehicle was there, an older, four-door car that had flipped onto its roof. As they drew closer to the crash, a woman appeared. She was on the side of the road, her body shuddering. "Help me! Help me!"

"Maddox…" Luna whispered.

"The cops are there." One patrol car, but he saw two officers trying to open the back door of the overturned vehicle. "They'll help her."

Luna rolled down the window. "I smell gasoline."

The woman had already whirled away from the road and raced back to the wreck.

"Someone is in the back of that car." Luna's voice was still quiet. "Trapped."

He'd slowed down the truck while he neared the patrol car's bright lights. No one else was around. Just a long stretch of road.

"The cops can't open the door," Luna said.

He could see them struggling, and Maddox knew what Luna was going to say even before—

"But we can," she added.

He slammed on the brakes. Shit. Shit! "*Stay here.*" Maddox jumped from the truck even as he heard Luna's soft voice calmly reply—

"No."

She slid out of the truck, too. And he growled at her as they hurried toward the wreck. The woman he'd seen before spun toward him. Tear tracks covered her face. She grabbed Maddox's arm. "My son is in the back! We can't get the door open!"

"Get back!" One of the uniformed cops barked at the same instant. A young, fresh-faced guy, with wind-tossed, dark hair. "The car is gonna blow. Don't need anyone else gettin—"

The mother had let out a sharp cry when he said *blow.* She rushed back to the vehicle, pounding on the rear passenger door. Screaming for her son.

Maddox's gaze flew over the scene. The front windshield was smashed. He was betting the mom had crawled out that way. The driver side door looked like a fucking accordion. The vehicle must have rolled several times before it stopped, and the doors were all hammered in and twisted. His nostrils flared as the scent of gasoline grew stronger.

The cop was right. The vehicle was going to blow.

He lunged forward. Grabbed the back door. "*Clear out, now!*" Maddox bellowed. And he yanked that rear door away with a fierce burst of strength. The metal shrieked as it tore loose, and he grabbed for the kid still in his booster seat. A little boy, one who was bleeding from his temple. A boy with red hair and pale skin. A boy who appeared to be barely four or five years old.

A boy who wasn't moving.

He snatched the boy out of the vehicle and ran, even as the car erupted behind him. The flames lanced over his skin, and he hurtled forward, but he made sure to keep a protective grip on the kid. Maddox slammed into the ground, but he rolled his body, curling around the child.

"Saul! Saul!" The mom shrieked her son's name as she rushed at Maddox.

Maddox carefully positioned the boy on the ground. "Get an ambulance," he ordered the cops. "*Now!*"

"Already on the way," the cop to the right said. The younger cop. The one who was staring down at the child with fear etched onto his face.

The other uniformed cop had dropped to his feet near the child. The guy was older, with a grizzled jaw. His hands went to the boy's throat. Seconds later, the cop's terrified gaze flew back to Maddox.

He'd already known, though, that the cop wouldn't find a pulse. Maddox hadn't heard the kid's heart beating.

"Saul?" The mom was trying to fight her way to him, but the younger cop was holding her back. "Saul, open your eyes! Saul, it's mommy!"

The older cop—face lined and grim—began CPR.

CPR wasn't going to help.

Luna slipped closer. She dropped to her knees before the boy. "He's not moving."

"I fell asleep—just for a second!" The mother's voice rang out, so desperate and ragged. "We'd been driving all day. I thought…oh, God, oh, God, I thought I could make it to the next exit, and we'd get a room, and it was so dark and I just—*Saul!*" Her pain-filled cry cut through the night. Maddox looked back in time to see the mom fall to her knees.

"What's wrong with him?" Luna asked. "I don't…I only see the blood on his temple." And her hand reached out to the boy.

"Luna!" Maddox snarled her name, but it was too late.

He'd seen this happen before.

Luna's whole body jolted when her fingers touched the child. Her eyes flared wide, and a low, keening cry escaped her.

Maddox tried to jerk her hand away from the little boy, but Luna was strong. So much stronger than most people realized.

"I can fix him," Luna said, and her voice was different. Ragged. Whispery. And Maddox knew she was already working on the little boy.

That was Luna's talent. Her psychic bonus that had come from Lazarus. She could heal.

But she couldn't bring back the *dead.*

"Luna, no," his hands closed around her shoulders, "he's—"

The cop who'd been doing the CPR jerked back.

The kid coughed.

Luna put her hands on the boy's head. "It's all up here." Her hands slid to his neck. "So much pain." She shuddered.

"What in the hell is she doing?" The grizzled cop demanded. He, too, reached for Luna. "What—Jesus Christ, she's burning up!"

Luna got hotter when she healed. Her body heated up.

"Get the cop away," Luna spoke with that whispery voice again. "The boy…he needs more…"

The cop looked up at Maddox. The fellow's hand went to his gun.

Maddox just snatched the weapon from him. "We aren't here to hurt anyone." His voice was flat. Low. "That kid isn't going to survive unless you let my friend work on him."

But the cop lunged toward him. Maddox touched the guy's chest, and the older cop fell, right there, crumpling on the ground.

The mother screamed again. Maddox whirled and saw the second cop was rushing at him.

Another touch.

The officer hit the ground.

The mother stood there, eyes wide and stark, her body trembling. The car burned behind her. And…

"M-mommy?" The little boy's quiet whimper.

Maddox looked back at the child. At Luna.

She pulled her hands away from the boy, and he sat up, his movements sluggish.

"Mommy?" A weak cry.

Luna rose, staggered a little, but stepped away from the kid.

The mother ran to her boy, scooping him into her arms as she cried.

Maddox glanced around the scene. One burning car. Two unconscious cops. And a boy that was gonna live. He tilted his head, and, in the distance, he could hear the sound of an ambulance's wailing siren.

He hurried to Luna. Swept her into his arms and didn't break stride as he rushed them back to the truck.

"Wait…" Luna's fingers grabbed his arm. "We can't…l-leave them. They need—"

He tucked her into the truck. Pulled the seatbelt across her chest. "He's okay. You fixed him, baby. But now we have to haul ass." His fingers slid under her chin as he tipped back her head. Her pupils were the size of pinpricks, and her skin was way too hot. "You're gonna crash, and crash hard, but I'll take care of you."

Her lashes drifted shut, but she blinked, jerking them open as she swayed in her seat. "Maddox?"

"I'll take care of you," he said again, knowing she didn't have long. "Trust me."

Her eyes sagged closed once more even as a low whisper slipped from her. "C-can't..."

Maddox stiffened. "Why not, baby?"

Her breath fluttered out. "You...scare me."

***

Maddox pulled the covers up to Luna's chest. His fingers slid over her forehead. She was still warm, but no longer blazing hot. She'd been out for the ride to the safe house just outside of Aspen. Luna hadn't stirred at all when he carried her inside. How much longer would it be before she opened her dark eyes and stared at him?

You...scare me.

Jaw locking, he turned from the bed — and found Jett propped up against the doorframe. He'd known the other guy was there, of course, and it was time to lay all of his cards on the table.

He didn't speak as he shouldered past Jett. Instead, Maddox stalked into the hallway, climbed down the staircase, and marched straight for the refrigerator. The place was kept well stocked, and ice-cold beers were inside the fridge. He grabbed one and downed it fast.

"Must have been some pretty bad injuries," Jett murmured from behind him. "If our girl is still out after all this time."

He rolled back his shoulders. "The kid's neck had snapped." He'd seen the unnatural angle in the car. "He wasn't breathing. Wasn't moving. A cop was trying CPR, and Luna—"

"Luna did the rest." Jett sauntered toward the fridge. Grabbed himself a beer. Saluted him. "You told her what she could do, so at the first opportunity, the woman was obviously going to use her talents on the kid."

"I didn't tell her that she could heal. I didn't tell her a damn thing about that."

A furrow appeared between Jett's brows.

"She just reached for the boy and did it."

Jett shook his head. "Guess some things can't be forgotten."

Maddox slammed the empty beer bottle down on the counter. "It's too freaking dangerous for her. You know it. I know it. If she tries to bring back someone who has injuries that are too severe—shit, she takes that pain into herself." She burned through the pain. That was what she'd told him, once, when he'd held her as she shuddered. *"Have to burn it off, then I'll be better."*

"You didn't want her to realize what she could do." Jett took a long drag from the beer. "Keeping secrets is some shady business. Especially with her."

"She's *died* healing civilians before." He glared at Jett. "She died healing you before."

"She comes back," Jett muttered.

"And loses every damn memory she formed! She loses herself, over and over again. Am I supposed to just sit back and watch it happen? We got lucky with that kid tonight. She healed him without killing herself. But it was a near fucking thing." He spun on his heel and paced to the window.

"Just take a breath." Jett's voice was low. Soothing. Like that shit was going to work with Maddox. "She's okay. The kid—according to what you told me—is okay, too. Happy endings all around."

This wasn't a happy ending. He closed his eyes. Blew out a hard breath. "She…did something to me."

"Yeah, man, I noticed. That woman has you all tied up in knots. I mean, I get that you were hot for her before, but this is like times ten level shit."

Maddox whirled to face him.

"You fucked her, didn't you?" Jett gave him a pitying glance. "I told you that was a bad plan. You know the subjects aren't supposed to be together that way. It's dangerous. That's what all the docs say. We can't—"

"I had memories." Maddox's flat announcement cut through Jett's words.

Jett put down his beer. Suddenly, his gaze was very sharp. "Want to run that by me again?"

"I had memories. Two flashes that I *think* were from my life before Lazarus."

Jett bounded toward him. "Don't you bullshit with me about that."

"I had the flashes come—each time—when Luna was touching me." No coincidence. "And her hands were hot. The way they get when she's healing someone."

Jett didn't say a word. Silence from Jett was unusual. It was also a bad sign.

"Tell me that I imagined it," Maddox finally snapped at him. "Tell me there is no way…" But his words drifted away.

"There's no way the woman could have shown your past to you?" Jett's Adam's apple bobbed. "Maybe she could have, though. She heals, we both know that. Our memories are gone, so that means our minds have to be damaged in some way. Maybe when she touched you, she was healing you. And the memories you'd lost came rushing back." His lip curled. "You lucky sonofabitch."

Maddox unclenched his jaw.

"What did you see?" Jett demanded. "Tell me."

"A beach." He swallowed. "I was standing on a beach." His eyes narrowed. "Gulf Shores." The name had come to him in that flash or memory or whatever the hell it had been. "The sand was like freaking sugar. White and soft, and

I was staring out at the waves." *Right before a blond asshole told me that he was marrying Luna.*

"And in the other flash?"

"I think I was dying. I got shot. And the wounds match up with the scars I carry."

"Holy hell." Jett rocked back on his heels. "What if she can give it all back to us? Every single thing that we've lost?" His head turned as he glanced toward the stairs. "She's been with us for months, and we didn't know what she could do. We could have gotten it all back!" What could have been anger sharpened his voice. His gaze flew back to Maddox. "You think the doctors knew?"

Maddox swiped his hand over his jaw, feeling the rasp of the stubble there. "I'm not sure. At this point, I can't even be certain she is restoring my memories. Maybe it was a fluke or something."

"One way to find out." Jett squared his shoulders. "Let's see what happens when she touches *me*." He bounded for the stairs.

But Maddox beat him. Maddox had always been a little faster. He put his body right in front of the staircase. "She's unconscious."

Jett lifted his brows. "Bullshit. We both hear her stirring right now."

Maddox did hear the soft rustle of covers.

"She's gonna be exhausted." Maddox didn't move. "You know what it's like for her when she first comes off a healing. She needs time to get her strength back."

Jett stepped forward, moving toe-to-toe with Maddox. "I have *nothing*," Jett gritted out. "No whisper of a memory. No dreams that come to me. My life before Lazarus is nothing but darkness. And now you're telling me…you're telling me that woman upstairs might be able to give me my life back?"

"I don't know what she can do."

Jett shook his head. "You told me all this because you *want* to know. You want to test her. You want to see if I have the same reaction."

Yes, he did. "It could be why Lazarus wants her dead."

Jett's brow furrowed.

"We're the government's perfect weapons because we have no ties to our past. No families that can look for us." He paused. "That *we* can look for. If our memories come back, all of that changes."

"Termination," Jett whispered.

They both heard the creak of wood from upstairs. The soft pad of footsteps.

Jett's gaze rose. "She's coming to us." His hands flexed at his sides.

"I'm talking to her first." Maddox locked his muscles. "Alone."

Tension rolled from Jett. "Fine, man, fine." His breath was ragged. "But, shit, don't leave me hanging too long, okay?"

He wouldn't. Maddox gave a jerky nod and turned to climb the stairs.

CHAPTER EIGHT

Luna opened the door, and she found Maddox standing right in front of her. Big, strong, *angry*-looking Maddox.

Her hands went to her hips as a sigh escaped her. "Okay. What's got you pissed now?"

He stepped toward her. She didn't back up. She'd woken in the bed, her body heavy with lethargy, and she'd glanced around, wondering where in the hell she was.

Then she'd remembered the car accident. The kid…

"You used too much energy." His words definitely held an angry edge. "You could have *died*."

Now she shrugged. "I just would have come back." Flippant words that she didn't really mean.

His gaze hardened even more. "Then you would have lost it all again. You would have lost *me*. You wouldn't know that we'd been lovers. You would stare at me like I was a stranger."

Her heartbeat kicked up. "I didn't die."

His hands closed around her shoulders.

"And *you* didn't tell me the truth." Her own anger was there, pulsing just beneath her skin. "I thought you were being straight with me. I mean, I'm giving you everything that I have, and you're holding back on me. That crap doesn't seem fair."

A muscle jerked in his clenched jaw.

"I healed that kid." She'd *felt* him mending beneath her touch. "Is that my psychic power? I heal people? Because don't you think that would have been something important to tell me?"

His hold tightened. "When you heal, *you* take the pain. You pull it into yourself. And you take too much. You won't stop, not if you think you can help someone. I've watched you kill yourself trying to save people who were too far gone. An IED took out a woman in Kuwait, and you…shit, you died in my arms because you wouldn't give up on her. *You won't stop*," he said again, biting off the words. "I've had to pull you away from scenes—fighting and screaming—because you were going too far. You don't know your limits. And I just thought, if you didn't know, then you wouldn't *die* on me again."

Her breath cased out. The raw emotion coming from him battered her. She'd never seen him like this.

Or, hell, maybe she had, and Luna just didn't remember it.

"I'm the commander of this team. I protect the team members." He let her go. "I was protecting you, and hell, yes, if it meant keeping you safe, I'd do it all over again."

A fine tension swept through her. "You'd lie to me?"

He met her gaze without hesitation. "In an instant."

Her lips parted. Fine. She'd definitely put that tidbit in the *must-know* file.

"Keeping you safe is my main priority. No matter what."

"Are you…are you lying to me now?"

His gaze swept over her. She was still wearing the green sweater. The jeans. But someone had taken off her shoes and socks when she'd been put in the bed. Luna was willing to bet that someone had been him.

"Maddox." She said his name deliberately. "Are you lying to me now?"

His stare slowly rose to her face. His eyes seemed to singe her. Such a gorgeous emerald fire. "Let's find out." He reached for her hand, pulling her through the doorway.

But she jerked against his hold. "The kid —" Luna cleared her throat. "Tell me about the kid. He's okay, right? I helped him?" Before anything else happened, she needed to know this.

"You almost killed yourself."

"The boy," she pressed, her voice thick.

"He's okay."

She could finally draw in a deep breath. Luna felt a smile curl her lips.

"That's why," he rasped.

She didn't know what he meant.

"That's why I lied. Because if you could, you'd save every person you saw. You'd save them until nothing was left of yourself. I can't let you do that. Someone has to keep you safe."

"And you're that someone?" Since when was Maddox her keeper?

"I'm in charge of—"

"Is that all I am? One of your team members?" Now she was the one to lean closer to him. To let her body press to his. "Because when you were inside of me, I thought we were lovers."

His pupils expanded. His gaze was so wild and dangerous.

She pulled from him and headed down the stairs. Her breath was coming a little fast and hard when she reached the first floor. Jett was standing near the fire, his broad back to her. "Guess the team's back together," she murmured.

He turned toward her. A careful mask covered his expression.

Luna instantly went on high alert.

The stairs groaned behind her as Maddox slowly descended.

"Any food around here?" Luna asked, turning her head to sweep her gaze over the place. "I'm starving." She realized that she had no idea when she'd last eaten. Absolutely none.

Things had been moving at super speed for her. She'd been rescued from that freaky hospital, she'd gone with Maddox, she'd *fucked* Maddox, she'd escaped a fire and—

"Got food waiting in the kitchen for you," Maddox told her. "Pineapple pizza."

She glanced toward him, her nose scrunching up.

His face softened, for just a moment. "It's your favorite, I promise."

Because he knew her better than she knew herself. That was…disconcerting. Without another word, she went into the kitchen. She found the box in the fridge, found some wine, too. Luna helped herself because, dammit, she figured she more than deserved some wine.

She hesitated with the pizza, but then she took a bite. The flavor was so good that she almost moaned. Her eyes closed and she just—

"Told you," Maddox drawled. "Your favorite."

Her eyes opened. She swallowed. Took another bite. He'd grabbed a plate for her and put it near the counter. She hopped up on the barstool and ate in silence for a few moments. Jett grabbed a beer from the fridge and downed it.

Then he crossed his arms over his chest, and his dark gaze slid from her to Maddox.

She ate four pieces of pizza before her gnawing hunger finally eased.

"Always like that for you," Maddox said with an incline of his head, "after you heal someone. You burn so much energy, you have to sleep and eat to get back up to your usual speed."

Her fingers curled around the wine glass. He'd poured more for her, but she hadn't seen him drink any. "It's…it makes me feel weird, that you know more about me than I know about myself."

Jett gave a low laugh. "Maddox is an expert on all things Luna."

Maddox cut him a hard glare. "*Jett.*" A definite warning edge.

Jett lifted up his hands. "Sorry. I just meant, he learns everything he can about his team members. Part of the job when you're the leader."

And there they were…back to her being part of the team. She didn't think Maddox had the same relationship with the rest of the *team* members that he had with her. "Who else is on the team?"

"We're core," Jett said, answering before Maddox could. "Then there's Andreas. The Greek is damn good at surveillance and infiltration. Josie's on the team sometimes, former sharpshooter, and—hell, the names don't mean a damn thing, do they? Our team is fluid. Can be just the three of us, can be as many as seven. Depends on the job we do."

"What sort of jobs do we, uh, take?"

"The kind that no one else can handle." Maddox's gaze was unwavering.

"The kind that normal folks don't expect to come back from," Jett added grimly. "And that's why they send in a team who can rise from the dead."

A shiver slid over her. "Don't think I'll ever get used to that part." She took a long sip of wine. Put the glass down. Flattened her hands on the bar top. "And I volunteered for this? To give up everything I'd had before? To take this new life?"

"That's what the lab coats say." Jett lifted one shoulder. "Course, not like we remember volunteering." He stalked closer to her. "Not like any of us can remember anything before we were given the Lazarus serum."

The tension in the kitchen had shot up. She glanced from Jett to Maddox, wondering about what was happening. She felt rather like prey that had just been caught between two dangerous hunters. She pushed away her plate. "What's happening?"

"We need to do a little…experiment," Jett explained, pausing only a bit.

She jumped to her feet. "I'm not really in the mood to be someone's experiment."

Maddox caught her hand. His fingers slid along her inner wrist, right over her racing pulse. "No one is going to hurt you, Luna. I promise." He rose, his body brushing against her. His warmth seemed to slide over her. "Something has happened to me — twice — when we touch." Once more, his fingers trailed up near her pulse. "I've had flashes. Memories."

She backed up a step. "What?"

"Never happened before," he murmured. "But then, I don't think you were trying to heal me before."

"I haven't tried to heal you at all!"

He raised her hand to his chest. "I don't think you realized what you were doing. Your hands heat up when you heal, and I could feel the heat against me."

"They…they heated when I was touching the little boy." Her hands had actually felt as if they were on fire.

Maddox nodded. "Right. You focus your energy, and you work your magic, baby."

Baby.

Jett cleared his throat. "We want to see if you can do that on me."

Her head whipped toward him.

"We want to see if I have a flash of my past, too. Maddox there, he thinks you might be healing our brains, restoring the memories. If you are…" A small shrug. "That fucking changes the game."

She didn't think she was playing a game.

"Rest more first," Maddox said, his words definitely an order. "You always need more recovery time after a healing. And with what you did for that boy—"

"I feel fine." She did. She'd eaten. She'd slept—Luna had no idea how long she'd slept. But she wasn't tired, and her mind was spinning. "If I've worked with you both before, wouldn't you have known I could do this? I mean—" Hell, she wasn't even sure what she meant.

"You healed me when I took two bullets to the chest once," Maddox told her quietly. "If I'd died on that field, the civilians we were there to rescue wouldn't have gotten free. You saved me, you healed my body, but I didn't have any memories come back to me." He seemed to consider the matter. "Maybe you were just working on the physical wounds you saw. Or maybe your power has gotten stronger. I know that I can focus my energy more, that I can take down more targets than I used to be able to handle in the early days."

"Or maybe I can't restore memories." A laugh escaped her. One that felt a little wild. "I mean, wouldn't I heal myself if I could? I'm the one who loses her memory with every rising!"

Maddox and Jett shared a long, silent look.

"Screw it," Luna muttered. There was one way to settle this. She surged toward Jett. Put her hands on either side of his head. Focused with all of her energy. If it was really that easy, if she just had to call up that heat that she'd used before on the boy...

I can do this.

She felt her hands begin to tingle. The heat spread slowly from her wrist down to her fingertips. Her head tipped back as she peered up at Jett's eyes. She didn't see any change of expression on his face, and she could feel Maddox easing closer behind her.

The moments ticked by. "Anything?" Luna whispered. This wasn't going to work. Maddox was wrong.

But then something happened. Jett stiffened beneath her hands, and his gaze seemed to go blank. The same exact way that Maddox's had changed when she'd touched him in the motel room. Jett's lips parted and a hard groan escaped him.

"Jett?" Luna didn't move her hands away from him. She could feel her touch heating more, and a shudder slid over her body. She trembled.

"*Enough.*" Maddox yanked her back.

Jett closed his eyes. His head sagged forward.

"Did I hurt you?" Luna cried, worried. He'd paled, and a light film of sweat covered his body.

As she watched, Jett's hand flew out and grabbed hold of the nearby counter. "I saw…my mother."

Luna's heart pounded hard in her chest.

"She was in a hospital bed, dying. Tubes were connected to her, and she was holding my hand." His head whipped back. He stared at her with a gaze full of grief. "She said she was proud of me."

Her own chest ached because there was so much pain in his voice.

"Then the machines stopped beeping. She died, and I was holding her hand." He gave a hard shake of his head. "What in the fuck? Why did you show me something so painful?"

Maddox pushed Luna behind his body. "You *saw* the memory."

"I fucking felt it." Jett's words were guttural. "I felt my mother dying again. Shit, *shit.* You don't know what loss is. Don't know…then it comes at you. It rips you open." His breath heaved in and out. "I need to leave. Got to get some freaking air." He shouldered past Maddox. Made a beeline for the door. He didn't look at Luna, and she just stood there, with her hands wrapped around her stomach.

"I'm sorry." The low words broke from her.

Jett's shoulders stiffened, and he finally glanced her way. "She was proud of me," he mumbled. "Proud." Then he was gone. Jett rushed out of the cabin and slammed the door shut behind him.

Luna didn't move. "I hurt him." Her stare was on the floor.

"No, baby, you just gave him a damn amazing gift." He moved toward her with his slow, gliding stride. His hand slid under her chin, tipping back her head so that she had to meet his gaze. "When he calms down, Jett will realize that."

Luna wasn't so sure. She'd just forced him to see one of the worst moments of his life. His mother…

"We lost ourselves when we joined Lazarus. You can give us our past back. Luna, that is *huge*. A game-changer." His touch was so gentle.

Another shiver slid over her. "I didn't shake like this when I touched you in the motel."

He scooped her into his arms. Held her against his chest. "That's because you hadn't just healed a kid who'd been at death's door. I knew you needed more time before you went at Jett." He was carrying her back through the cabin. Holding her while he climbed up the stairs. She put her head against his chest because she did feel weary. Bone deep. Soul deep.

Soon they were back in the bedroom. He put her on the mattress, eased her down like she was breakable.

But she wasn't, right? Wasn't that the point of Lazarus? He started to rise, but her hand flew out, and she grabbed his wrist. "The memories I made you see…" Luna cleared her throat. "Were they bad, like Jett's?"

He stared back at her. "I saw my death."

Her eyes widened. "I'm so sorry!"

He looked away. "You don't ever have any flashes of your life?"

"I don't even have flashes of last week."

His gaze shot back to her. Luna tried to smile at him. "I was…attempting to lighten the mood."

"You *don't* remember last week."

No. Her smile vanished as she felt very foolish. "You do, though." They were sitting on the bed together. His warmth was reaching out to her. "Tell me what happened last week."

Maddox swallowed. "We were training at the Lazarus facility. Doing our normal exercises. Pushing our limits."

"What does the facility look like?"

"It's a huge place. State of the art. Only the best for Uncle Sam."

There was something about his voice… "Maddox?" Luna prompted.

"We're watched, twenty-four seven. And we're kept separated in rooms that we aren't supposed to be able to escape, not even with our enhanced strength."

Her stomach twisted into thick knots. The pizza suddenly wasn't sitting so well. "I thought we'd volunteered."

"And once we did, it seems we sold our souls away. We don't make a move without the lab coats knowing about it." He seemed to make some sort of decision. "There's something you need to hear, baby."

He was making her feel even more nervous.

"I'm not taking you back to the facility. I'm not *ever* taking you back there. Because if you go back, they'll kill you."

A dull ringing filled her ears. "What?"

He stared straight in her eyes. "You're under termination orders, Luna. If you step foot inside the Lazarus facility again, you'll die, and you won't come back from the dead."

***

Jett rushed away from the safe house. He'd jumped in his ride and hauled ass as fast as he could. And when he thought he was safe, when he thought he was far enough away...

He yanked out his phone and called his handler. The guy picked up on the second ring.

"Are they in position?" the guy asked in his cold, nasally voice. Henry fucking Danwith. The guy looked like a prick and sounded like one, too.

"No," Jett said quickly. "They aren't." He'd screwed up, and he had to fix this thing, now. "Maddox wasn't at the safe house. I have no idea where he and Luna are. They must have changed plans on me." His words were coming too fast. He needed to slow them the hell down.

Silence.

"Did you hear me?" Jett demanded. "They're not in the cabin near Aspen. I'll keep looking for them, and I'll update you as soon as—"

He heard a whistle, something shooting through the air. He jerked to the side even as the windshield in front of him shattered. *Sonofabitch!* The tranq missed him, lodging in the driver's seat. "What in the hell?" Jett snarled into his phone.

"We know they *are* here," Henry said, voice smug. "And you'll all be coming back to the facility immediately."

The hell he would. Jett sprang out of the vehicle.

And a barrage of tranqs fired at him.

CHAPTER NINE

Her eyes were so deep and dark. He could fucking get lost staring at her.

"They were going to terminate me?" Her voice was a husky whisper.

Shit. He crowded closer to her as they sat on the bed. "That's what you told me, the night you vanished. You and I—we were communicating telepathically."

Her eyes widened. "Do we do that a lot?"

She'd often reached for his mind, in the middle of the night. And he'd felt her, as if she'd been right in front of him. "Yes." *Tread carefully.*

"And I told you I was going to be killed?"

"You said they were coming to terminate you. I tried to get to you, I swear I did, but they tranqed me." His rage had overwhelmed him. Rage and a cold fear. He'd been desperate to get to Luna. He should have thought things through. Planned his attack better. If he'd kept his cool, he could have used his psychic power to take out those bastards who'd stormed at him. But his control had been shattered. He'd been like some kind of wild beast. The guards had swarmed after he'd burst out of his cell. He'd taken two men down, sending them crashing to the floor, but the other guards had kept coming. The tranqs had taken him out, and he'd lost her. No, he'd *failed* her.

He wouldn't make the same mistake again.

"I think they knew what you could do." It was the only thing that made sense to Maddox. "They found out that you can give us our memories back."

"Why would it be so bad to have them back? Bad enough that they want to kill me?"

"They won't. I swear it." He wouldn't let that happen.

She bit her lower lip. His body immediately tensed because his gaze dropped to her mouth. Such a sexy mouth. *She* was sexy. Luna had starred in more fantasies than he could count. And, now, the fact that he'd known her before Lazarus…

What happened back then?
Why the hell did I have the knife on me?

He'd stabbed the blond. The man who planned to marry Luna. Maddox knew that shit. The weight was cold in his gut. After Maddox had stabbed him, the blond guy had fired those fatal shots.

He killed me.
And Luna.

Darkness stretched inside of Maddox. A fury that consumed. For an instant, the scene changed. He could feel Luna in his arms, smell her blood, see her falling...

"Why do you look that way?"

He blinked.

"You looked...like you could kill."

He could. He had. But not her. Not—

I've been obsessed with her since I woke up in the Lazarus facility.

Maddox let out a slow breath. "You should rest. We both should." He'd driven for hours to get them to this safe house. "We'll make a plan when we wake up, okay? I'm thinking we'll head to Canada." He slid from the bed. "Start fresh there."

Her hand caught his. "Will you stay with me?"

"I'm not just going to send you off to Canada on your own—"

Luna shook her head. "No. Right now. Will you stay with me, right now?"

His chest ached. So did his cock. "Probably not a good idea." A very, very bad idea.

"Why?" Her hair slid over her shoulder as Luna stared up at him.

"Because you need rest. You don't need me to fuck you." There. Couldn't get more honest and brutal of a truth than that.

But she smiled. *Smiled.* "How do you know what I need?"

Oh, sweet hell. She liked to play with fire. "Luna…"

"Everything in my world is insane. Nothing makes sense to me. The only time I stop being scared and stop feeling like I am absolutely lost…it's when we're making love."

He tried again, "Luna…"

"So, yes, I do need you to fuck me. I'd like it very much."

Was he supposed to be able to walk away after those words? His dick shoved against the front of his jeans, and he wanted to pounce on her. To take and take until the past and any memories there—they didn't matter. Maybe the past was better dead and buried. Maybe he and Luna could just go the hell forward.

She didn't need to know about his sins.

"How about we just start with a kiss?" Luna asked.

Her voice was sexy, husky, sweet. Maddox found himself leaning over the bed. He put his hands on either side of her, and he lowered his head until their mouths were just inches apart. "*Kiss me, Maddox.*"

It was her voice, but she hadn't spoken, not out loud. She'd used the mental communication link they'd shared so often in the past. A link that he'd missed with her. Her mental touch seemed to slide through his whole body. His mouth took hers in a hot, open-mouthed kiss. His tongue stroked against hers. Her taste drove him crazy, made him desperate for so much more. And she still had the mental link open between them. It was as if she'd lowered a barrier in her mind, and Luna was wide open to him.

As he kissed her, he could feel her need. Her hunger. He pulled away from Luna just long enough to yank her sweater over her head, and he dropped it to the floor. He unhooked her bra. Sent it flying someplace, and then his hands were on her breasts. Teasing her tight little nipples, caressing her. Kissing her because he loved her taste. He liked the way she moaned into his mouth. Loved the way she arched against him.

And this…this was different. Having her mind open to him. She wasn't holding any part of herself back from him. She loved what he was doing to her. The desire she felt was real and hot, rising and surging more with every touch.

His hand slid down her stomach. He touched her through the jeans. She'd jerked up to her knees on the bed so that she could put her hands on him, so that they could reach each other easier. He pushed his fingers against the crotch of her jeans. She rocked her hips back against him.

This is wrong. I should stop —

"Nothing is wrong," Luna whispered, obviously picking up on his thoughts because the link between them was so strong. "Nothing that feels this good can be wrong."

He closed his mind to her. Shut down fast because she didn't know what he'd been holding back from her, and Maddox couldn't risk her finding out the truth. Not then.

But she gave a little gasp and pulled back. Her nails bit into his shoulders. "You left me."

And he missed the link, too. Missed the way that she'd burned right through him.

"I want it back," Luna said. "I wasn't alone."

"Baby, you'll never be alone." He tumbled her onto the bed. Managed to yank off her jeans. Lost her panties with them. He kissed his way down her stomach. Fucking perfect Luna. Moaning and arching beneath his touch.

His Luna.

I don't care what the sonofabitch in my past said.

He parted her thighs. Stroked her clit. Got ready to taste what he'd wanted for so long—

The growl of an engine reached him. Maddox's shoulders stiffened.

Luna moaned.

He wanted to put his mouth on her. Fucking heaven was waiting right there but—

A rustle of sound. Sound that didn't belong. Footsteps? "Someone is outside," he snarled.

Luna's breath heaved out.

His instincts were screaming at him. "Baby, baby, stay right here." Leaving her was hell, but protecting her was his priority. He pulled away from the bed.

"Maddox?"

He hurried for the door. "I hear something…"

"Probably Jett coming back." Her words tumbled out.

No, he didn't think so, because Maddox could have sworn that he'd heard more than one person's footsteps. But now there was only silence.

"I don't hear anything," Luna whispered.

He glanced back at her. She'd pulled on her green sweater. She stared at him with her wide eyes, her flushed cheeks, and her red lips — lips red and swollen from his mouth.

He wanted to return to that bed. To put his mouth all over her. But they had enemies, and he knew someone was outside.

"I cut out the tracker." Luna's hand went to her side. The wound had healed. "They couldn't have found me."

Maybe. But he had to be sure.

His phone vibrated. The phone he'd forgotten was even in his pocket. Maddox yanked it out, staring at the screen. A text from Jett had just appeared.

Come outside. Big fucking problem.

Maddox narrowed his eyes. He didn't text back. Instead, he sent out a fast, psychic message—one that he targeted right to Jett. *"Why the hell are you texting? Too lazy to talk this way?"*

Maddox waited, but…nothing.

The phone vibrated in his hand again. *I'm right outside. Shit. I don't want Luna hearing this. We can't trust her.*

"What's happening?" Luna asked.

He could still taste her on his mouth. Maddox crept toward the window. Glanced out. Sure enough, the vehicle Jett had used earlier was outside. He could even see Jett in the driver's seat, his body slumped down low. "Something bad."

She jumped from the bed. Grabbed her panties and her jeans and hauled them on. "Maddox?" Luna shoved on her shoes.

Jett should have been communicating with him psychically. The fact that the guy wasn't— *bad.* Very bad. "We've got company," Maddox told her grimly.

Luna nodded. She squared her delicate shoulders.

He caught the rustle of more movement. Knew the place was being surrounded. But how, *how* had he and Luna been located so quickly? "We've got to go." Out the back. They'd run as fast as they could. And he'd take out anyone in their way.

The unit outside was assembling quickly. He could hear them coming. Closing in. More vehicles were rushing to the scene. And a chopper's blades beat in the distance.

Sonofabitch.

He caught Luna's hand. "Come on." He had weapons downstairs. They'd get armed, and then they'd get out.

They raced down the stairs. He went into the den and hurriedly opened the trunk that he'd used as a weapons storage area. Armed, ready, they rushed for the back door. He yanked it open, heading out first—

"Good job, Agent Kane."

A tall, brown-haired man with pale features stood in front of armed men. Maddox instantly recognized the speaker. Dr. Henry Danwith. The doc who led the group of lab coats at the Lazarus facility.

"You found her." Henry smiled broadly, revealing his perfectly white, perfectly capped teeth. His hair had been slicked back away from his forehead. "I knew you would. When Jett called to tell me that the mission had been a success, I couldn't have been more pleased."

Maddox lifted his gun. Aimed it at Henry. He counted easily two dozen men out there. And he *should* have heard those bastards. The very fact that he hadn't heard them assembling until it was too late told him that Andreas was there.

There was a reason Andreas was the super soldier so good at infiltration and surveillance.

The guy could cover the whisper of movements. Mute the approach of an enemy team. A talent very helpful in the field.

A talent that was a pain in Maddox's ass right then.

Because there were too many men for him to take out. Henry had come well prepared. Too prepared. And Maddox was betting that all of the guns currently aimed at him were loaded with tranqs.

If I attack, I'll take out some of them, but they'll tranq me. Their fingers would squeeze the triggers before he could knock them all out. There were just too many guards there. If he fought, Maddox had no doubt he'd wake up in a cell. And Luna...where the hell would she be then?

He'd freaked out before when she'd been threatened. Attacked first, then lost her. He had to think. And fast.

"*Trust me, Luna.*" He sent the message on their psychic link. Escape wasn't an option, not right then.

He felt her fingers on his back. "*Maddox, what's happening?*"

But Henry had just given a slight motion with his hand. A motion that Maddox understood because he'd seen the bastard give that same signal plenty of times. *Prepare for attack.* One wrong move, and all of those armed men would be firing.

"Finding her wasn't hard," Maddox called out as he stepped away from Luna. His gaze swept the men, looking for strengths. Weaknesses. *"Andreas, where the hell are you?"* He fired off the question on the telepathic link that should have linked him to Andreas.

But the guy didn't answer.

"You are the best hunter we have," Henry said, his hand frozen in the air. He hadn't given the signal to fire, not yet.

Maddox shrugged. "That I am." He turned his head toward Luna. "Sorry, but you need to go back to the facility. We have to find out what was done to you."

Her lips parted. Shock flashed on her face. "Maddox?"

He focused on Henry once more. "She doesn't remember anything, of course. Typical Luna. But someone's been dogging our steps. Someone who wants her very badly. There were signs they'd been experimenting on her, doing surgeries." He bit back the rage and kept his voice cool. "We need to figure out what's happening. Project Lazarus is being threatened."

Fear flashed on Henry's face. "What?"

"Let's go inside for a briefing," Maddox motioned back toward the cabin. He needed Henry to take a few steps away from all of the bastards with guns. "I'll tell you what I discovered."

But Henry's smile stretched. "Nice try, but you think I don't know?"

I think you don't know plenty.

"You weren't going to bring her back to me," Henry added with a sad shake of his head.

"Of course, I was." He could lie without hesitation. "I had to ditch the bastards after us, and then we were coming home." Like those cells were really home.

"Maddox?" Luna whispered. "They're still aiming all of their guns at us."

Yes, they were.

"You were going to keep Luna. You thought she was going to be all yours." Henry glanced away from Maddox, and his stare softened as it landed on Luna. "Luna, it's all right. You're safe now."

What the actual fuck?

"My men will tranq Maddox, and he won't be a threat to you any longer."

Oh, hell, no, that slimy bastard wasn't going to spin—

A sad sigh escaped Henry. "I'm very disappointed in you, Maddox. I thought you would put the team first. It's a good thing Jett understands the value of loyalty more than you do." His lips tightened. "You should have just brought her back, Maddox. It would have been so much easier."

"Screw easy," Maddox snapped.

"Maddox…" Luna's voice was high.

"Run, baby," he growled.

Henry's hand came down in a hard slash. The signal to fire. *Fuck.*

Maddox sent out a hard, psychic blast, an absolute wave that blew from his mind as he roared his rage. Ten men immediately fell. The closest ten.

The others — they fucking fired.

The tranqs slammed into him. And he heard Luna scream.

CHAPTER TEN

"Hold your fire!" The guy with the slicked back hair and chilling smile bellowed.

The men stopped firing.

Maddox had fallen to the ground, and Luna dropped to her knees beside him. She kept her right hand curled around her weapon, even as her left went to his chest. "Maddox?" He'd been hit at least five times, maybe six. But not with regular bullets.

Her hand pressed to his chest. She felt the tingles begin in her wrist. She could help him, heal him…

"Luna, step away from Agent Kane."

Her weapon immediately lifted and locked on the bastard.

His smile did *not* reassure her. "You don't remember me."

"I sure as shit don't." There were *so* many men there. Humans? Or Lazarus subjects like her?

"I'm Dr. Henry Danwith, and I'm here to help you."

"Your men just shot Maddox!" That wasn't helping her. Her fingers burned as she pressed them to Maddox's chest.

"Maddox was the immediate threat to you. I needed to take him down so that you'd be safe. I was afraid he'd try to take you away from me. I couldn't let that happen." His smile was gone. He took a step toward her. "I do not want to hurt you. I know Maddox may have fed you a different story about me, but I assure you, I am not a threat."

"Says the man who just had his men shoot Maddox over and over again."

Henry's face tensed. "Stop healing him. Now."

Her breath sawed from her lungs. "Or you'll shoot me, too?" She kept her hand on Maddox's chest.

A long sigh came from Henry. "If necessary, I will have to tranq you, but that isn't what I want."

From where she was crouching, it sure seemed to be what he wanted. All of those men still had their weapons pointed at her.

"He's brainwashed you. Only to be expected, really, since you had no memories to go on. But Maddox has been a threat to you for a very long time." Henry took another careful step toward her. "It's my fault. I didn't realize...I didn't know that the two of you had been connected before Lazarus."

Wait, *what*?

Maddox let out a low groan.

"We'll just tranq him again," Henry told her flatly. "It must be done for transport—and for your protection."

Her temples were pounding. "Maddox knew me before Lazarus?"

"Um, he didn't tell you that, did he?"

"He wouldn't know!" She threw back. "All of our memories are gone!" Anger beat in her. "Because of *you*!"

"Don't blame me," Henry fired right back. "You're the one who volunteered." His hand lifted. The men behind him seemed to tense. "I'm sorry, but if you won't listen to reason, I'll have to tranq you, too. It's necessary until you can calm down and talk rationally with me."

Reason? "Reason my ass," Luna snarled, and she lunged up.

The tranqs hit her, slamming into her chest, knocking her back. She'd expected the tranqs to burn, but they didn't. They felt like chunks of ice in her chest, and the cold slithered through her body.

Her knees gave way, and Luna crumpled, landing next to Maddox. As she fell, she saw his eyes open. His stare locked on her, and his lips parted.

"Maddox is back!" Henry yelled. "Subdue him, *now!* Andreas, get your ass over here!"

Andreas…that name was familiar…had Maddox or Jett mentioned him? Wait, yes, Jett had…part of their team…

Luna heard the sound of gunfire.

But she couldn't see anything. Her eyes had sagged shut, and the cold consumed her completely.

***

Her breath left her in a whoosh, and Luna jerked upright, sitting on the narrow cot as awareness flooded back to her. Her heart raced, and her gaze jumped frantically around the small room.

Stone walls on three sides…a mirrored wall right in front of her. *One-way mirror.* Because if she squinted just right, Luna could see through the glass. She could see a long, stretching corridor beyond her room.

Beyond her *cell.*

She jumped to her feet. Then Luna realized that her clothes were different. She wore jogging pants and a t-shirt. Her feet were bare. Frantic, she did a sweep of the room again. There was a dresser to her right. A desk to her left. A pile of books. Some clothes were discarded near a basket.

She whirled around and saw a small video camera positioned in the upper corner of her cell. A red light glowed from the bottom of that camera. "Where is Maddox?" Luna snarled.

Then she charged for the door. The only door in the damn room. There were no windows, just the one door that was located in the middle of all that stone. A big, metal door. And, of course, when she grabbed the handle, the door didn't open. She yanked it hard, pulling with all of her strength, but the door didn't budge. A scream broke from her as she turned her attention to the damn mirror. Her fists pounded against it. She'd break the glass. She'd get out of there. She'd —

"You're going to hurt yourself, Luna." A voice drifted down to her from speakers that she hadn't even noticed, not until that moment.

She pounded harder on the glass.

"It won't break." She knew the nasally voice — Henry Danwith's voice. The voice of the bastard who'd let those shooters fire at her. "There is no use trying to shatter the glass."

She spun to face a speaker positioned near the top of the right wall — and Luna spied the second camera right next to it. She knew he was watching her. "You locked me up."

"Only for your safety. I know how confused you are right now, and I needed you to wake in a safe space."

Bullshit. "I don't feel safe. I feel like your prisoner." *Termination.* Oh, God, was he about to kill her? She had to get out of there. Had to find Maddox, had to—

"Luna." Henry sighed her name. "I am not your enemy."

Again...*bullshit.* "If that's true, then get in here and talk with me face-to-face."

Silence. The red dot kept glowing on the camera. She whirled back to the glass. Drove her fists into it as hard as she could. Again and again and—

She saw him. Henry Danwith appeared in the long corridor beyond the glass. He wore a white lab coat that fluttered around him almost like a cape. Luna stilled as he approached. She saw his eyes narrow on her. An armed guard was right behind him. Henry paused at her door, typed in some kind of code, and then he walked inside.

She was on him before he'd even cleared the threshold. Luna grabbed him, spun him back against the mirror, and shoved her hands under his throat. The guard's footsteps rushed toward her.

"Drop your gun," Luna snapped at the guard, not taking her gaze off Henry. "Or I'll break his neck."

Henry's gaze jerked to the guard. "D-don't..." Henry wheezed.

Luna laughed, and it was a cold sound. "You think I won't snap your neck before that guy can get to me? You need to think—"

The guard grabbed her. He yanked her back in a movement that was *too* fast for a normal human, and now he held her against him, held her with a strength that was greater than her own.

Henry sucked in a breath. "Th-thank you, Andreas…"

Andreas. That name again. Luna stopped struggling, for the moment. "You're one of us," she accused the guard.

Henry had braced his hand against the mirror. "Yes." He was breathing easier. She'd barely choked him, but the drama queen was acting like she'd shown him death's door. "Andreas is Lazarus."

Andreas released her. Immediately, she spun and faced him. Tall, muscled, with curly black hair and bright blue eyes. "Way to be a sell-out," she muttered to him.

His lips thinned. "You don't understand."

"Jett said you were on our team." Her heart was still racing, and she knew Andreas had to hear its wild beat. She could certainly hear his low, steady heartbeat. "He never mentioned you were muscle for this jackass." She jerked her head toward Henry.

"Maddox didn't mention a lot to you." Andreas held her angry stare. "Maybe you should calm down and listen to what the jackass has to say."

Or maybe she should plan an escape attempt right the hell then.

"Luna." Henry drew out her name, long and winding.

She huffed out a breath and positioned her body so that she could easily see both him and Andreas. She knew Andreas was the bigger threat.

"Maddox has deceived you." Henry delivered this line with a sad air.

"Really?" She let her brows rise. "So you *didn't* send him to find me? You didn't send him and Jett to hunt me—"

"Originally, yes, I did." Henry's cheeks flushed. "But then I did some digging, and I realized that Maddox Kane *is* the greatest danger to you."

He was trying to mess with her head. Not working.

"I think his memories are coming back," Henry added, watching her carefully.

Her hands knotted. "Good for him."

"Perhaps, but bad for you."

"Are you *threatening* me?" Luna demanded, rising on the balls of her feet.

Beside her, she felt Andreas tense.

But Henry gave a hard, negative shake of his head. "No, no, Luna, I'm trying to warn you. Maddox isn't the man you think he is. Hell, we were all misled by him. He was such a decorated soldier. A former Ranger with a success rate that you wouldn't believe. He seemed to be the perfect candidate for the program. But we missed his…problem."

Uh, huh. "What problem would that be?"

Henry licked his lips. "You."

He was lying to her. Manipulating her. Why?

"You and Maddox were killed together."

What? Her face seemed to turn icy, then burn red hot.

"You two were shot. Luckily, our operatives were close by, so we were able to get to you and institute the Lazarus preservation process before your bodies—"

She held up one fisted hand. "Who shot us?"

Henry took a step toward her. "We believe it was your ex."

What? Luna sucked in a shocked breath.

"He'd been selling government secrets. The agents in charge knew the traitor was in Maddox's unit, and Maddox was tasked with unmasking the guy. Maddox found him, all right. The traitor was another ranger named Adam Brock."

The name meant nothing to her.

"Maddox was supposed to bring the traitor in, but instead, Adam wound up dead. Maddox was dead. And so were you."

Her breath was coming a little too fast. "Is this Adam...Lazarus?"

"No." Henry shook his head. "The guy was a traitor to his country. You think we'd want him enhanced?"

She had no idea what Henry wanted.

"But, once you were here at the facility, I noticed the way Maddox acted around you. At first, the shrinks and I — we thought it was a good thing. I mean, especially considering your issues."

Her issues. "You mean my repeated memory loss."

"Exactly." He smiled at her as if he were pleased she'd been the one to put that on the table. Saved him some awkwardness. "Losing your memory every time you die is very hard — hell, it's extremely difficult to retrain you, to explain Lazarus protocol, to get you up to speed with a team — "

"I'm so sorry to inconvenience you," she cut in, her words dripping with ice.

"Yes, well, you can't help it."

Andreas was quiet beside her.

Henry cleared his throat. "Maddox seemed to steady you. So we started bringing him in after all of your risings."

Jesus—how many times had she died?

"But we noticed he seemed to be growing too attached to you, and that set off alarm bells for us."

Us. Him. The shrinks.

Henry licked his lips. "So we did some digging. And things weren't quite as black and white as we'd originally been led to believe."

She glanced toward the door. It had shut behind Andreas.

"Maddox wanted you."

Her gaze flew back to Henry.

"It seems that he and Adam actually fought about you, several times. You'd all grown up together, something I did *not* realize, and Maddox…" Henry's cheeks stained. "From the accounts we received, he'd become quite jealous and possessive where you were concerned. When you ended your engagement to Adám—"

She'd been engaged? To the man who'd shot her? To the traitor? No way. *No. Way.*

"Well, it was only after your engagement ended that the suspicions started to fall on Adam Brock. Suspicions that were first reported by Maddox."

She didn't like where this was going. Actually, she didn't like *anything* that was happening. "What are you saying? That Maddox was lying about the guy?"

Henry's stare didn't waver. "I'm saying I've seen Maddox in action. I've supervised him for the last few months. When Maddox wants something badly enough, then nothing will stand in his way." A pause. "He wants you, more than I think he's ever wanted anything."

She pulled in a deep breath. Tried to think.

"His memories are coming back. He remembers *you*. He remembers losing you to someone else. And Maddox will go to any extreme to make sure that doesn't happen again." Henry's hands shoved into the pockets of his lab coat. "Yes, Maddox is the best hunter we have, so when you went missing, he was sent to find you. Sent *with* Jett. Jett had orders to keep a close watch on Maddox. But Maddox went off mission operative. He was going to take you away. He had no plans to ever bring you back to this facility."

No plans to bring her back to her cell. She focused carefully, picking up Henry's heartbeat. Listening to his breathing. Catching the scent of his sweat.

"I am sorry," Henry told her, face haggard. "I'm in charge of this facility, but I didn't realize just how much the past would matter. As a result of this situation, I will be changing experimental protocols. I'll require a *full* history of all potential Lazarus test subjects. The past was supposed to be gone, but for Maddox, it isn't. I will not make this mistake again." His shoulders straightened. "I won't allow him to be a threat to you. Maddox is going to be transferred to another Lazarus group. You won't see him again."

She didn't let any expression cross her face.

Henry wasn't done talking. "I think…I believe he was the reason you fled before, and I didn't even realize it. You'd expressed some hesitation about going in to the field with him again, and I should have listened to you. I *won't* be making that mistake again."

The guy seemed so sincere. Saying he was going to keep her safe. Apologizing. But she didn't like him. And she damn well didn't trust him. "Am I free to go?"

Henry blinked.

"If you're just trying to help me, then when you leave this room, will the door stay open?"

His gaze darted to the door. She heard the acceleration of his heartbeat.

"Not yet," Henry told her. "I'm sorry, but there are tests that must be done. You ran away from the facility, but something happened to you out there. If Maddox's story is to be believed, you were experimented on in some sort of hospital. Your captors came after you when you escaped—"

"All of that happened. You can believe that story, one hundred percent."

A quick nod from Henry. "Right. Right. Of course. But…we have to find out what was done to you. We'll need to examine you thoroughly."

She didn't like the sound of that.

"After the examination, we'll reevaluate." His gaze cut to Andreas. "I think we're done for now. We'll come back after we've handled Maddox."

That was something else she didn't like the sound of…Just how was Henry going to handle Maddox?

Henry turned for the door. Andreas shadowed his movements. Protecting him?

"Termination," Luna tossed out that word.

And she was rewarded by the fast jerk of Henry's heartbeat.

"You aren't planning to terminate Maddox, are you?" Luna asked.

"Of course not." She couldn't see Henry's face. "He's my best hunter." The door opened. Henry filed out. Andreas started to follow him—

Luna leapt forward. She grabbed his arm. "Why are you helping him?"

Andreas looked down at her hand, then back at her face.

"*Why?*" She fired that fast, hard thought right at him.

"*Because things aren't what they seem.*" His answer, one delivered straight in her mind.

Then he was gone. The door clanged shut, and Luna was trapped in her cell. Her chest ached as she made her way back to her bed. More like a cot, really.

Henry's words spun in her mind. And she tried to figure out what had been real, what had been lies, and what in the hell she could to do next. And all the while, two words seemed to replay in her head.

Trust me. Maddox's order to her, right before things had gone to hell.

Her hands wrapped around her stomach. She tried to still her racing thoughts and reach out to him. He was still in the facility, at least, for the moment he was. He had to be close by. *"Maddox? Maddox, are you there?"*

Henry wanted her to fear him. Henry wanted her to turn on Maddox.

Henry wanted her to believe that Maddox was a monster.

But she wouldn't.

"Are you there?" Luna asked again.

***

He recognized the fucking cell.

Maddox paced the confines of his cell like a caged tiger. Rage pounded at him. He'd woken on the floor, probably in the same spot the guards had dumped his ass. They'd dragged him back to the facility, locked him up, and taken Luna.

Hell, no.

He heard footsteps approaching. Could tell by the slightly uneven gait that it was that dick Henry. But he wasn't alone.

Andreas.

Shit.

Why was the Greek working with him? But the fact that he was — well, that was trouble.

The door opened a few moments later. Maddox didn't attack, not yet. But every single part of him wanted to leap forward.

Plan. Control the fury. Hold on. Do it for Luna.

Henry peered at him as if Maddox was a bug under a microscope. "You recovered from the tranq dosage very quickly." His lips pressed together. "Too quickly."

"I'm a fast healer."

"Especially when Luna aids you. We had to dose her just to get her to take her hand off you."

You sonofabitch. I'm going to rip you apart.

Henry waited, expectant, as if he thought Maddox would do something.

So Maddox didn't do a damn thing.

Henry's eyelids flickered. "Aren't you going to ask where she is?"

"She's here. In the facility." He shrugged. "Probably on the level above me, if you put Luna back in her old cell."

Andreas glanced up, a slight movement of his gaze that was telling.

"What do you remember?" Henry asked.

Maddox scratched his chin. "Let's see…you and your men shot me. Five, six times? Even though I was out on the mission you'd assigned." Now his stare cut to Andreas. "Even though we were on the same team." He knew Andreas had been responsible for cloaking the movements of the humans. If Andreas hadn't helped them, Maddox would have heard the bastards coming from miles away.

"You went AWOL, soldier," Henry snapped. "Don't feed us those lies. And I know *why* you did it." A nod. "For her. Because your memories came back. Memories of life before Lazarus."

"We don't have memories of that time." Again, Maddox kept his gaze on Andreas. "None of us."

Henry stepped forward, but caught himself before he came *too* close. "Bullshit. There's no other reason for you not to follow orders. You remembered her. Did you remember how much you wanted her before Lazarus? How you were willing to do anything, even kill, to have her?"

Maddox's heart raced.

"He remembers," Andreas said quietly. Fucking ass.

"So you thought you'd just take her. Vanish with her." Henry shook his head. "Not happening."

Maddox shot a disgusted glance at the doc. "You want to terminate her."

Now Henry's eyes widened. "That's preposterous! Why would I send you after her if I just planned to kill the woman?"

Henry was a good liar. World class. Maybe because deep down, he was a psychopath. "Because you couldn't risk her running free on the outside. Not with what she can do."

Henry's stare was absolutely avid now. "And what is it that you think she can do?"

And Maddox realized he was part of Henry's latest experiment, too. Had the leader of the lab coats wanted to push him and Luna into desperate circumstances and see what happened? See what she could do when she was out of the lab? Maybe Henry had wanted to test Luna's healing powers and determine what she could do when it wasn't just about saving a life on a mission.

Luna had restored Maddox's memories. Fuck, he'd even gotten her—foolishly, now, he saw that—to restore Jett's memories, too. Henry and the lab coats would know what she could do. He'd played right in to their hands. "You sonofabitch…" Maddox could only shake his head. "Was any of it real? The termination order?

Her escape? Or was it all a set-up to see what she could do once she was outside of these walls?" And he'd tracked her so well. "What *I* could do?"

A faint smile curled Henry's lips. "Some experiences just can't be recreated in the lab."

Andreas stiffened his shoulders.

"She gave you memories back, didn't she?" Henry murmured. "I thought that would happen. She started with Andreas over there." He pointed to the silent soldier. "Gave him some flickers on the last mission when he took the knife to the chest, and Luna stopped the bleeding. I watch my subjects very closely, you see, so I knew what was going on. And I realized more study was needed."

It had all been an experiment. Her so-called *escape,* the termination. Hell, what about that old hospital? Had it—

"You were supposed to bring her back, though." A furrow appeared between Henry's brows. "When you went against protocol, I had to do more digging. That's when I realized just what memories might be playing in that head of yours."

"Fuck you."

"You remembered her from before Lazarus, didn't you? The two of you grew up together. I didn't know that, of course, because I don't make a habit of learning all of the details about a subject's life before Lazarus. Normally, it's just not relevant."

"You listening to this shit, Andreas?" Maddox shoved the mental jibe at the soldier.

Andreas didn't so much as flicker his eyelashes.

"But it became relevant with you." Henry laughed. "My, what interesting things I learned. You and Luna grew up together. You were best friends. And then Luna met a man named Adam Brock. She fell in love, and she left you."

Something happened inside of Maddox. He could feel it. Cracks breaking open. Rage building.

"You couldn't handle it, could you? You killed her lover. But in the middle of that love triangle, he fought back. Luna died, too. So did you." Henry's gaze didn't waver. "Only you and Luna were both lucky enough to be preserved and brought back."

"I'm supposed to believe your bullshit story?" Maddox kept his voice flat with an extreme effort.

"Primitive emotions." Henry enunciated very slowly. "That's what drives Lazarus subjects. That's why we have to be so careful about your interactions. Lust. Jealousy. Rage. They get a tight hold on you, and they don't let go. Darker emotions fester and grow inside of Lazarus subjects. I think they've been growing within you for quite a while, Maddox. And I think that the more you're around Luna, the more dangerous you become."

You have no idea.

"Since waking here, you've tried to reach her, psychically, right? But you can't make contact. It's because Andreas has many hidden talents. You all seem to be able to do so much more than I originally suspected. Andreas can block you from reaching Luna. From reaching any of the others. He's a shield that will keep this facility protected...at least, until your transfer is complete."

Oh, hell, no. "I'm not leaving Luna."

"And I'm not giving you a choice." Henry's smile was far too smug. "You're too important to lose. After all, you really are an incredible hunter. But you can't be allowed to stay near Luna. It's okay, though, she'll have forgotten you long before you even leave the facility. Then we can start fresh with her."

She'll have forgotten you —

"No." The one word came out as a growl from Maddox. "You won't kill her."

Henry rolled his eyes. "I'm not going to permanently terminate her. It will be purely a standard death. I'm prepping my lab now. It will be a painless, temporary end, I assure you, and she'll come back, good as new."

"Andreas, you gonna let this happen?"

"When she wakes up, we'll continue the experiments. We'll see how much of his past Andreas can recover with her help."

So Andreas was selling Luna out so he could get his memories back.

"Why the hell did you even bring me here?" Maddox snarled. "If you were going to send me away, why did you—"

"Because I need you, of course. I'm not quite ready for your transfer just yet." Henry had started to sweat. Unusual for him. The guy typically did a much better job of hiding his emotions. "I put the plan—the experiment—in place, but someone else intervened. Someone changed *my* damn plan."

Maddox raked a disgusted glare over the doctor. "You're not making any sense."

"Before she could escape, someone *took* Luna. Someone who seized control of my surveillance systems. Someone who must have worked here, at the facility. And that bastard covered his tracks so well that I couldn't find him." Henry drew in a quick breath. "And *that's* why you're here right now. Because I want you to find the bastard. Do your job, *hunt* him."

Maddox laughed. "Go screw yourself. I'm done being your attack dog."

"This man *hurt* Luna. Jett told me about how you found her in the rundown hole of a hospital."

Jett. Right. Another betrayal Maddox would get to deal with—later.

"Someone cut her open. Someone abused your Luna, and you're going to stand there and tell me you don't care? That you don't want to find the person and rip him apart?" Now Henry's disbelief was plain to see. "I don't buy it. You loved her before Lazarus. Loved her so much that you died in her arms. And you love her still."

Maddox just stared at him. "Nice story." He acted as if he were considering the matter. "I think I like it better than the version where I kill her fiancé."

Henry's smile crept over his face. "Never told you that she had a fiancé. You *did* remember, didn't you? You remembered killing Adam Brock."

Shit.

"If it makes you feel better, the man was a traitor to his country. He sold government secrets, and if you hadn't killed him, someone else sure as hell would have."

Maddox didn't blink.

Henry coughed. "Of course, that's *not* the story Luna now knows."

Fucking jerk.

"As a precaution—since you are both in the same facility right now and I do need your services—I may have told Luna how obsessed you are with her. Until she dies and wakes, that's the story she'll believe. As far as Luna is concerned, you're enemy number one. So see, it's really better for us both if Luna just starts fresh."

Maddox smiled.

Henry's body tensed. "Why are you grinning?"

Because I'm thinking about all of the ways I'm going to hurt you.

Henry gave a sharp, negative shake of his head. "Never mind. I don't have time for your shit." He pointed at Maddox. "Andreas will accompany you on the hunt. You find the man who took Luna away, and I'll end him." Henry turned for the door. "Or maybe I'll let you do the honors."

Because Henry didn't like getting his hands dirty.

"If Maddox turns on you, Andreas," Henry directed, "just shoot him. Not in the head, though, I do want him rising again. We need him."

"You like hurting people, don't you, you sonofabitch?" Maddox's voice was low. Savage.

Henry's shoulders stiffened.

"'Cause there really is no other reason for you to have lied to Luna. You just wanted to hurt her." *And no one hurts my Luna.*

Henry spun on his heel. "Primitive instincts remain. All Luna should have are those primitive responses. But when I told her about you, I could see the pain flaring in her eyes. If all of her memories were gone, she shouldn't have responded that way."

"So what—by hurting her, you were doing another freaking experiment?"

"Pain can teach us all so much."

I'll be sure you learn that lesson.

"Luna is an amazing subject. I'm not even sure she realizes her own potential. Don't worry, though. I'll make sure that, before I'm done—I'll understand every secret she possesses."

Then Henry was gone. Maddox knew several armed guards stood just beyond the doorway. He could smell their sweat and fear. But he didn't focus on them. Not yet. He let his rage blast at Andreas. "You're selling Luna out?"

"I'm following orders. The way we're supposed to do. The way *you* should do."

He'd followed orders plenty. And all he'd gotten for his efforts was a cell. Maddox closed the distance between him and Andreas, standing toe-to-toe with the guy. "They're not ever going to let us go. You understand that, don't you? We're their lab rats."

Andreas didn't change expression.

"You want your past so you're willing to do anything that Henry wants." Disgust deepened Maddox's voice. "How the fuck do you sleep at night?"

"I don't. Haven't slept in weeks." For a moment, his gaze blazed. "Not since Luna gave me a vision of myself standing at my wife's grave."

What?

"I want more than just the memory of her death." Andreas put a hand to his chest. "More than just gut-wrenching grief that tells me I lost my whole world. I want more. I want her *back*." He swallowed. "And, yeah, if I have to follow orders and hurt your girl in order to do it…then so the fuck what? My soul is already gone. As for my heart, Luna gave me the memory of burying it in a pine box."

Sonofabitch. Andreas wasn't going to help him.

That meant that Maddox was on his own.

Fine. He'd hate to destroy his former teammate, but there was no way — no way on earth — he'd leave that facility without Luna at his side.

CHAPTER ELEVEN

"Get on the exam table, Luna."

Armed guards were all around her. They'd escorted her out of her cell and down a narrow corridor that had led to a big lab. An exam table waited in the middle of the room. An instrument tray was beside it. She didn't like the look of those instruments at all. The whole set-up reminded her of the blood-soaked hospital room that she and Maddox had found.

"I don't think so," Luna murmured. She flashed a smile at the guards near her. They didn't smile back. "I'm really not in the mood for an exam."

The guard closest to her — a blond fellow with broad shoulders and a bright gaze — cast a quick glance at the table. His stare seemed to linger on the straps that were attached to the table. For a second, she could have sworn sympathy flashed on his face.

"You don't have a choice, miss." This was the sharp answer from the second guard. A big, burly fellow with a buzz-cut. He had his tranq gun out and trained on her. "Get on the table. The doctors will be in soon."

She kept her smile in place as she turned toward that guard. And then—

Luna attacked. She jumped on him, kicked the gun right out of his hand. Then she drove her fist into his throat. He gasped, gurgled, and his eyes went wide as he struggled to breathe. He backed up, stumbling, unable to cry out for help. Luna's fist hit him in the jaw, and he crumpled in a heap.

She snatched the gun from the floor and turned toward the blond guard.

Even as she did…an alarm was sounding. Echoing all around her.

She heard the clicking of the door's metal locks engaging. "No!" Luna yelled.

She ran for the door, but when she got there, it was too late. She'd been sealed inside.

"You can't get out," the blond guard told her, his voice quiet and oddly calm, given the situation. "That door is reinforced, just like the one in your cell."

Whirling toward him, Luna aimed the gun right at the fellow.

He had his weapon trained on her. "You're faster than I am," the guard said, still calm.

Damn straight she was.

"But you see those vents above us?" he asked.

Her gaze darted up.

"If I fall, the guards watching us on the security feed will just send in gas. It will knock you out." He shrugged. "It will probably kill me, but hey, that's a risk of the job, right?"

The people there would kill their own guards?

Why not? They play God with the Lazarus subjects.

"I don't want to die, though," the guard continued. His gaze was grave. "Because I won't come back, not like you do."

They continued their armed stand-off. The alarm kept shrieking.

"You won't be terminated, Luna. That's not what's happening here. Just get on the table. That's all you need to do."

Did she look like a fool? "If I get on that table, I'll die."

"But you'll come back."

At least he hadn't denied the fate that waited for her.

"My memories will be gone." She'd be back to nothing. Absolute blankness.

"That has to happen. Maddox screwed things up. He got in your head. Henry said he told you all kinds of lies. We need you fully committed to the program, and the only way to do that is to push you back to being a blank slate."

"I'm not a blank slate," she whispered as her finger squeezed the trigger. "I'm a fucking person." The tranq fired, shooting right into his chest. He jerked back, heaving, twitching, and then falling.

And a moment later, the soft *hiss* of gas began to fill the lab.

***

Maddox stalked down the hallway, conscious of the guards behind him, their weapons trained on his back, and Andreas at his side. "So I'm supposed to search this facility with you assholes shadowing my every move?" he snapped at the humans.

"Yes, sir," one of the guards responded. "That's the plan."

Maddox rolled his eyes. Damn fool plan. "I need to interview every guard here." Now he was just talking to distract them as he tried to figure out what move to make next.

"I spoke with them all before," Andreas replied. "None of them were lying. I believe Henry is wrong. The person who helped her *isn't* on staff here."

Now Maddox stopped. "Did you talk to all the docs and nurses, too?"

Andreas nodded.

"Then you missed something."

Andreas adamantly shook his head. "I heard their heartbeats, their breathing, their—"

"Some people are just good at lying," Maddox cut in flatly. "Like your buddy Henry. He only lets us see what he *wants* us to observe. You think he's going to help you, but he's just stringing your dumb ass along. Don't you get that? He doesn't want you to know your past. He doesn't want *any* of us to know. If we know…" Now he switched to silent communication. "*If we remember what it was like to be human, then we won't be so happy living in cages anymore. Why the hell don't you get that?*"

Andreas looked away from him. "You're the better hunter, so…hunt."

Before Maddox could respond, the alarm began to blare. Loud, echoing.

Behind him, the soldiers swore.

The alarm *wasn't* a good sign.

One of the guards barked, "Back to your room! Now!"

Oh, how amusing. The human was giving him orders?

Maddox turned toward the fellow. "Why the hell would I go back? It took too fucking long to get out of that cell."

The guard's eyes widened. "But you—you're cooperating. You're—"

Screw this. Maddox snatched the weapon from the man. Without a second's hesitation,

Maddox tranqed him, then hit the second guard. Barely taking time to aim, he fired at the third man who'd been running down the hallway.

Seriously, too easy.

He turned the gun on a silent Andreas. "You didn't stop me."

"I thought you might use your psychic power on them. Kept waiting for you to just knock them out. Henry figured you wouldn't risk it, not with their weapons trained on you, but I suspected you were simply waiting for them to be distracted."

Maddox grunted. "I used the tranqs because I'm saving my energy." He studied Andreas as the alarm blared. "Who the hell's side are you really on?"

Andreas shrugged. "I'm just supposed to make sure you hunt the man who took Luna away. Protecting those guards..." He waved toward the fallen men. "Not on my to do list."

The alarm kept blaring.

"I'm pretty sure that alarm is coming from Lab Four." Andreas raised his brows. "Luna is in Lab Four. Sounds like someone might be trying to take her away again. I think we should hunt the bastard, don't you? Going back to your cell wouldn't exactly accomplish that goal."

Maddox was already lunging down the hallway, racing for the stairs that would take him to Lab Four. And to Luna.

***

Luna fell. The gas filled her lungs—a sickly sweet taste and smell that engulfed her world—and she collapsed on the floor, falling far too close to the blond guard's body. Tears leaked down her cheeks because the gas burned her eyes. She coughed, contorting, hating that she was trapped. She'd tried to force open the door.

But the gas had made her so weak.

Footsteps shuffled toward her. She squinted and saw two people in white uniforms with big, heavy masks over their faces. They grabbed her. Hoisted her up. Put her on the exam table. Straps slid over her body, locking her in place.

The hiss of the gas faded, but the heavy lethargy didn't leave her body.

"She took enough to kill an elephant." That voice—*Henry?*

And she could see his face behind the clear mask he wore.

"The guards are dead," a woman responded. She stood just beside Henry, and she was reaching for the exam tray with her gloved hand. Like Henry, a mask covered her face. A gas mask of some sort? Had to be.

"Occupational hazard." He didn't seem concerned. "Their families will be compensated." He leaned toward Luna. "You should have just gotten on the table. It would have made this so much easier. Everything was going to be painless for you."

She tried to shake her head.

"Thought if I told you that story about Maddox's obsession, you'd cooperate more. Didn't work out so well, did it?"

Luna couldn't speak.

Henry sighed. The sound carried through the mask. "So much for that plan. But at least we won't be disturbed any longer. I've shut off the security feed while I complete this procedure. Don't want any record of what's happening here."

He didn't want a record of killing her?

"Here's the scalpel, Dr.—" The woman's words ended in a gurgle.

Luna didn't understand what had happened, but she heard the soft thud as the woman's body hit the floor.

Henry whirled around. "What in the hell? *You're dead!*"

"No," a low voice told him. "But you are…"

And then Luna saw Henry's body jerk. Once, twice. He slammed back into the exam table, hitting her, and blood bloomed on his chest. He stared at her a moment, his eyes wide and shocked, before his head slowly turned to the left. He stared at his attacker. "Y-you…"

Another shot. The bullet never made a sound as it fired, but she saw the hole that appeared right in the middle of Henry's mask. A shot had been fired straight to his head.

Henry fell and crashed onto the floor.

Luna's head was clearing now that the gas had stopped filling the room. She realized Henry and the woman were dead. And...

"I can't believe you shot me."

It was the guard. The blond guard she'd shot with the tranq. He edged toward her. Stared down at her with a glittering gaze. "I'm the fucking one who saved you the first time...and you *shot* me."

"Tranq. It was a tranq." She twisted against the metal straps that held her in place, but there was no give to them.

Sighing, he lifted his hand. He put the gun to her forehead. The gun was equipped with a silencer. "There isn't a tranq in here."

She stopped twisting.

"My cover just got blown to hell and back. You realize that, don't you? I can't stay here any longer. I'm going to vanish, and you — well, not like I can leave you behind."

Her breath came faster.

"It was easier getting you out the first time," he muttered. "You trusted me then. I'd spent weeks building that trust. Getting you to think that I sympathized with the subjects. Now, though, we can't exactly work on trust, can we?"

He had a *gun* to her head. Trust wasn't an option, no.

"It will be easier for me to transport you if you aren't fighting me."

Transport her? "Why?"

He blinked. Leaned in closer. "Oh, right. You don't remember any of that, do you? Must really suck to be you. Never knowing who you can trust. Never knowing if you're with a good guy or the freaking villain." He put his index finger to his lips. His blue eyes were ice cold. "Here's a tip. I'm one of the villains."

She strained against the straps.

"Not that you'll remember that later."

"You're...Lazarus." He had to be, right? He'd survived the gas. He'd recovered so fast from the tranq—

"Yeah, I am. Escaped a facility in Arizona after that bitch burned to the ground and my *team* left me for dead." His face hardened. "Then I realized just what a pot of gold I was. The US military thought they were so smart, making us. But why should they be the only ones with super soldiers? I knew I could sell these secrets to the highest bidder."

Her temples throbbed. There was something...familiar about him.

About what he was saying.

"You're the weak link. I can get you to believe any freaking story I feed you." He smiled at her, still with the gun pressed to her head. "And that's why you and I will be walking away with all of the intel I managed to hack. The rest of the bastards here can burn."

What?

"Something I learned from the place in Arizona. If the fire is big enough, hot enough, then no one looks for survivors." His Adam's apple clicked as he swallowed. "My team sure as shit didn't look for me. The others left me and never glanced back."

Maddox had told her there were other Lazarus soldiers out there...

"But you know what my *team* didn't understand? I can feel others—the other Lazarus subjects. I can home in on them. I can find them, anywhere. Just like I found you. Just like I found my partner, Sam. I found this whole freaking facility, and now I'm going to tear it down." He laughed. "Everyone was so focused on you. They didn't even notice what I was doing in here. Didn't notice what I stole. Didn't notice when I planted explosives." He leaned closer and whispered to her, "But they'll notice when they're blown to hell and back."

"Let me go!"

He moved the gun to her chest. "When you wake up, we'll be best friends. Hell, maybe we'll even be lovers."

She couldn't get away. "No!" Luna screamed.

"Adam," he said softly.

Luna felt her heart squeeze.

"That's my name. But don't worry, I'll tell it to you again...when you wake up."

"Don't do this," she cried. "Don't!"

He pulled a phone out of his pocket. Swiped his fingers over the screen. "Boom, baby, boom."

What?

"We've got only minutes to leave here, and since I don't want to be fighting you the whole time, you're going out." His fingers tightened around the gun.

"Adam, don't!" Luna cried.

A furrow appeared between his brows. "It'll only hurt until you die."

"Get the hell away from her!"

Her breath heaved at that enraged bellow. Maddox?

Adam stiffened. "Who let you out of your cage?"

Her head jerked to the side. Maddox was there, standing just inside the doorway, with Andreas at his back. Maddox gripped a tranq gun in his right hand.

Adam immediately yanked his gun up—and put it next to Luna's temple once more.

"Who let me out?" Maddox took a slow, stalking step into the lab. "That would be the dead asshole at your feet. Henry wanted me to find the traitor in his group, and I guess I just found him."

"This isn't your fight!" Adam screamed. "Get out of here, and I won't put the bullet in her head."

"Don't leave me, Maddox!"

"I…know you." Maddox's voice had gone flat and cold.

Adam gave a rough laugh. "Yeah, yeah, you freaking do. I'm the guard who has been at your side for weeks, I'm the—"

"He's Lazarus," Luna yelled.

The gun shoved harder into her temple.

"Don't hurt her," Maddox snarled.

Andreas was right at his side.

"He set the place to blow," Luna gasped out. "We only have minutes!"

"That's right." Adam didn't look particularly worried. "Time's running out for us all. So how about you two just walk the hell away? Save your own asses. The humans are all going to die here, so no one will ever know you even exist. You can be free. Consider that my gift to you."

Maddox didn't move. "I'm not going without Luna."

Adam shook his head. "See, I'm afraid that's a deal breaker. 'Cause Luna is staying with *me*. She's far too valuable to lose."

Maddox took another step closer. "I *know* you."

"Yeah, asshole, we covered that, I'm—"

"Adam Brock. *I know you,*" Maddox said again. "You're the sonofabitch who killed me before. You shot me in a seedy motel room. You *killed* me."

Adam wasn't laughing any longer. He also wasn't making deals. For an instant, Luna could have sworn she smelled his fear.

"Only fair, though," Maddox added, "because I also killed *you.* You were fucking bleeding out even as you fired at me."

"How about I kill you *again?*" Adam demanded, and he yanked the gun away from Luna's temple as he focused on Maddox. "Goodbye, you—

Before he could fire, a tranq blasted into Adam. One, two, three. Maddox fired the tranq gun over and over until it just clicked.

Adam swayed, but *didn't* go down.

"The tranqs don't work the same on him!" Luna yelled. "He got right up after I hit him with one. I thought I'd knocked him out, but I think he was just faking, he was—"

Maddox bounded forward. He grabbed Adam's neck. Snapped it.

Adam fell. Dropped like a stone.

The sound of his breaking bones absolutely chilled Luna. Maddox turned toward her. His face was twisted with rage and something inside of her—

Splintered.

The lab vanished. The table vanished. The dead bodies vanished.

She was outside of a motel room door. Fear beat within her. She had to stop Maddox. Adam was wrong, Adam was so freaking evil and twisted, and she hadn't seen it. She'd been blind, but the blinders were off. She and Maddox could turn Adam over to the authorities. That was what they would do.

She shoved open the motel room door.

Maddox whirled toward her. He had a bloody knife in his hand. His face was twisted with rage. So much dark rage. And behind him, she could see Adam on the floor. Adam was bleeding, struggling to sit up. Adam was whispering her name, begging for help.

Adam. She knew him. He was her fiancé. And Maddox —

Maddox reached for her just as Luna felt pain burn through her side. She tried to speak, but she couldn't manage any words. The pain twisted and grew, and her blood pumped out as she fell forward. Maddox grabbed her, holding her tight.

His frantic gaze was the last thing she saw.

"Luna!" His hands were around her shoulders, shaking her.

Luna blinked. The motel room was gone, fading like mist, and the lab was around her once again.

"Baby, shit, what happened to you?"

She pointed to the vents. Her mind was still a little foggy. "Gas…"

Maddox scooped her into his arms. The metal straps had been ripped away. Had he done that? "We're getting the hell out of here," Maddox told her. "Right now." But when he turned for the door, Andreas was blocking it.

Andreas held a tranq gun in his hand.

"I don't have time for this shit," Maddox bit off. "I don't want to kill you."

Andreas lowered the gun. "What happens when we leave?"

"I don't know, but I'm fucking ready to find out."

They *all* had to leave. Luna coughed and said, "He set explosives…that's what…what Adam said. I saw him activate them with his phone. We don't have much time left!" They needed to haul ass. "I can walk," she told Maddox shoving at his arms. "We need to run, now!"

"We need to evacuate the place." Maddox lowered her to the floor. "The humans — hell, we can't let them burn."

"Jett's in detention level two." Andreas whirled for the door. "I'll get him."

They had to get *out.*

They rushed into the hallway. Maddox ran to the right, and he pulled hard on a red fire alarm. A loud blaring filled the facility.

Luna glanced back. What about Adam? Maddox had broken his neck, but that wouldn't stop a Lazarus soldier. "Maddox —"

And then she felt the explosion. A distant roar that seemed to come from beneath them. The walls trembled.

Screams reached her. Screams that came from the floor below her.

"Jett's down there!" Andreas yelled.

Maddox grabbed her shoulders. Spun her to face him. "Go upstairs, baby." His eyes glittered. "Haul ass. Get to safety."

She grabbed his arm when he would have barrelled away. "Not without you!"

"Jett is on my team. Whatever else he did, he's mine." He yanked her close and pressed a hard kiss to her lips. "Get to safety. I'll be right behind you, I swear."

"Maddox—"

But he was already gone. He'd raced away with Andreas.

Another explosion rocked the building. This one—this one came from above her. She heard voices rising, falling. Guards rushed by her in the hallway and she tensed, thinking they were going to attack her, but they didn't even look at her. They were all too intent on living.

She could hear fire crackling.

Bombs had exploded above her, below her. Maddox had headed down below. He'd gone into the fire to get Jett.

And she…she was just supposed to run away?

She heard the faint gasp from far too close by. She spun around, staring back at the lab she'd left behind only moments before.

The gasp came again.

She hurried inside. Stepped over the body of Henry Danwith.

The gasp had come from Adam. As she watched, his body started to jerk and twitch.

He was coming back.

Her gaze flew around, and she saw the weapon he'd had before — the gun with the silencer on the end. It was about five feet away. She lunged for it. Her fingers curled around the weapon just as she felt hard hands grab her shoulders. Luna was yanked back around.

She came face-to-face with Adam. She pointed the weapon right between his eyes.

"I know where all the bombs are." He licked his lower lip. His pupils were huge. "I can get us out. I'm your only hope."

"Maddox is downstairs. He's getting Jett — "

"They're dead. Both dead." A rough laugh. "I set the most explosives down there. You need to start at the bottom. Destabilizes everything. Maddox is dead. Fucking dead, he's gone and he's — "

Another explosion rocked the building.

And the gun fired.

CHAPTER TWELVE

Maddox had thrown Jett over his shoulder.
The flames were all around him, the heat lancing
him. He didn't take a breath because when he
did, he just tasted fire. Maddox rushed forward,
searching for an exit. The smoke was thick,
smothering him. He'd lost sight of Andreas.
Didn't know if any guards were still down there.

Jett was unconscious. Maddox knew that if
he didn't get them the hell out of there, soon,
they'd both be dead. The flames would get them,
and there would be no rising after that. You
couldn't come back when your body was just ash.

Luna. You need to get out for Luna. If he could
survive, then he could see Luna again.

What if she didn't get out? The fear slid
through him as the flames flared higher. He'd
told her to go, but what if she hadn't made it?
He'd left her, he'd —

A hand grabbed him, seeming to burst right
through the smoke. He looked up and stared into
Luna's dark eyes. She didn't speak, probably
couldn't with all of the smoke, but she turned,

and, keeping her grip on his arm, she led him through the flames. They barreled into the stairwell, and the heat followed them, the flames crackling and blazing. The smoke rose fast in that stairwell, but Maddox climbed determinedly.

"Fire on the next level." Luna's voice. In his head. That meant whatever block Andreas had put in place before was gone. Was Andreas gone, too? The Greek had been right at his side until they'd gotten Jett out of his prison. As soon as they'd broken down the door, and Maddox had grabbed Jett, Andreas had seemed to vanish. Since the guy could cloak himself so well, Maddox had no idea where the bastard had gone.

"Have to go this way," Luna continued. *"Follow me."*

And he did. She took him through a maze of rooms, past fires and smoke. Then they were bursting outside, leaping into the night, as they flew through a broken window. They plummeted down, and he landed easily, with Jett still tossed over his shoulder.

Maddox sucked in a deep breath. He tasted clear air and coughed, shoving the smoke from his lungs.

Chaos reigned around him. Guards in ash-covered uniforms and staff in green scrubs were running and desperately trying to escape the flames.

"There's an SUV waiting—let's go," Luna said, her voice sounding hoarse.

Once more, he followed her. She went straight to a vehicle that had been hidden far away from the flames. They jumped inside, and she grabbed keys from under the seat. Luna slid into the driver's seat, while Maddox pushed Jett down in the back seat. Then he hurried into the front with her right before Luna sped away from the flames.

"Not that...I'm not grateful..." Maddox coughed again. "But how did you find this ride? How'd you know how to get us out of there?" He'd been lost in the smoke and flames. The scents had been overwhelming, and he hadn't been able to escape.

Luna's delicate jaw hardened. "I did what had to be done."

He wasn't sure what that meant. "Luna..."

A big, wrought-iron gate waited up ahead. Luna sped up, and the SUV crashed right through it. The guards fired shots at them, but Luna didn't stop. The SUV's engine growled as they burst through the gate and raced into the night.

"*Andreas?*" Maddox shoved out the mental call with all the power he possessed. "*The others —*"

And he got an answer. "*None of the other super soldiers were here. They were all out on missions.*"

Maddox sucked in a deep breath. *"Where are you?"*

"Going to face my past."

What in the hell did that mean?

"Don't look for me." The connection ended.

Maddox glanced back. The facility was burning. No damn way to stop those flames. "How many bombs did that bastard set?" Hell had seemed to explode around him.

"Ten." Her hands tightly gripped the steering wheel. "He didn't want to take any chances. He wanted the place *gone*."

Maddox narrowed his eyes on her. "Luna…"

"He said we were lovers once. That I loved him." The SUV hurtled forward. "It should have been harder to do."

His gut clenched. "What should have been harder?"

"He said you were going to die. That you wouldn't come back. I couldn't let that happen."

"Luna…"

"I trusted you. You told me to trust you, right? That was what you said before they took me from the safe house."

Her voice was too brittle. Her body was shaking. He wanted to pull her into his arms and never let go.

"He was going to kill you," she said again. "Kill you, then *sell* me to someone. I couldn't have ever loved a person like him. Adam must have been lying about that part. That's why it was so easy to do." She swallowed. "I made him tell me how to get out. I made him tell me where all the bombs were. He thought...he thought I was going to let him get away."

Maddox could feel her pain, and it seemed to rip him apart. "Baby..."

"He thought I was going to let him get away," she whispered once more. A tear leaked down her cheek. "But I didn't."

Maddox looked back. In the distance, he could still see the light of the flames.

"I didn't," Luna repeated. "And what does that make me?"

***

Adam Brock dragged himself toward the door. Blood poured from the side of his head where that bitch had shot him. He had wounds all over his body because of her. But he wasn't out of the game, not yet. He threw up his hand, curled his fingers around the knob, but the damn door wouldn't open.

He staggered to his feet. Yanked hard on the door.

Locked. She'd *locked* him in there?

Smoke shot in from beneath the door. Drifted in from the vents above him. Filled the room. He could hear the crackle of flames outside. How many bombs had gone off? How many were left?

His fists pounded into the door. No, no, he wasn't going out this way.

The flames crackled louder.

His fists drove into the door. "You fucking bitch!"

***

Luna wasn't sure where they were going, but that didn't seem to matter. Blind instinct had her steering the vehicle.

Maddox didn't talk. Neither did she. She was too afraid to speak.

I killed a man. A man who said I loved him.

A groan came from the backseat. Her gaze immediately jerked to the rear-view mirror. She'd just repositioned it a few moments ago, and she had a perfect view of Jett. With her enhanced vision, she could see him easily in the dim interior of the vehicle.

A finally *awake* Jett.

"What hit me?" Jett muttered. "And what in the hell *burned?*"

"We nearly did," came Maddox's growled reply. "After you fucking betrayed us and turned our asses over to Henry Danwith."

"Oh, *fuck.*" Jett lunged upright.

"Stop the vehicle, Luna," Maddox ordered. *"Now."*

She slammed on the brakes. Even before the vehicle had come to a full stop, Maddox was out of the ride. He'd yanked open the back door and hauled Jett out of the SUV. Luna jumped out of the driver's side and ran toward them.

By the time she got to them, Maddox had Jett pinned to the side of the vehicle. Maddox's right hand was drawn back into a fist, and Jett wasn't fighting.

"Do it," Jett said, the words making Luna still. Wind beat against her. "Punch the shit out of me. I deserve it."

Maddox didn't hit him, but he also didn't lower his clenched fist. *"Why?"*

"Because I was given orders! Because I was told after this mission—after this one, we'd be free! We just had to turn over Luna. They said she was damaged..." His gaze cut to her.

Her shoulders stiffened. *I'm not damaged.*

"Henry said she had to come back so he could fix her. But I swear, man, once we got to the safe house near Aspen, everything changed, okay? When I realized what she could do..." His lips thinned. "I knew how valuable she was. I knew I couldn't just turn her over to him. *We* couldn't. So I was going to throw him off. I was going to help hide you both. *That* was my plan, but the jerk got to me first."

Maddox still didn't lower his fist. "I trusted you."

Jett flinched. "You saved me, didn't you? Whatever the hell just happened — why I smell like someone tried to cook me and I'm covered in ash — *you* saved me."

"Henry ordered you pumped full of tranqs and put in containment. You were going to fucking be unconscious while they *killed* Luna."

"I swear, I wasn't going to sell you out! I was going to lead Henry away! But he was watching me. He tracked my phone. I was…shit, I was supposed to give him updates, but I promise, I was going to lead him away."

Luna glanced down the road. A long, narrow stretch of road that was deserted. Stars glittered overhead. "We can't stay out here." Her voice was too flat. She wrapped her arms around her stomach. "Adam said he'd taken all tracking devices off the SUV, but we still need to get another ride. We need to keep moving in case someone comes after us."

Maddox slowly turned his head toward her. "Adam told you a whole lot."

She wouldn't let tears fall again. "A man will say plenty when his life is on the line." She couldn't hold Maddox's gaze.

"Who the fuck is Adam?" Jett demanded. Then he frowned. "Wait, isn't he one of the guards at the facility? Blond dude?"

A shiver slid over her body. "He was one of the guards."

"Was?" Maddox asked.

Luna swallowed.

"Look, man," Jett spoke quickly, "I'm sorry. I didn't mean to—shit, it's not like I wanted to—"

"I saved you. We're done." Maddox motioned to the SUV. "Luna, let's go." He stepped away from Jett.

Jett grabbed his arm. "What?"

"I can't fucking trust you," Maddox gritted out. "You betrayed us once, and I can't risk her life again. They were going to wipe her memory away. If she loses her memory…" Fury and what could have been fear flashed on his face. "I lose her."

I lose her.

"So I'm getting her to safety." Maddox's body was tense with determination. "And you can't know where we're going."

Jett flinched.

"Andreas got out, too." Maddox's gaze swept the area. "He's someone else you might not want to trust too much, if he finds you. Because he's the sonofabitch who helped pump us both full of tranqs so Henry could take us in."

"Henry," Jett growled the name. "That's a bastard I want to get my hands on."

Luna cleared her throat. "No need for that. He's gone."

Jett blinked, and his head immediately craned toward her. "You killed him?" His brows shot up as he studied Luna.

"No, Adam did."

"The guard?" More confusion from Jett. "Jesus, how long was I out? How did I miss so much?"

She marched toward the driver's side of the SUV. "Adam wasn't just a guard. He was Lazarus." Luna jumped in the SUV. Revved the engine. With the door still open, she called, "We need to go!" Because she wasn't going back to that facility. She *couldn't* lose her memory. Not again. It couldn't happen. She'd be helpless.

Helpless in a world full of freaking super soldiers.

They needed to keep using the cover of darkness. They had to move. To flee.

"I won't betray you again." Jett's voice was low, but it easily reached her ears as he spoke to Maddox. "I'll prove it, I promise, I will."

Maddox didn't speak.

"But you're right, man," Jett added. "We need to part ways here. Because if they are hunting us, I'll lead them away from you. I swear it. I'll distract them. Get their attention. And you can disappear."

"Watch your ass, Jett."

A rough laugh was Jett's answer. "Watch yours…and hers."

Then she saw Jett run back the way they'd just come, heading into the darkness of the night and vanishing quickly.

Maddox jumped into the SUV with her. In moments, they were rushing down the road, driving as fast as they could. Her hands wanted to shake, so she just held the steering wheel tighter.

"Luna…"

"He'll be okay, right?"

"He's strong."

That wasn't a good enough answer. "Maybe he should have stayed with us."

"No." His immediate denial. "Jett…hell, he was working with Henry, Luna. The guy was reporting in, telling Henry every move that we made." Maddox's voice roughened. "Being a fucking good soldier."

The SUV hit a pothole, bounced. "Isn't that what you were doing, too? Finding me at first, because that was what you'd been ordered to do?"

"I don't take orders any longer."

No.

Silence. More darkness. A road that didn't seem to end.

"What did Henry tell you about me?" Maddox finally asked.

Her hold jerked on the wheel. They swerved, just a bit, but she steadied them quickly.

"Luna?"

"I got it," she whispered. "It's fine." Adrenaline had flooded her system. She was shaky and her heart wouldn't stop racing and her whole body felt too tight and tense.

"You trusted me."

Her breath came faster. "You told me to." And she'd obeyed. *Being a good fucking soldier.*

"What did he tell you?"

"H-how do you know he said anything?"

"Because the asshole came to me and bragged about how he was turning you against me. He was planning to kill you and wipe your memories away, so there was no need for him to lie to you...the only fucking reason he did it was because the guy wanted to see your reaction. Wanted to see *my* reaction. Every damn thing was an experiment to him."

"I don't understand..." And she didn't. "Why not just kill me at the safe house?"

"Because there were too many witnesses there. Too many guards who might report to the wrong person. But once he got you to the Lazarus facility, he could bring you into the exam room. He could shut off the cameras when he went to work, and no one would be the wiser about what he'd done. *He* had control there."

Henry hadn't been in control when he'd been dying.

Maddox swore. "Dammit, he got to you, didn't he? The lies he told you…they're between us."

Nothing was between them.

"I can feel your fear." Anger was there, making each word almost a growl. "You're not sure you made the right decision with me. And the fear is pumping through your veins like wildfire."

"I'm not afraid of you," Luna denied.

A mocking laugh came from him. "Oh, Luna, you know I can tell when you lie."

Her own anger flared to life. "Then you need to look again." She didn't take her gaze off the road. "Fine. You want to know what Henry said? He said that we knew each other, before Lazarus. Before the first time we died. That you knew me, you knew Adam. And that—that you wanted *me*."

Maddox didn't spit out a denial. He said nothing at all.

"Henry said you wanted me more than you wanted anything. He said he'd learned that you'd gotten possessive and jealous when I-I got involved with Adam." She stumbled there, still confused about how she'd been so wrong about Adam. "You probably don't remember any of that, of course," she added quickly. "I mean, you don't have all of your memories, and Henry spinning the story about you wanting me had to be just a mind game that he was playing—"

"I wanted you from the first moment I saw you at Lazarus."

Her heart seemed to shove into her chest.

"I felt a connection, fucking felt like you were *mine*. And every time you died, it tore out a piece of me. You'd wake up, and everything we'd shared would be gone. We did that shit over and over, and it was a knife cutting into me again and again."

Her throat had gone desert dry.

"Yeah, we knew each other before Lazarus. I had a flash of us—when we *died* together. I told you I died, that I remembered that, but I didn't say that *you* were there, too. Didn't say that the last thing I saw was you. The last thing I remember was holding you. A bullet went through me and into you. Adam was there. I'd stabbed him."

Now she flinched.

"Yeah, I remember stabbing him, but I don't remember *why* I did it. Henry said the bastard was selling government secrets, but we both know Henry can lie as easily as he breathes. The guy wasn't an easy read."

Henry wasn't breathing anymore. Adam had seen to that.

"I remembered," she said, voice soft. "I remembered dying with you."

"What?" His surprise filled the car. "You remember your past? Baby—"

"Just a flash." She wished there was more. "I just...I was going into a motel room. I was going to talk with you. I wanted to turn Adam over to the authorities. I knew you were so angry at him. But I was sure we could just turn him over." Her voice broke. "Then I opened the door. I saw you. And I felt something burn into my body." The one memory she had was the worst memory of her life. Figured. "Henry lied."

She could feel Maddox's stare on her.

"He told me..." Luna licked her lips. "He said that only you and I were brought into Lazarus. That Adam was too dangerous to be included. A traitor to his country. So he hadn't been put into the program." She risked a quick glance at Maddox. "Henry *lied.* Adam was enhanced, just like we are."

"He didn't know." Maddox spoke slowly, as if considering. "There's no damn way he knew. Henry wouldn't have put a Lazarus soldier on guard duty at the facility. He didn't *know* Adam had been kept alive. Shit, *shit.* You get what this means? Adam must have been one of the rogue test subjects that I overheard the lab coats talking about one day. A subject who escaped from his facility and handlers."

Yes, she'd already realized that. "Adam was at a lab in Arizona. He said the place got blown to hell." Goosebumps rose on her arms. "That's where he came up with the idea to set the bombs. If the fire is big enough, Adam said no one looks for survivors." Once more, her gaze cut to the rear-view mirror.

Are they going to look for us?

"Did Adam say how many more of us there were?"

She swallowed. "He told me that his team left him behind."

"I don't think Henry knew the guy had been resurrected. That's how Adam slipped right past his radar. The government is holding secrets, playing games with us."

"We aren't going back," Luna vowed.

"No, we damn well *aren't.*"

He didn't understand. "I can't go back to not knowing. To being helpless." She exhaled slowly. "Don't let me go back to that, understand? If something happens to me, if I lose everything—"

"You won't."

There was something she wanted to do. Something she wanted to try. "Will you trust me?"

"Baby, I do. Don't you see that?"

"I don't know how to bring up my own memories. But I think I can give your life back to you. You can remember everything. And if you do, then we can know all about Lazarus. We know what we signed up for. We know what we're up against." She could do this. She *would* do this. "Let me heal you. Let me give you everything *back*." No more secrets. No more lies. He'd have his past. Every single bit of it.

And since he'd known her before Lazarus, he could help her to discover just who the hell she'd really been, too.

"Henry wasn't lying about one thing." A rough, deep growl rumbled from Maddox. "I do want you more than anything."

She could feel her cheeks heating.

"And I think I wanted you that way, even before Lazarus. When another man had a ring on your finger. *I wanted you*." A warning note. "So when we explore my past, shit, it might not be pretty. Maybe I am the jealous bastard Henry described. Maybe you'll need to get the hell away from me as fast as you can."

***

The fire hadn't gone out easily. Even as the sun rose with the dawn, firefighters still fought to control the blaze, but it just kept flaring up. Jett watched from the shadow of the trees, his gaze sweeping the area. He'd journeyed back to the scene deliberately. He hadn't been lying to Maddox. He *was* going to make things up to his team leader. He was laying out a scent trail, making it damn obvious that at least one Lazarus soldier had survived. He'd stolen a motorcycle from the facility's garage, and he was sure that the lab coats would be able to track it down. He'd deliberately left the GPS tracker on the vehicle. They'd spend their time hunting him, and while they did that, Maddox and Luna would be safe.

It was time to go. His gaze swept the area once more, and he revved the bike's engine.

"You're going to attract too much attention."

The voice was low, deep, and far too close.

Jett's head whipped to the left. He could see a figure there. A guy who hadn't made a sound as he approached through the trees.

"Every good soldier knows you don't let the enemy see you. You keep a low profile."

"You don't know I'm good." He bent, reaching for the knife he'd acquired when he'd taken the motorcycle. With a careful move, he slid the knife out of his boot. "And you just let me see *you*, buddy."

"That's because we don't have to be enemies." The guy stopped, with his hands loose at his sides. "You and I—we have a lot in common."

"Really?" Jett challenged. "And just what the hell would that be?"

"*I think you can guess.*" The guy's words slid right into Jett's head.

Fucking hell. Another Lazarus subject.

The fellow raced forward just as Jett threw his knife.

CHAPTER THIRTEEN

It was easy to disappear in Sin City. When they hit Vegas after driving for far too freaking long, Maddox knew they could get lost in the pool of people. Money had been stashed in the SUV. Plenty of cold cash because obviously Adam Brock had been planning ahead for his escape with Luna.

They used the cash to get a room. He picked a small motel on the edge of town, one that would be far enough off the radar that he didn't think their pursuers would be able to find them. It was just a pit stop for him and Luna. They needed to crash. Shower. Get new clothes and food.

Then they could hit the road again.

At that moment, Luna was in the shower. He could hear the water pouring down over her body. He'd wanted to join her in there, but, hell, with everything that had happened, he wasn't quite sure how Luna would feel about picking up where they'd left off in the safe house.

She trusted me.

She could easily have thought he was the monster. The bastard who'd hunted her down. But she hadn't. She'd gone into the fire to pull him out.

He stripped off his shirt. Tossed it across the room and rubbed his chest. Did she realize he'd been telling her the stark truth? Every time they'd had a mission that had taken her life, he'd felt ripped open. He'd had to fight the clawing darkness in his head.

Because when she woke up, he lost her.

She stared at him as if he were a stranger. Because to her, that was exactly what he was. He lost Luna over and over. And he nearly went mad.

Henry hadn't been wrong when he said that Maddox wanted her so badly. There was nothing in the world he wanted more than Luna.

Not his past. Not the life he'd once had.

Nothing.

The shower had shut off. When he focused, he could hear the faint *drip, drip, drip* of water. He turned toward the bathroom door.

It opened a moment later. Luna stood on the threshold, a white towel wrapped around her body, and her dark, wet hair fell around her shoulders. Faint drops of water clung to her skin.

Arousal hit him hard. His dick jerked eagerly even as Maddox found himself advancing on her.

"Shower's all yours." She stepped to the side, waving her hand. "I know you want to get the ash off."

No, he wanted to get her towel off. Wanted to rip it aside and put his hands all over her. But when Maddox glanced down at his hands, he saw the dark marks on them. "Shower first."

He'd get his hands clean, and then—

"First?" Luna repeated.

He brushed past her. "Then we'll get you something to eat." *Take care of her.* He cleared his throat. "You must be starving."

"I am."

He started to shut the door.

"But I was really hoping we'd fuck before we eat."

Maddox whipped around to face her. He'd misheard. Must have. Absolutely.

"Did I say the wrong thing?" Her gaze searched his face. "I thought you might join me in the shower, but you didn't—"

"You still want me." After everything...after Henry, after Adam, after learning that he'd lusted for her before Lazarus—

"Of course." Luna wet her lips. "Don't you want me?"

"Only every time I draw a breath."

Surprise flashed on her face. Okay, shit, his voice had been guttural. And he smelled like fire and had ash and soot all over him. He needed to shower and get his control in check. Because if he was going to touch her again, he'd make sure he used every care.

He headed fully into the bathroom. Stripped. Yanked on the shower. The water that came down was ice cold, and he couldn't get the hot water to work. *Screw it.* He climbed into the shower. Let the cold water hit him. He washed his body, and then he turned off the water with a jerk of his hand. Maddox shoved a towel over his body, his thoughts all on *her*.

He stalked back into the bedroom. Her back was to him as she stood near the bed, but she quickly whirled, her eyes widening. "That was fast."

"The water was ice." He dropped his towel to the floor.

Her gaze immediately dropped, too. But not to the floor.

"Didn't help anything," he muttered as he reached for her towel. "Still want you just as badly."

"Good."

She had no clue of the danger that was right in front of her. "Wanting you this much…it isn't safe." He let her towel fall. Sweet hell, but she was beautiful. Tight, dusky nipples. Round breasts. Curving hips.

His hand lifted toward her.

And his finger brushed the scar on her side.

"Maddox?"

He slid to his knees before her. Put his mouth on the scar. "I don't want to hurt you." For just an instant, he could see her—in that other motel room, her eyes wide with shock as she stumbled.

She didn't stumble right then. Instead, her hands settled on his shoulders. "I'm not afraid of you."

Maybe you should be. He kissed a path across her stomach. Slid his hands to her thighs.

"I thought I was."

His hands stilled.

"Then I realized that I was...I was afraid of how you make me feel."

His fingers trailed up her inner thigh. He was so close to her sex. So close. "Maybe that's a bad thing."

"No." He heard the soft click of her swallow. "Because without you, I'm not sure I'd feel *anything.*" Her nails bit into his shoulders. "I want you. My whole body seems as if it's about to rip apart. My heart is going crazy. I can't draw in a breath deep enough."

Adrenaline rush. Shit, he needed to get his control in check and help bring her down. "It's because of everything that happened. It's because—"

"It's because you're touching me. Because I like it when you do. I don't know what happened before Lazarus. I don't know why I was with someone else."

He stared up into her eyes.

"I can't ever imagine wanting anyone else…*this* way."

"Luna…" A warning. Because his need for her was about to rage out of control.

"I'm afraid of how I feel about you. And I'm afraid that I *won't* feel without you. You're inside of me."

Not fucking yet. But he was sure about to be.

"You came for me in that lab. You *saved* me when Adam was going to shoot me." Her gaze was so deep and dark. "And then you went for Jett. Even though you knew it was dangerous, you still went to save him after he'd turned on you. I don't care what you *think* about yourself. But I know you're a good man. With or without the memories."

And his control shredded. The trust she was showing him… The way Luna stared at him… As if he were some kind of hero when he felt like a monster.

The fact that she was looking at him, knowing him…

I'm no stranger to her. She wants me, she knows me.

He tumbled her onto the bed. He spread her legs and his mouth went to her sex. He kissed her, he licked her, he stroked her, he devoured her. Maddox wanted to give her so much pleasure that she went insane.

Then he wanted to give her even more.

He worked her with his fingers and his mouth, going wild for her taste. Her hips bucked up against him as she called out his name. Need was in her voice, and her nails raked over his shoulders.

He rubbed her clit. Applied just the right amount of pressure.

She came. An explosion that shook her whole body. She came against his mouth, and he *loved* it. He licked her core, wanting every last drop of her.

Then he surged up. Spread her legs wider and drove into her. For a moment, the whole world seemed to go still. She was tight and hot, his personal heaven, and her eyes were wide with pleasure. Pleasure he'd given to her.

Then she smiled. Whispered, "Maddox..." And her legs locked around his hips.

He was a goner.

He surged into her, withdrew, and drove deep even harder. Over and over again because he was frantic for release. The bed groaned and squeaked, and it rammed into the wall, but he didn't care. He rolled them over. Brought her on top of him so that her knees were on either side of his hips. Oh, hell, yes, he liked this position because he could reach her breasts. Could lean up and lick them. Suck her nipples. So he did. And she moaned and arched against him. She rose and fell in a desperate rhythm to match him.

He put his hand between their bodies. Even as he surged up into her, Maddox was strumming her clit. Her head tipped back, and she gasped out his name. He felt her release all along the length of his dick. Squeezing. Contractions that didn't end.

Contractions that drove him right into oblivion.

Her body shuddered above him, and her hands flew down to press against his chest as she braced herself. The pleasure kept rolling through him, through every cell and nerve.

Her head lowered. Her mouth pressed to his. The kiss was hot, open, and it just made him want more.

Who the hell was he kidding? Maddox knew the truth. When it came to Luna, he'd *always* want more.

***

Luna trailed her hand over Maddox's chest. He'd pulled the curtains closed, trying to shut out the day, and only a sliver of light slid into the motel room.

They'd eaten. He'd brought in some take-out for her, and she'd discovered that she was wild for noodles and chicken. He'd just smiled at her, and Luna had realized that he knew those were her weakness.

She didn't remember her life, but he seemed to know everything about her.

He'd made a point of knowing everything.

She'd had one flash of her past, just one, and she was so hungry for more. She didn't know how to unlock her own memories, but she could help him.

Luna eased out a slow breath. Her hand slid up, moving to his head. Her fingertips pressed lightly to his temple. It was their brains that were different, right? All of the memories were up there? So she just had to focus on healing his mind. Her eyes closed as her fingers began to tingle.

"You don't have to…" Maddox's deep voice told her.

"Yes, I do." Because if she could help him, then she would.

Her fingers grew even warmer.

Luna suspected she'd do just about anything for Maddox.

***

She was trying to heal him. Trying to fix a brain that had been in a dead man's body. Maddox's hand rose because he was going to tell her to stop. It didn't seem fair for him to have memories when she didn't. When she could wake up and have everything gone. He was going to stop her—

"Maddie, Santa was here!" A woman stood in a doorway, a woman with dark hair and green eyes just like his. "Come and see!"

For an instant, he had a fast impression of a bedroom. Superheroes and football players were on the walls. He leapt out of the bed and ran toward the woman. But he didn't rush past her, ready to get to the presents below. He grabbed her. Held her in a tight hug. "Love you, Mom."

The vision vanished, but the memory stayed, shifted, grew stronger in his mind. Maddox's breath came faster as another vision hit him.

A girl with long, dark hair strolled on a beach, near the water's edge. She wore a pair of white shorts and a black t-shirt. She turned toward him, flashing a wide smile. A smile that lit her dark eyes.

She was the most beautiful thing he'd ever seen. At fifteen, he fell in love. Lost it for —

"I'm Luna," she said, holding out her hand to him. "My family just moved here."

He took her hand. Held it so carefully. "Maddox." His voice cracked when he said his name.

But she didn't seem to notice. Her warm smile stayed in place. "Have you lived here all of your life?"

He was still holding her hand. "Yes."

"You are so lucky."

He absolutely was. The waves crashed as he stared at her.

Maddox sucked in a sharp breath as that bittersweet memory flooded through him. He'd met Luna on the beach. They'd become best friends. He'd spent every summer day swimming, fishing, or boating with her. They'd been so close.

As if a floodgate had been opened in his mind, more memories slammed into his head.

He could see his dad and his mom — they were hiking in the mountains.

His dad was teaching him how to drive.

His mom was teaching him how to do the box step.

And Luna...Luna was there, so many times. His date for the senior prom. She called him her best friend, and he'd wanted so much more. He hadn't pushed, though, because he didn't want to lose Luna. He'd waited, waited too fucking long because —

"I'm going to marry Luna."

Maddox froze at that announcement. He'd been staring out at the beach, enjoying the sound of the waves crashing into the shore. He loved the beach, always had. He'd been one lucky asshole to grow up in Gulf Shores. But at his buddy Adam's words, he whirled around. "What?"

The guy nodded, his blue eyes hard and determined. "I'm going to marry her. So I'm telling you right now, she's mine. Keep your hands — "

Off her. Maddox lunged up in the bed, and Luna's fingers slid away from his head. "Maddox? Are you okay?"

His head seemed to be splitting open. Too many memories. A whole lifetime. Suddenly battering at him like angry waves hitting the beach right before a storm.

Keep your hands off her.

"Adam moved to Gulf Shores my senior year. You and Adam were both juniors, one year below me." His breath heaved out. "He was my friend. Your friend." Until Adam had wanted to be more. And then he'd closed in on Luna. "Said he loved you from the first moment he saw you." Maddox climbed out of the bed, pacing. Fuck, fucking hell. The memories were all cramming into his head. He could see himself playing football with Adam. Laughing at the guy's dumb jokes. Adam could be a funny sonofabitch. He'd been so good at charm, and he'd charmed his way right into Luna's heart.

"Adam and I were on the beach when he said he was going to marry you." The memory he'd first gotten was so much clearer now. "He was just talking—we were freaking kids, but he was warning me off you because he knew how I felt about you, too." He looked back at her.

Luna was in the bed, with the covers pulled up near her chin. She stared at him with her dark eyes. The girl he'd first met on the beach. The girl...

I fell in love with her when I first saw her, too. But he hadn't said anything. Not to her. Not to Adam. He'd waited too damn long. Why? Why?

I was a kid. And I thought I had forever.

Until someone else had come too close and tried to steal the girl he wanted.

"You fell for him." He swallowed. "Since I was a year ahead of you, I went into the military, and when I came back..." He rubbed a chest that burned. "I didn't ask you to wait. Didn't tell you how I felt but I fucking should have told you. I *should* have told you everything."

She shook her head in confusion. "Maddox?"

He grabbed his temples. They throbbed and ached and the memories were blasting through him. They were absolutely ripping him apart.

"*Traitor,*" he gasped out that one word. "He was selling government secrets. Had to stop him. You were gonna marry him..." His eyes squeezed shut. "Didn't mean to stab him. He attacked me. Said he wouldn't go to jail. Said..."

"Luna has been working this scene with me. You think she's so innocent? Why the hell do you believe she's marrying me? Because of the money we make together. Because Luna has been working this con from day one with me."

"No," Maddox growled. But the memory wouldn't stop playing in his mind.

"She was never as innocent as you thought. That's why she chose me, and not you. Luna didn't want the fucking good guy." Adam's eyes had gleamed as he yanked out his gun. "She wants me."

Adam was going to fire his weapon.

Maddox leapt forward, stabbing fast with the knife…

A soft hand touched his shoulder. "Maddox?"

He grabbed Luna, pulling her close, but that wasn't good enough. His hands flew over her, down to her side. She'd put on a t-shirt, and he yanked it up so that he could touch her bare flesh.

So that he could touch the scar on her skin. "Maddox?"

His head whipped up, and he stared into her eyes.

A faint furrow appeared between her brows. "Are you okay? I just—I want to help you."

And once more, he could hear Adam's words in his head. *"She was never as innocent as you thought. That's why she chose me, and not you. Luna didn't want the fucking good guy."*

He'd always played by the rules. His whole life. Never stepped out of line. Never took any risks. Adam had been the risk taker. Adam had been the life of the party. Adam had been the one to put his ring on Luna's finger.

"I did something wrong."

Her words had him sucking in a hard breath.

"Didn't I?" Her gaze searched his. "I'm sorry. I just wanted to give your memories back to you. But I didn't really know what I was doing." She bit her lip. "I hurt you."

Luna was so beautiful. And she owned his heart. Then. Now.

Had she been working with Adam? If that bastard hadn't shot them both, would Maddox have been forced to turn Luna over to the authorities?

"I'm trying to be good," Luna whispered. "I get so confused sometimes. Everything seems so messed up."

His head was about to explode. Her scar was beneath his fingertips. The constant reminder of death. Of life.

A tear leaked down Luna's cheek. "I hurt you, when I just wanted to help you."

Fuck it. Maddox realized it didn't matter what she'd done or hadn't done in the past. *She is mine.*

He grabbed her, lifting Luna into his arms and holding her tight.

"Maddox?"

Memories were driving him mad. Tearing apart his mind. Pushing him to the brink of sanity. But Luna wasn't a memory. She was real. Flesh and blood. In his arms. *His.* "The past doesn't matter."

Pain flashed on her face.

He pressed her up against the wall. His cock shoved toward her. She hadn't put on underwear, and he was still buck-ass naked. "*You* matter."

Luna licked her lower lip. "You matter to me, too."

He kissed her, swiping his tongue over the lip she'd just licked. Then he was thrusting his tongue into her mouth, tasting her, even as his cock thrust into her body. Deep and hard. There was no holding back. There was no *going* back. The past—dammit, he wasn't going to make the same mistakes. He wouldn't do it.

Her fingers dug into his arms. He thrust harder and deeper as he kissed his way down her neck. He licked her throat, bit her lightly, wanting to mark her. Wanting to own her.

Just wanting her.

She came, crying out with a fast, hard release, and it was his name that she called. His body that she held.

He emptied himself into her. Shuddering as he came, filling her completely even as Maddox knew that he would never, ever get enough of her because...

"I love you," Maddox rasped.

Her breath caught. Her eyes flared wide. And he just said it again. "I love you."

CHAPTER FOURTEEN

Night had fallen again. Maddox had told her it was safer for them to travel at night, that they'd be harder to spot under the cover of darkness.

He'd stolen a different car. Nothing flashy. A small sedan that wasn't going to attract too much attention. He drove it now with single-minded determination, his body tense. His gaze was focused on the road that just stretched and stretched before them.

"Did it work?" Luna asked, breaking the silence that had settled heavily in the car. She hadn't been able to bring herself to ask the question before even though she'd suspected the result. They'd spent the day fucking. Sleeping. Eating. Not talking. Not much talking at all. Except for…

I love you.

Her hands twisted in her lap. She hadn't responded to his declaration because she wasn't sure how she was supposed to respond. His gaze had been blazing, his face so hard and fierce when he growled those words to her.

And she'd…she'd liked hearing them. She'd felt ice melting inside of her. Ice she hadn't even realized was there — ice around her heart. She'd warmed up, and Luna had found a smile curving her lips.

To be loved by Maddox…

She liked that idea. She liked him.

Did she love him, too?

She wasn't sure. Mostly because she didn't understand love, not fully. She knew fear. She knew fury. But love — what did it mean, really? That she trusted him? She did. She'd put her life in his hands, and he hadn't let her down.

Did it mean that she wanted him?

Absolutely. She couldn't imagine wanting someone else the way she did him.

He made her feel safe. Strange, since the first time she saw him, Luna had been utterly terrified.

"It worked." His deep voice filled the car.

Her breath exhaled in a rush. "You don't seem very happy." And she was confused. She'd wanted to make him happy.

Was that love? Wanting someone else to be happy?

"Not all memories are good, Luna."

"Oh." Yes. Of course. Luna cleared her throat. "Some are though, right? Some have to be good."

Now he glanced at her. His gaze seemed to heat. "Some are."

She tried to smile for him, but he'd already looked away. She searched for something to say. "I think it would be better to have the bad memories, too. Better them than nothing." Considering the only memory she had was a bad one.

"You might be better not knowing some things."

The road twisted up ahead. They'd left Vegas. Those bright lights were far behind them now. The desert surrounded them.

Maddox glanced in the rear-view mirror.

Automatically, Luna glanced back, too. The road was pitch black behind them, but—

"I hear an engine," Maddox said, his voice tense.

She strained, and, yes, she could hear an engine, too, in the distance. But she didn't see anyone.

"The driver isn't using lights because he doesn't want to tip us off that he's there, but I hear the engine. He's not hiding well enough." Maddox shot into the curve up ahead, and when he came out, the car lunged forward even faster—as fast as the sedan could go—as Maddox shoved down the gas pedal. The sedan's engine snarled.

She was still looking back. Still not seeing anything, but definitely hearing the other vehicle approach. "Maddox, no one followed us from the motel." She was sure of it.

But the car was there, right behind them. And the fact that the headlights were off...*not a good sign.*

Up ahead, the road twisted again.

"Big rig is about to pass us," Maddox growled. "I can hear it coming from the north." He slowed down, just a bit, as they took the twist in the road.

When they came out of the curve, she could see the big rig's lights, too. Bright and shining. Such a stark contrast to the vehicle tailing them. The sedan shuddered as it hurtled ahead on the road, staying in its own lane as it swept past the big rig and —

The big rig whipped toward them. The movement happened so fast that Luna didn't even have time to scream. The big rig careened into their lane, slammed into their sedan, and a terrible crunch of metal filled her ears. The rig hit hard on the driver's side, and glass exploded through the sedan.

The impact tossed the sedan off the road. It hurtled through the air, and Luna fought to suck in a deep breath so that she could call out to Maddox.

Her hand was reaching for him when the sedan slammed into the ground. It hit, rolled and rolled. The impact whipped her head back and forth. Air bags exploded around her. She shoved the bags out of her way even as she felt blood trickling down her cheek. Her heart thundered in her chest, and she clawed at her seatbelt, ripping it out of the way. The top of the sedan had crumpled onto her. The passenger side door was bent and twisted, and Maddox—

The car stopped moving.

There was a terrible silence, one punctuated only by the ragged gasp of her breaths. An airbag hadn't deployed near Maddox. His upper body was crumpled over the steering wheel, and the driver side door appeared to be cutting into his side. The coppery scent of blood filled her nostrils.

"Maddox?" Her voice was a whisper as she reached out her hand to him.

He didn't move.

She strained, fighting to get to him as she shoved the dashboard out of her way. And she focused *hard,* trying to use her enhanced senses to pick up his heartbeat or the rasp of his breath. But…

No beat.

No beat and no breath.

Maddox wasn't breathing. His heart wasn't beating.

"No." She touched him, his skin was still warm, but there was blood, a whole lot of blood all over him. "Maddox!" Her fingers slid down his neck, but there was no pulse. Of course, there was no pulse. How could there be a pulse when there wasn't a heartbeat?

The scent of gasoline reached her, burning her nose. Oh, God. Maddox was dead. They were trapped in the car, and gas was leaking from the wreck. *Just like the scene before!*

For one wild moment, she remembered the mother and son that she and Maddox had helped. The boy had been trapped in the car, and she'd smelled gasoline just like this. If Maddox hadn't moved so fast, the boy would have died in the explosion.

Luna knew she had to move fast, too. She had to get Maddox to safety.

"You wake back up, do you understand me?" Glass cut into her arm, but she didn't care. The steering wheel and front dash had crumped into Maddox, and she pounded them with desperate fury. "You hurry up and come *back!*"

Footsteps rushed toward her. A man's voice shouted out, "Please tell me you're alive!"

She was.

Maddox…

Will be.

"Oh, God, oh, God…" The man's frantic mutters reached her as she heard him hurrying toward the wreck. "I just…I was reaching for the glove box. Swerved. Not used to driving that rig. First freakin' time out. Didn't mean to hit you…please be the hell alive!"

"I am alive!" Luna called. "But we need help!" Maddox did. Even with her Lazarus strength, she couldn't get him out of the sedan from that angle. She turned her body and kicked hard at the passenger door. Once, twice, and the door flew off.

Not that it had been held on very well, not after the crash.

She leapt from the car and saw the man who'd just ran to the vehicle. He wore a baseball cap, a big coat, and loose jeans. The cap was pulled down low over his face. He grabbed her, and his hands ran down her arms. "You're okay. Thank Christ! I was afraid I had killed you!"

Not her. Maddox. "We have to get my friend out." She yanked away from him and started to run around the wreckage.

But the guy grabbed her once more. "You smell that gasoline?"

She did. All the more reason that they had to get Maddox out of there, right then. She'd seen exactly how a scene like this could end already. Maybe the car would blow, maybe it wouldn't. But she wasn't going to take any chances with Maddox. "We have to get him out." She yanked free and ran to the driver's side. So much glass.

So much twisted metal. And the scent of blood was almost as strong as the acrid odor of the gasoline.

She grabbed the door handle. Heaved. The door was smashed in tight, and she knew Maddox's side had taken the worst hit when the big rig had collided with the sedan. She pulled harder. *Harder.*

"You're not getting that open," the guy in the baseball cap said in a cracking voice. "We need to call nine-one-one."

They didn't have time for nine-one-one.

She pulled harder. The door groaned but didn't move.

"You need the freaking jaws of life," the guy groused. "Oh, shit. Wait, that guy—" He shoved his hand through the broken window. Touched Maddox's neck. "He's dead."

"Only for the moment!"

The guy's shoulders stiffened. "What?"

"He's only dead for the moment. He'll be fine soon enough. I just need to get him *out.*"

The fellow backed away. His cap was pulled low over his face, so she couldn't see his expression, but, voice shocked, he announced, "Lady, you're crazy."

The door groaned again. She could feel it giving way. She could get it off, get Maddox out, and then the fire could do whatever the hell it wanted to the sedan. "Hold on, Maddox, please,"

Luna begged as blood dripped into her eyes. "I'm going to get you—"

Something hard swung into the back of her head. Big, heavy, and the hit sent her slamming into the wrecked side of the sedan. Her hands flattened against the metal, and she whirled around.

The fellow in the baseball cap had a tire iron in his hands, and he was holding it like a baseball bat.

"You...hit me?" Luna gasped.

He smiled. His head angled up, and she finally got a good look at his face. And she caught sight of the red hair that had been hidden beneath his ball cap.

I know him.

"Sure as hell did hit you, sweetheart. And I'm about to knock your pretty ass out."

He was—oh, God, he was the guy who'd shot at her when she'd been trying to escape with Maddox from the inferno that had been the first cabin! The fellow who'd moved too fast, the guy who'd hidden when Maddox took everyone else out. The guy who was—

"Lazarus?" Luna whispered.

"That's right, and you're my key to getting my life back. So, sorry, but the guy in the car is staying dead, and you're coming with me." He swung the tire iron right at her head.

She ducked. Drove her fist into his chest as hard as she could. He grunted and jerked, but he didn't let go of the tire iron. Instead, he slammed it into her back. Pain burst through her body. Luna hit the ground, rolled, sliding away from the car. Away from the bastard with the tire iron. "You've been…hunting me."

She could hear the crackle of flames coming from the sedan.

"Hell, yeah, I have been. And you made it easy. Hell, you even gave me the idea for this attack. You just *had* to stop and play the hero, didn't you? Help that mom and her kid? Heard all about the story when I was tracking you." He once again gripped the tire iron as if it were a baseball bat. "Here's a tip. When you're on the run, don't pull some dramatic rescue shit that has local cops talking like they just witnessed a miracle."

"I don't want your tips. I want you to get the hell away from me!"

"You should have stayed in the old hospital. We weren't done with you. But after you attacked the doctor, we had to get her to safety. She was the best we had, so we couldn't risk her. Don't look at me like that. I cleaned you up, didn't I? Got all the blood off you. Sure, I broke your neck because I needed you out for a while, but I didn't leave you a bloody mess. Even gave you a new hospital gown. I'm a gentleman like that."

He was between her and the sedan. Her and Maddox. And the flames were getting bigger.

He smiled. "If he burns, he won't be coming back now, will he?"

Her hands fisted as she rose to her feet. "I'm not letting him burn."

"You don't get a choice. I wasn't hired to bring him in. Only you." He rolled back his shoulders. "So I'm afraid this is going to hurt." He lunged at her, swinging the tire iron.

She caught it in her hand. Held it inches from her head. "You too used to hurting regular humans? Did you forget that I'm strong, too?"

He laughed.

She didn't. Luna rammed the tire iron back at him, aiming for his collar bone. He howled in pain, and she zipped past him, throwing the tire iron as far as she could. Luna grabbed for the sedan's door.

And the bastard grabbed her. He curled his hands around her waist and heaved back. She didn't let go of the door, and when he pulled her—

Hell, yes.

The driver's door finally broke loose. It crashed into the ground even as her attacker threw her down. Luna surged up, but he drove his fist at her. And the hit was so powerful it felt as if he'd hit her with the tire iron again. For a moment, everything seemed to go dark.

"You're coming with me, sweetheart."

Did she look like his freaking sweetheart?

"The doctor thinks you're the next level. The way to make us stronger without losing our memories. You're the key, the fucking key to it all, just like Adam said. And you're worth more money that you can imagine."

He knew Adam? Wait — had he been *working* with Adam? "You…you were working with Adam." She tried to think. Tried to remember what Adam had said in that lab. He'd mentioned a partner. Said the guy's name was — "Sam?"

He stiffened. "How the hell do you know my name?"

"Because…" A rasp. "Adam told me, right before he died."

"No!" A fierce denial. "No way! No freaking way!"

She heard doors slamming. Oh, dammit. Was that his backup? His team?

He bit off a curse. Then she felt a knife at her throat.

"One wrong word," Sam snarled into her ear, "and I will cut off your head. Do you understand me?"

Bullshit. Sure, he might be strong enough to do it, but he'd just said she was his money train. And without her…*no way are you riding on any train.*

Footsteps rushed toward them. Two men, both big, strong, and wearing dark coats. Their faces were locked into tense lines.

Behind her, the fire burned hotter. She could hear it. Smell it. The car hadn't exploded, though. Not yet. *Not yet.*

"That car is going to blow!" One of the approaching men yelled. "You need to get the hell away from it!"

"Right!" Her captor yelled. "We're coming your way, we're—"

She drove her elbow back into him, as hard as she could. But when Luna attacked him, the blade cut across her throat. She felt the blood pour out as the pain sliced right through her.

She sagged onto the ground, falling to her knees. She'd been so certain he was bluffing. So sure—

"Bitch," he growled, "now you can't say a word. Not a damn thing." He smiled at her.

And a bullet tore into his chest. He staggered back, his eyes flaring wide, and then he let out a roar. He turned for the man who'd just fired— one of the men in the thick coats. He lunged for the shooter—

Another bullet hit her attacker in the head. He went down, and he didn't get up.

But Luna got up. With one hand at her neck, she ran for the sedan.

"It's going to blow! Lady, we need to get out of here!"

She grabbed for Maddox. So still. Too still. With one arm, she started pulling him from the wreckage.

But in the next instant, Luna found herself yanked away from Maddox. Yanked by a guy who seemed far too strong.

"I'm saving you!" He barked at her. "Look, don't fight me, okay? My name is Sawyer, and I just want to help you."

"She's bleeding like crazy," the other guy muttered.

"Yeah, Flynn, I *see* that. She needs a hospital right the hell now." Sawyer held her with his hands on her shoulders. "I'm sorry, lady, but your friend in that car is dead."

No, he wasn't. She tried to speak, only the knife had cut her too deeply. Her body was swaying.

"She's losing too much blood," Sawyer snapped. "We need to stop the blood loss *now,* or she's going to die."

Dizziness burst through her. Sawyer tried to lift her into his arms.

She punched his nose. Luna was pretty sure she broke it because she heard the crack of bones and felt a spurt of blood beneath her fist. He let her go, and she flew back to the car.

"She's fast," Flynn's low voice easily reached her ears. "And strong."

She grabbed Maddox. Hauled him out. Held him tight even as she swayed.

"That's because she's one of us," Sawyer replied, voice wary. "And I'm guessing so the hell is he."

One of us.

No, oh, no.

They were in front of her. The burning car was behind her. "Get…away…" Oh, damn, but it *hurt* trying to say those words. And they barely came out. Mostly a gurgle just emerged from her.

"We're here to help you," Sawyer said again. "Just trust—"

Behind her, the sedan exploded. The force of the blast sent her hurtling forward. *Just like before. But the little boy lived. He got to stay with his mom. Maddox will be okay. We'll both make it. We'll —*

She lost her grip on Maddox. And when her head slammed into the ground, everything went dark.

CHAPTER FIFTEEN

Maddox jerked upright, sucking in a deep gulp of air. The scent of fire and ash immediately filled his nostrils, and for a moment, Maddox thought he was somehow trapped once more at the Lazarus lab. Burning in the flames…

"Ah, well, he's back."

His head whipped to the right. He saw a man he didn't recognize. Tall, muscled, with a hard stare that said the fellow had seen shit and lived to tell the tale. The fellow's dark hair was tousled, and a faint stubble covered his jaw.

"Welcome back to the land of the living." He gave Maddox a faint smile. "I'm Flynn, and I—"

Maddox lunged at the bastard. He slammed the fellow to the ground, and then Maddox's hand went for the knife that he kept in his boot—

"Not…there," Flynn gasped. "Took it…in case you…came back…like this…"

Came back. The sonofabitch knew what Maddox was. He put his elbow on the guy's neck. "Where is Luna? If you've hurt her, I will destroy you."

The guy shoved Maddox—hard. Hard enough that if Maddox hadn't been enhanced, he would have gone hurtling back. Instead, Maddox just shoved down harder.

"Shit," the man gasped. "You're...stronger..."

"Luna," Maddox snarled right back. "Where is she?"

"Over here!"

At that call, Maddox's head whipped up. He looked to the left and about fifty yards away, he saw a black Jeep parked near the edge of the road. Jett was there, crouching beside—

"Luna!" Maddox roared her name. Then he was surging toward Jett, running to Luna, and falling to his knees beside her.

Some stranger had his hands on Luna's neck, and the man's fingers were covered in her blood.

"She's going to die," the guy muttered. "We just need to let her go. It's not like she won't wake up again."

Oh, hell, no. "She can't die." Maddox's frantic gaze flew up to Jett. "She *can't* die."

And the guy trying to stop the wild flow of blood gave a low whistle. "Wait. She's not Lazarus? Jett, dammit, you said she was—"

Maddox stiffened. Had Jett betrayed him again? In a flash, he was up—and he'd snatched the gun that Jett had holstered on his hip.

Maddox pointed the weapon at Jett and the bastard with him. "Get the fuck away from her."

Jett didn't attack. He just held up his hands. "It's not what you think, Maddox. I swear, it's not."

Maddox kept his gaze on the man kneeling so close to Luna. The man who had her blood on his hands. "Get away from Luna, or I'll put a bullet in your brain."

He heard footsteps coming up behind him. The dick who'd called himself Flynn. Maddox didn't look at him, not yet. If necessary, though, he'd put bullets into the heads of all the bastards trying to hurt Luna.

"If I move my hands, if I let up on the pressure, she'll just bleed out faster." The stranger's bright blue gaze didn't waver from Maddox's face. "Look, calm down a minute, okay? My name's Sawyer Cage, and the guy behind you is Flynn—"

Maddox growled. He didn't want more introductions. "You hurt her." He could see the twisted big rig. And flames were crackling nearby...from the sedan?

"I didn't," Sawyer denied quickly. "That was another guy. A redhead with a death wish because your lady here is a definite fighter. He wanted to leave you to burn in that car, but Luna didn't let him. She fought him. She got you out."

A redhead?

"We put a bullet in his brain," Flynn said. "Then the bastard went flying when the sedan exploded. His body's a bit down the road."

Maddox shook his head, trying to follow everything even as a terrible, numbing fear swept through him. *So much blood.*

"He sliced her throat. She's strong, though," Sawyer added quickly. "Hasn't given up." He looked down at Luna. "Why haven't you given up? Why are you still fighting?" His expression showed his confusion. "Just let go. You can wake up in a few minutes, and you'll be strong again."

"No!" Maddox yelled.

Jett stepped toward him. "Luna's different." He spoke quickly as his gaze jerked around the small group. "Sawyer, Flynn—you don't understand her. If Luna dies, then she'll lose her memories. That's why she's fighting. Because when she wakes up, she'll be in a world she doesn't know. With people she doesn't know. Maddox doesn't want that happening. He doesn't want Luna to lose herself again."

Sawyer's calculating stare had slid back to Maddox. "He doesn't want to lose *her*."

Maddox stalked toward Luna. Maddox put the gun to Sawyer's temple as he crouched next to Luna.

"What the fuck, man?" Flynn burst out. "Get that gun away from him! We are *helping* you!"

"Maddox isn't the trusting sort." Jett was sweating. "And, um, he has reason."

Maddox glared at Sawyer. "You make one wrong move, and I'll end you."

Sawyer's eyes narrowed.

Maddox held his stare a moment, then glanced down at Luna. Her body was trembling, tears leaked from her closed eyes, and the blood…

"Baby…" Anguish ripped through him. "Baby, I need you to heal yourself."

"What the hell is he talking about?" Flynn's growling voice demanded. A hint of Texas slid through his words.

Maddox ignored him. He leaned toward Luna, but kept the gun on Sawyer. "Luna, baby, use that heat of yours. If I were the one on the ground, you'd be healing me, I know you would. You can heal yourself. Use your power, baby. Turn it on yourself. You can do it, I know you can."

Her eyes flew open. She stared up at him. *Mad…dox?* Her lips formed his name, but she didn't speak.

He caught her left hand in his. "I'm here. They just told me that you saved my ass." His last memory was of the big rig plowing into them. "Now save yourself. You hear me? Save yourself. Turn that heat on, use it to heal your wounds. Stop the bleeding. Keep *fighting*."

Her lashes slid closed.

His heart was about to jump right out of his chest. Maddox brought her hand to his mouth. Kissed her knuckles. He could feel her skin starting to warm. Or at least, he hoped he did.

"I've got a chopper en route," Sawyer said, his voice low. "A doctor will be on it. If you can keep your girl with us a while longer…"

"I'm going to always keep her with me." No, he'd always stay with her. No matter what. Memories or no memories. He slid her hand up to her throat, putting her fingers on top of Sawyer's. He didn't know if this shit would work, if she *could* heal herself with such a terrible injury, but he had nothing to lose.

Luna. Luna is what I have to lose.

And Luna wasn't nothing. She was everything.

So he started talking to her. He wanted her to hear his voice. Wanted her to know he was there. That he would always be there.

"The first memory I have is of my mother."

He felt Sawyer tense.

"Christmas morning. She came into my bedroom to tell me that Santa had been at our house."

Luna shuddered.

"I remember meeting you."

"What in the hell?" Flynn had closed in on him. "How do you remember all that?"

Luna's eyes opened again, just a faint slit. Her breath heaved in and out.

Maddox didn't respond to Flynn. Instead, he kept talking to Luna. "You were walking on a beach. The wind was blowing your hair. You had on white shorts. A sexy little top, and I took one look at you and knew my whole world had changed."

A tear leaked from her eye. "*I don't…I don't want to forget you…*" Her voice whispered through his mind.

"You aren't dying." He swallowed. "Baby, you're going to keep focusing that heat of yours inward, got me? I can hear the chopper coming." He couldn't. Not yet. "You just have to hold on a few more minutes. Then a doctor will be here. Your body heals faster than any other super soldier I've seen. You get past the rough part, and it's smooth sailing."

Her breath came faster.

"We used to go sailing," he told her, struggling to keep his voice easy. Reassuring. "We'd go out into the Intracoastal Waterway, and the sailboat would cut right through the water. I taught you to sail, but you were soon better than me. We'd stay on the water for hours. God, you had this little red bikini…I thought you'd give me a heart attack every single time you wore it…"

He kept talking.

She kept breathing.

And soon, he did hear the sound of the helicopter coming to them. The chopper landed right there on the highway. They loaded Luna on a stretcher, got her onboard, and a woman with a long braid of dark hair went to work on Luna.

They all piled in the chopper.

"Cops will find the wreckage eventually," Flynn said to Sawyer. "Do we need to worry about the body?"

Sawyer shook his head. "I shot him between the eyes. He's gone."

The chopper rose. Jett was beside Maddox, and Maddox—

"Gonna give back that gun anytime soon?" Sawyer asked him.

Maddox had kept that gun pointed at the fellow's head until the chopper arrived. Now the gun was still in Maddox's right hand. Surrender it?

Nah. He just tucked it into his jeans.

"I'm going to help her." Sawyer exhaled as the chopper began to rise. "I'm going to help you both."

Maddox wasn't ready to be besties with the bastard. He wasn't ready for anything…but for Luna to get better. For her to heal.

"I've been looking for you a long time," Sawyer continued.

Jett cleared his throat. "Maddox, you need to hear this guy's story."

Yeah, he did. But *after*. "After Luna's better." Because until her pain stopped, his world was fucking wrecked. He leaned close to her. The chopper was loud now, vibrating. But he kept talking.

"When I was a senior, you were my prom date. I bought you the ugliest corsage that you've ever seen…The thing looked like a pile of weeds, but you told me it was beautiful…"

***

Luna opened her eyes and found herself staring up at a white ceiling. Everything seemed so bright around her. White and bright. She was on a bed, a soft mattress, angled a bit so that her upper body was reclining and she—

Green hospital gown.

She was wearing a green hospital gown.

And a white, hospital ID bracelet circled her wrist. She lifted her hand, staring at her wrist as tremors began to roll through her. The antiseptic scent of the place flooded her nostrils. She was in a hospital.

The door opened. A dark-haired woman bustled inside. She saw Luna and came to a quick stop. "You're awake!" Surprise flashed on her face. "I thought you'd be out longer."

Luna realized she had been taken again. She'd been taken, experimented on, and put in a hospital. Only this hospital wasn't some closed down wreck. They'd found a new place for her.

Luna jumped from the bed. She put her back to the wall. Her hands tightened into fists as an animalistic growl built in her throat.

"Oh, no," the woman whispered. She wore a white lab coat.

Just like Henry used to wear…

The lady lifted her hands, holding them — palms out — toward Luna. "It's not what you think."

Luna glanced toward the window. She could jump out. Run. How high up were they?

"I need *help* in here!" The woman's shout seemed to echo around Luna. "She's awake. Now, *now, I need —* "

Luna lunged at her, mostly to stop the woman's shouts because they were hurting Luna's ears. But before Luna could knock the lady out, strong, warm hands grabbed her and whirled her around. Familiar hands.

And she was pulled against a familiar body.

His smell was masculine and rich. Reassuring. She tilted her head back and stared into Maddox's green eyes. Such gorgeous eyes in a face that was so hard and handsome.

"I've got you," he told her.

She smiled at him. He did have her. And if he had her, then everything was going to be okay. "Maddox."

"Yes, baby, it's Maddox." His head lowered. His mouth brushed over hers. The kiss was soft, gentle. Soothing.

Her hands were fisted in his shirtfront. Her body pressed hard to his. She was holding tight to him, and Luna never wanted to let go.

She'd woken up, and she'd known him. Woken up to a life she *remembered*.

She and Maddox were lovers. They'd escaped the Lazarus facility together. They'd been on the run. Made love in a cheap Vegas motel. They'd raced down the highway. They'd been hit by a big rig—

"I'll, um, give you a few moments alone." The woman cleared her throat. "I'm Elizabeth, by the way. And I swear, I don't mean any harm to either of you."

She was supposed to just buy the stranger's words?

Elizabeth slipped away, and the door clicked closed behind her.

As soon as that door closed, the kiss changed. Maddox stopped being soft and soothing. He became absolutely wild. He kissed her with a sudden desperation. A raw hunger. A savage need. And she responded the same way. Her hands flew over his shoulders as she pulled him even closer. Her heart thundered in her chest as she kissed him desperately.

I remember.

"Baby…" He pulled his mouth from hers and growled the endearment. "You scared the hell out of me."

She tried to smile for him, but her lips barely curved. Fear was still too heavy within her. "I was afraid I wouldn't get you out of the car in time. I kept thinking about that boy and his mom, how close he'd come to dying, and I knew if you were in the sedan when it blew—*I'd lose you*."

"You got me out." A muscle flexed in his jaw. "But next time, leave my ass, okay? Because they told me what happened. They told me how close you were to burning right with me."

A shiver slid over her. She didn't let him go. She wanted the warmth he offered far too much. "They?"

A grim nod. "Sawyer and Flynn. They're the ones who got us off that godforsaken road and to this hospital."

Sawyer and Flynn's images drifted into her mind. "You…trust them?"

"Hell, no, but I didn't have a choice. You were going to die, and Sawyer had a freaking helicopter. He could get you medical help."

"I would have come back," she whispered. "If I'd died." Her gaze searched his.

Maddox's stare heated. "You wanted your memories."

Yes. She would have done anything to keep them.

"So I wasn't going to let them go, wasn't going to let *you* go, not without one hell of a fight." He pulled her tightly against him once more, wrapping her in a hug and holding her against his heart. "Jesus, but you scared the hell out of me."

It felt good to be in his arms. She could feel his heart racing against her. He was big and strong and solid. She hadn't woken alone, to a world she didn't know. Maddox was there with her. Maddox was holding her tight.

Maddox loves me.

Warmth spread within her. "I hated when you left me." Her arms had curled around him. "You were so still and silent in the car. I kept asking you to come back."

He eased away a few inches so that he could stare down at her. Her chin tipped up as she met his gaze.

"I will always come back for you." His voice was clear. Strong. "There is nothing on this earth — nothing in heaven or hell — that could keep me from you."

And her smile wasn't weak this time. Wasn't forced. It was absolutely huge because she was surrounded by her big, bad Maddox.

She believed him.

His gaze fell to her mouth. "I fucking love your smile."

She was starting to think that she might fucking love him.

But Maddox cleared his throat. Stepped back. She immediately missed the warmth of his body.

"They're like us." His expression hardened.

"I-I remember." They'd moved so fast.

"Sawyer Cage seems to be the leader. He told me that he escaped from a lab in Arizona a while back."

Her heart jerked in her chest.

One dark brow rose. "Sound familiar?"

He knew it did. "Adam was in an Arizona lab." She'd already told Maddox that before. "You think it was the same lab?"

"Yeah, I do. Sawyer said when he and Flynn escaped, the place was turned to ash."

That sure fit with what Adam had told her. Goosebumps covered her arms. She really missed Maddox's warmth. "Did you ask him about Adam?"

"Not yet. I was waiting for you."

She nodded. Her gaze slid to the door. "If they're like us, are they listening to what we're saying right now?"

"Maybe."

So she needed to be careful what she said.

"Jett brought them to us. They found him near our Lazarus facility—or, what was left of it."

Now she didn't understand. "Why was Jett there?" Why go back to the scene of hell?

"Jett said that he was trying to create a new trail for the lab coats and their guards to follow. A way to lead them away from us. Only he stumbled onto Sawyer and Flynn instead."

Okay, now she was getting very, very nervous. "I haven't exactly had the best track record with other Lazarus subjects. Adam was a nightmare, and the guy who was driving the big rig? He was a test subject, too." She tried to keep her breathing under control. "Adam—he told me that he could find other Lazarus subjects. Like he was some kind of homing device. He could lock onto them."

Maddox's face was a hard, angry mask.

"The redhead was Adam's partner, a guy named Sam. Sam told me that he was at the old hospital when I was taken. Said he'd only left because I got loose and attacked the doctor who'd been working on me."

Maddox swore.

"I don't know what happened to the doctor." She bit her lower lip. "He said the doctor was a she, but I don't know anything else about her."

"Well, I know what happened to the fucking truck driver. *Sam.*"

Her eyes widened. She remembered his ending. "Bullet to the head."

Flynn had fired the shot. Or had it been Sawyer?

"They saved our asses," Maddox continued, "so I think we should hear them out." A pause. "If you don't like what they have to say, then we leave. They won't stop us. I won't let them."

"We won't let them," Luna corrected.

His mouth lifted into a half-smile. "You ripped the doors off the car, huh?"

"I kicked one off." She smiled back. "Ripped off the other."

"Baby, have I ever told you that you're the sexiest woman in the world?"

She felt her cheeks stain. "No, but I do like hearing—"

Footsteps. Coming their way.

Maddox's shoulders stiffened. "You ready for this?"

Not quite. She walked to his side. Caught his hand in hers. Felt his warmth slide through her as their fingers twined together. "Yes."

"Good, baby." His voice whispered through her mind like a caress. *"And if you want to leave, at any point, tell me. Because I will do whatever the hell you want."*

What a sweet promise.

A knock sounded at the door. A moment later, Elizabeth pushed open the door and poked her head inside. "You two ready to talk?" Her voice held a nervous edge.

Luna nodded. "And, um, I'm sorry for attacking you."

"I just hope you don't do it again," Elizabeth mumbled as she stepped inside, "especially when you hear what I have to say."

Luna's brow furrowed. That had hardly sounded reassuring.

Three men followed Elizabeth inside. The men spread around the room. Sawyer stayed right at Elizabeth's side. His hand went to her shoulder. Elizabeth glanced at him, and for a moment, her face softened.

Lovers.

Luna was sure of that fact.

"You met Sawyer before," Elizabeth announced, waving her hand. "And Flynn."

Flynn stood near the window, with his arms crossed over his chest.

"I remember them," Luna murmured. "I don't know the suit near the door."

The suit near the door — a tall, blond-haired man with brown eyes — straightened. "I'm Jay Maverick."

He announced his name like it was supposed to matter. It didn't.

So she focused on Elizabeth.

"I'm Dr. Elizabeth Parker." Elizabeth released a long, slow breath. "And I'm the woman who created the Lazarus serum. I came up with the preservation process, the entire procedure for bringing back the dead." Her face paled as she confessed, "I made Lazarus."

Well, damn.

CHAPTER SIXTEEN

After Elizabeth's confession, Sawyer immediately moved even closer to her, as if he expected Maddox or Luna to attack.

Luna didn't move. She just stared at the other woman. "Why do you act as though I should hate you for that? We volunteered for the program."

Sawyer and Elizabeth shared a long look.

A look that sent off warning bells in Luna's head.

"How do you know that?" It was Flynn who asked the question. "Were you told that you volunteered? Told by the doctors at your lab? One of the doctors who — according to our new friend Jett — issued a termination order on you?"

"It was a test," Maddox snapped. "Henry — the bastard doctor — wanted to see what Luna would do when she was outside of the lab. He staged the scene for her escape, only an asshole named Adam Brock intervened. He *took* Luna, and Henry's grand plans went up in smoke."

Literally. The lab had burned and burned.

Flynn's eyes had turned to slits. "Just what is it you can do, Luna?"

"Heal," she blurted.

"That certainly makes sense." Elizabeth gave a quick nod. "I've never see anyone heal at the rate you did. Your recovery was absolutely amazing."

"I-I can heal other people," Luna added. "It's not just—"

"*Stop, Luna.*" Maddox's voice flew into her head. "*Don't tell them anything else about what you can do.*"

But she saw the ripple of surprise that had flashed on Sawyer's face. Luna stepped forward. "You just heard what Maddox told me, in my head."

"We *both* heard," Flynn announced. "Like we said, we're Lazarus. And we've had more practice at the psychic communication than you two obviously have. If you want your messages private, then put up a shield."

Maddox's hand curled around her shoulder. She could *feel* the burst of his rage. "Keep the hell out of her head, you understand me?" Maddox's words were low and lethal.

Sawyer immediately held up his hands. "Sorry. Just ease up, okay? We aren't here to be enemies."

"Not unless we need to be," Jay muttered from his position near the door.

Luna tilted her head as she studied him. "You aren't Lazarus."

His eyes widened. "No, I'm not. So if this scene turns into a fighting frenzy, how about you leave me and Elizabeth out of things, hmm? I'm the money man. I'm the guy who funds the hunt for people like you."

Maddox took a lunging step toward him.

But Flynn appeared in his path almost instantly. "We *weren't* hunting you. Or at least, not in the way you think. Sometimes Jay just gets carried away. He's used to playing with tech all day, not dealing with other people."

"I'm offended by that," Jay snapped.

Flynn shrugged. His gaze darted from Luna to Maddox. "Trust has to start somewhere." His shoulders rolled back. "Sawyer and I were originally told we volunteered for the program, too. Then we were shown videos that even had us *saying* we agreed, but the thing is…that shit was manipulated. We were *killed* and placed in the program. Things were not what they seemed, and we never agreed to be Lazarus guinea pigs."

Jay advanced, clearing his throat. His gaze darted from Luna to Maddox, then back. "My intel indicates that you two did not volunteer, either. Luna, you were Air Force, an amazing pilot, while Maddox had spent years proving himself with the Rangers. You were both killed during the course of a classified investigation, and because your bodies were discovered so soon, you were placed in Lazarus."

"Along with the bastard who *killed* us," Maddox snapped.

Jay tensed. Anger flared in his eyes. "My *intel* didn't tell me that part. Tricky bastard. Hiding his secrets even now."

"I don't know who the hell your source is, but the man who killed us, Adam Brock, he was in the Arizona Lazarus facility." Maddox's voice was cold and hard. "Said he escaped when the place blew. And guess what that psychopath did after his release? He came for Luna."

"Psychopath," Jay muttered. "Perfect word choice, and that brings me to why we sought you out."

"*Jay.*" A hard, warning edge had entered Sawyer's voice.

But Jay just shrugged. "I'm not about dealing in lies with these people. So let's just put the truth out there." He inclined his head to Elizabeth.

She swallowed and seemed to search for the right words to say. "As you've probably realized by now, darker emotions are *amplified* in Lazarus subjects. You get lots of bonuses—super speed, enhanced strength, faster reflexes—but there is a price to be paid."

"Memory loss," Flynn tossed in.

"Yes, that's the price that is immediately obvious. But the other is the darkness."

Luna didn't like where this was going.

With sympathy on her face, Elizabeth added, "Unfortunately, we've seen that this darkness can manifest too strongly in certain test subjects. Those subjects go over the edge. They lose all sense of right and wrong. You combine that with all their new powers…and you have a recipe for disaster."

Silence.

Luna shifted from one foot to the other. Her feet were bare, and the floor felt cold beneath her toes. She absorbed what Elizabeth had said…and what she hadn't.

"We've been searching for all of the test subjects. Most of the labs were already shut down." Sawyer's stare was unreadable. "Except for yours. But, well, guess that one is gone now, too."

Gone. Turned to ash. Same thing.

"We've been trying to find the subjects," Sawyer continued, seeming to choose his words just as carefully as Elizabeth had. "Because we want to help."

"No, you fucking don't." Maddox's angry denial. "You *want* to see if we're psychotic. If we've been eaten alive by the darkness because if we have…then you're ready to put a bullet in our brains, aren't you?"

Luna feared Maddox was right. "A bullet to the brain." She shivered. "Just like you did last night."

Flynn's eyes narrowed. "He'd sliced your throat. The guy was ready for your lover there to die. He wasn't listening to reason, and if I hadn't put that bullet in him, Maddox would be gone."

An alternative she didn't want to think about.

"It's apparent that you two haven't given in to the darkness." Elizabeth spoke in a low, soothing voice.

"What makes you so sure?" Maddox's question was instant.

Sawyer stiffened.

"Because you two are so obviously connected," Elizabeth answered with a considering nod. "Your connection is serving as an anchor for one another."

Sawyer cast a quick glance at her. "Elizabeth is my anchor. Without her, I would have lost my sanity."

She smiled at him. But her smile faltered as she glanced back at Luna and Maddox. "When you share a strong connection with someone else, that connection can serve to trigger memories of life before Lazarus. That connection is the key in awakening a bit of the past but…" Now her stare turned assessing as she studied Maddox. "It seems that you retrieved far more than a *bit* of your past."

Luna's shoulders stiffened.

"When Luna was fighting to survive," Sawyer said, tilting his head to study Maddox, too, "I heard what you were telling her. You went over your entire life before Lazarus. Your life with Luna. How the hell did you do that? How the hell do you remember all of that?"

Maddox just smiled. "Like I'm supposed to share with a Lazarus soldier I just met?"

"I *saved* you and Luna. I got you off that road."

"And I'm not ripping off your head," Maddox replied evenly. "I'm giving you the chance to talk. I think that makes us square."

Flynn swore. "Not fair, man. Why do you get to have your memories while the rest of us face darkness?" He pointed to a very watchful Jay Maverick. "His lover — she lost *everything*. She fought for months to remember a single piece of her past."

Luna felt the rage building in Maddox. His hold on her hand tightened as he growled back, "And my Luna loses everything each time she dies and rises again. She comes back to a world she doesn't know. So don't dare talk to me about how hard something is. How bad it is not to have memories, because I damn well know."

Elizabeth's eyes widened. She stared at Luna in shock. "You...you lose it every time?"

It. Her memories. Her life. Luna nodded. "Yes."

"Don't you see? We have to work together!" Flynn burst out. "We can *help* each other. You don't keep secrets from us, we don't keep secrets from you. That is what being a *team* is all about."

Maddox made a show of looking around the room. "This isn't my team." His gaze slid to Luna. "Luna *is* my team."

He was going to protect her secrets. But…

These people were hurting. She could feel it. Sawyer and Flynn's memories had been stripped away. She knew what it was like. Oh, God, did she. And because of that, because it happened to her so much, Luna released a slow breath. "Who gave you the intel?" Her gaze was on Jay.

He straightened.

"You want no secrets between us?" Luna demanded, surprised her voice was so steady and strong. "Then give us something to go on."

He nodded. "Does the name Wyman Wright mean anything to you? To either of you?"

Luna shook her head.

But Maddox said, "Fucking hell. That bastard?"

Once more, Jay nodded.

"Who is he?" Luna whispered.

Maddox glanced down at her. "He *was* the government. Or rather, the puppet master pulling all the strings behind the government's curtain.

He's the one who ordered me to track down the traitor who was selling government secrets from my unit."

Her chest felt tight and she knew Maddox was going to say—

"He's the one who put me on the mission that ended with me stabbing Adam Brock and the bastard shooting us both." He raked his left hand through his hair. His gaze darted back to Jay. "So, wait, let me get this straight, Wyman was—"

"He was the one setting up Lazarus. Pulling in the subjects," Jay filled in quickly. "Since he knew about you—and about Luna—he figured you'd be perfect candidates. He put you in the program when your bodies were discovered."

Luna shuddered. "Adam wasn't perfect for the program." For a moment, she was back in the lab room. Staring at Adam as she pointed the gun at his head.

"Tell me how to get out of here."

"Put the gun down, Luna. We both know you can't shoot me. You fucking love me."

"Wyman didn't tell me about this Adam," Jay spoke carefully. "Though it certainly wouldn't be the first time he neglected to reveal all the facts."

Flynn's hands fisted at his sides. "Yeah, and it wouldn't be the first time Wyman put a man who was a monster in the program. He thought darker personality traits might give the Lazarus soldiers an advantage. Since they were going to lose their memories, he thought what they'd done before didn't matter. They wouldn't remember the bad stuff they'd done, and he could…" His words trailed off.

"Reprogram them," Jay said quietly.

This just got worse and worse. Luna's temples ached. "Adam wasn't kept in the facility with me and Maddox. Like Maddox told you already, he was in Arizona—"

Sawyer and Flynn shared a long, hard look.

Flynn's head inclined toward Luna. "Describe Adam. Physically," Flynn added. "As clearly as you can."

Since his image was branded in her head, she could describe him plenty clearly. "Six-foot-two, two hundred pounds, blond hair, blue eyes, a faint scar on his left cheek—"

"Four," Sawyer muttered.

"For what?" Luna demanded.

"No, the number four. As in Subject Four. I remember him." He blew out a rough breath. "We had numbers at that place, not names. We weren't given that particular luxury. I was One, Flynn was Two, and your Adam—"

"*He's not mine,*" Luna cut in fiercely.

"He was four," Sawyer finished.

Her hands pressed to the front of the hospital gown. She felt far too vulnerable, just talking to them in that paper covering. If she turned, she'd be mooning them all. She wanted clothes. She wanted armor. She wanted *away* from that place.

"We, ahem, convinced Wyman to tell us where the other subjects were. Or at least, the last place he *knew* of them being," Jay explained as he cleared his throat. "That's what led us out here, to you. When we got to the facility, it was blazing. Then we found Jett, and, well, the rest just happened."

"Just happened?" Maddox repeated. "You got to us damn fast considering that Luna and I had such a lead on you all."

"I have faster rides," Jay said. "Private planes, helicopters…"

Her gaze darted around the room. "Where is Jett?"

"In the lobby," Sawyer answered immediately. "He wanted to stand guard because he wasn't sure who might be showing up. He's not exactly the trusting sort. After the attack on the highway, he wanted to make sure someone was keeping watch." Sawyer's right shoulder moved in a small shrug. "It seems he thinks you might be targeted again."

"Why are people after *you*, specifically, Luna?" Flynn wanted to know.

Elizabeth was just watching her, the other woman's dark stare considering. Luna felt like a bug under a microscope. Far too exposed. Far too— "I want to get dressed," she blurted. "Where are my clothes? I need clothes." She sounded frantic, but so what?

"Clothes are in the closet." Elizabeth's voice was soothing. "Flynn, Sawyer, Jay...let's give them a bit of time, okay? Luna probably wants to shower, too. We've just dumped a whole lot of information on them."

Flynn's body seemed to lock down. "But we still don't know how he got his memories back." He pointed right at Maddox.

Maddox didn't speak. He was still protecting her. Luna knew he would always protect her. That was just who Maddox was.

Elizabeth gave Flynn a shove. "Let's go outside. They need to process what we've said."

Luna's eyes narrowed on the other woman. Elizabeth was almost at the door, when Luna called out, "Was it you?"

Elizabeth stiffened, but glanced back. "Was what me?"

"I was told a female doctor had been experimenting on me." She licked dry lips. "You see, my life has been really, really crazy lately. A few days ago, I woke up in a rundown hospital, pretty much wearing the exact same get-up I have on now." Her words were coming too fast, but she couldn't slow herself down. "Maddox and I did some exploring in that place and down in the basement, we found an exam table. Turned

out I had been strapped to that table.
Experimented on. But I broke loose. I hurt the
doctor who held me, and she had to be taken
away from the scene." Her stomach was in knots.
"Not that I remember any of this, of course.
Because I died in that hospital. I woke up,
absolutely terrified, but the asshole super soldier
who tried to kill me just *last night?* Sam? He filled
me in on a few missing pieces. And now here you
are. A female doctor who knows plenty about
Lazarus."

Elizabeth turned to fully face her. "It wasn't
me."

She wanted to believe the other woman. "*You*
made all the Lazarus subjects—"

"I made the formula. Wyman took it from
me. He used it on others without their
permission. I want to make things *right*. I want to
help the men and women who've been hurt."
Elizabeth swallowed. "I would do anything to
make it up to them. To give them back the lives
they lost."

A lump rose in Luna's throat but she choked
it back down. "That's what I'm afraid of."

A furrow appeared between Elizabeth's
brows. "What?

"You doing *anything*." Luna shook her head.
"I'm just one big experiment, right? To Henry. To
you. To everyone."

Elizabeth's eyes widened. "No, that's not what I meant."

"*Out.*" Maddox ordered, as he moved protectively in front of Luna. "Now."

They went out. Maddox shut the door behind them. Fury was stamped on his face. "We listened to what they had to say. Now I think we need to get the hell out of here."

***

Flynn and Jay remained in the hospital corridor. A private hospital that they'd cleared out because Jay had more money than God.

Elizabeth and Sawyer stepped into the elevator, and she waited until the doors closed, waited until the elevator was descending, before she turned to her lover and whispered, "It's her."

Sawyer's brows rose. "What about her?"

"You told me…you heard Maddox say that she was a healer. That if someone else had been injured, Luna could easily fix the person's wounds."

He nodded.

Her hands were shaking with excitement. "She fixed him."

"I'm not following, babe."

"She *fixed* him. I mean, all the Lazarus subjects have different psychic gifts, so why not the ability to heal? And the memory loss is a physical issue. A difference in the brain. She'd just need to focus on the injury, then she could repair the damage and—"

"Slow down." He caught her shaking hands. "You're saying Maddox has his memories because Luna healed his mind?"

It was sure what she suspected. "*Yes.*" And if Luna could give Maddox his memories back, then maybe she could give memories back to all of the super soldiers.

Sawyer blinked. Once. Twice. "Shit. That's why that other bastard was after her. The guy at the wreck—he wanted *her.* He didn't care if Maddox lived or died. He was only interested in Luna."

"If all of the Lazarus subjects got their memories back, it would completely change the program." She knew Wyman had liked the fact that the soldiers lost their memories. The bastard thought the loss made them easier to handle. But when those men and women remembered their families, their lovers...*They won't be controlled any longer.*

"There are people who'd want her dead because of what she can do." Sawyer's expression had tightened.

"And Lazarus subjects who'd fight like hell to get her for the same reason," Elizabeth whispered.

The elevator dinged. Bottom floor. They'd planned to send Jett upstairs, thinking he might reassure Maddox and Luna. But… "He's going to run with her," Elizabeth predicted. "I saw Maddox." You didn't have to be a shrink to figure out that man's priorities. "He's not going to let anyone use Luna. He's going to make a break at the first opportunity."

Sawyer's jaw locked even as he nodded. The doors opened. She stepped forward.

"We can't let her go, Elizabeth."

She'd feared he would say that.

"If she can do that, if she can give us our lives back…" Sawyer raked a hand over his face. "How the hell are we supposed to let her just walk away?"

CHAPTER SEVENTEEN

Luna stepped out of the bathroom, dressed in jeans, a dark sweater, and a shiny pair of white sneakers. Her hair fell over her shoulders.

He walked toward her. Lifted her right hand. Ripped off the damn hospital tag on her wrist. He tossed it into the garbage can. "We're leaving."

"Maddox, I can help them."

"They want to *use* you." And he was afraid of just how they'd do that. "I don't know who our enemies are. I don't know who I can trust. When it comes to *your* life, I can't make a mistake." His fingers twined with hers. "I won't." Didn't she realize how important she was to him? Nothing, no one was more important. Never would be.

She'd owned his heart since she was fourteen years old. She'd own it until he left the earth.

"Maddox, do you remember volunteering for Project Lazarus?"

Dammit. "No." He led her into the hallway. Jay and Flynn were there, leaning against a nearby wall, and when they saw Maddox and Luna, the two men stiffened.

Maddox leveled a hard glare at them. "You don't want to get in my way."

Flynn raked his gaze over Maddox. "You need to calm down."

"No, I need you to back the hell off."

Flynn took a step toward him, but Jay shoved his hand against Flynn's chest. "Sawyer is downstairs. Let's just all ride the elevator down together, okay? Everyone *breathe*."

Breathing wasn't a problem for Maddox. Stopping himself from kicking their asses was harder. They loaded into the elevator.

He could knock these two out right now.

"Don't." Luna squeezed his hand.

He sucked in a hard breath. For her. For *her*.

"I'm in love with a woman named Willow," Jay suddenly announced as the elevator descended. "In some ways, she reminds me a lot of you, Luna."

Maddox moved closer to Luna. "She's not your Willow."

"No, of course not." Jay shook his head. "I love Willow, and I want to help her. Her past is gone, her father is dying, and I just want to make things a little better for her."

The elevator dinged.

"Good luck with that," Maddox muttered as he pulled Luna from the elevator.

"Maddox…" She frowned at him.

"Baby, your heart has always been too soft."
It's why you fell for that bastard Adam. And he
knew now, knew with absolute certainty since his
memories were back…Luna hadn't been
betraying her country. She hadn't been working
with Adam to steal secrets. That just wasn't who
Luna was. Luna had always been good and kind.
So intelligent. So caring. Too caring.

That's why I have to get her out of here.

They hurried down the hallway. The place
was freaking deserted. They rounded a corner,
and bam — there was Sawyer. Elizabeth. Jett.

A wide smile crossed Jett's face when he saw
Luna. "Hell, yes!" He hurried to her. Yanked her
into a big hug. "They said you were all right, but
I wanted to see you with my own eyes."

Luna squeezed him back. "I'm okay."

Jett let her go, and then he turned,
positioning his body subtly closer to Maddox.
"What exactly is the plan?"

"To get the hell out of here," Maddox
answered.

But Sawyer shook his head. "No." His hands
were loose at his sides. Flynn immediately moved
into position near him. *Everyone is picking a side.*

Sawyer's gaze slid to Luna. "You do it, don't
you? You give the memories back. That's how
your boyfriend there can remember his whole
life. You did that for him."

Luna opened her mouth —

"Get the fuck out of our way," Maddox directed, voice flat and cold. "I won't ask twice."

Sawyer gave him a grim smile. "Doesn't sound like you're asking right now."

"He's not," Jett fired back as he stiffened his spine. "Maddox is telling you, *move*."

Sawyer slanted a quick glance at him. "And here I thought we were all getting along."

"You said you were going to help me and my friends. You're Lazarus like us, so I wanted to give you the benefit of the doubt. But my loyalties will *always* lie with Luna and Maddox. I won't screw up with them again." His smile was as grim as Sawyer's. "So do what the man says. Get the fuck out of the way. If you don't, you won't like what happens next."

"Don't be so sure about that," Sawyer tossed back. "Don't be—"

"Just let them *go,* Sawyer," Elizabeth said, her voice sharp and high.

He whirled toward her. "What?"

Anguish showed on her face. "I know you want the past back. Don't you understand how much I want to give it to you? But we can't *make* her help us. We can't make them do anything. If we do that, God, aren't we just like the Lazarus bastards who kept you locked up for so long? Who took away your choices?" She came to him, put her palms against his cheeks. "It's not right. It's not who we are. They aren't dangerous.

Aren't psychotic. And they just want to disappear."

Sawyer held her gaze.

Tears filled Elizabeth's eyes. "I'm so sorry. I will keep working. I can find a way to do this. If she healed his brain, see, it's physical. It's science. I can do science. And I won't give up. I swear, I won't ever give up. I'll give your memory back. I'll get Flynn's back. I'll get—"

"Stop." Luna's voice was calm when Elizabeth's had been too high.

Maddox immediately pulled her closer. "Baby?"

She smiled at him, making his heart ache. "They're not bad."

But that didn't mean they were *good,* either.

"You always protect me, don't you?" Her head tilted as she studied him. "In all those memories you've got, are you protecting me in most of them?"

When they'd first gone sailing, she'd slipped off the edge of the boat and fallen into the water. She hadn't been wearing a life vest, and he'd nearly lost his shit. He'd jumped in after her, held her so tightly.

Sworn that he'd never let her go.

When they'd been walking home one night in high school, a drunk driver had come barreling down the road. The car had been coming right at them. He'd grabbed Luna, roaring for her, and he'd tumbled them both off the road—

"See?" Her smile stretched. "I kind of think it's just what you do. Like you're some kind of programmed protector. But I don't think I need protecting, not from them."

He wanted to protect her from the whole freaking world.

Luna turned to face Sawyer and Elizabeth. "I gave Maddox back his memories."

"Fuck me." Flynn took a step back.

"No, thanks," Luna immediately replied. She waved her hand toward Jett. "And I was able to restore some memories for Jett, too."

Jett gave a jerky nod. "She did."

Luna licked her lips. "I heal. That's what I do. We all have our gifts, don't we? Mine is healing. I can heal wounds fast…"

"Your neck healed at a phenomenal rate," Elizabeth mused. "It's something *in* you, isn't it? An accelerated healing rate that is stronger than anything I've ever seen before."

"I can't heal myself completely." Now Luna sounded sad. Maddox hated her pain. "If I could, I'd make sure that each time I died, I didn't wake up as a blank slate." She shivered. "Because that is the worst nightmare I have. A nightmare that has come true over and over. Waking up. Not knowing who I am. Where I am. If I could stop that, I would." Her shoulders lifted, fell. "I can't change that." Her gaze darted around their group. "But I can give memories back to you all. And I will."

"Thank you," Elizabeth whispered.

"We can help you, too," Jay added quickly as he hurried forward. "Money is no fucking object, and I mean that. I can give you all any houses you want, as much cash as you want. New identities. I can help you to disappear and escape from the bastards who were after you before."

"When I was in the lab, Adam told me that Sam was his partner. Sam—he was the bastard who slit my throat. The one Flynn killed."

Maddox wished he'd been the one to kill the bastard.

"There was a doctor working with Sam and Adam, but I don't know who she is. I got the feeling that Adam was the one in charge of their group. He seemed to be the one with the master plan."

"And what in the hell happened to Adam, exactly?" Flynn groused.

Luna raised her chin. "I happened to him. I killed Adam after he set bombs all over our facility. He's gone."

Maddox wanted to pull her into his arms and hold her tight. So he did. With Luna snug against him, he added, "Adam's dead, and so is Henry Danwith."

"Danwith?" Elizabeth's eyes narrowed. "I know that name. I even studied with him in med school. Henry is an expert on genetics and—"

"He *was* an expert," Maddox corrected. "He's dead."

Luna shivered, and his hold tightened on her.

"He'll never hurt you again," Maddox promised on their link.

Jett started to pace. "The guy was the lead lab coat at our facility, and from what I glimpsed when I went back to the scene, the people on his team were already lost without him."

Maddox would love for their enemies to be history, but he wasn't ready to let down his guard just yet. Not when Luna's life was on the line.

"The female doctor is still missing," Luna said. She pressed her body to his. "The one who was doing experiments on me. But I don't remember anything about her. And I have no idea what she did to me."

Elizabeth's gaze swept over her. "I can find out."

Maddox didn't like where this was going.

"Let me examine you." Elizabeth squared her shoulders "If I examine you, I can find out what she was doing—or trying to do."

Luna glanced up at Maddox.

"He can stay with you every moment," Elizabeth was quick to reassure her. "But we should do a thorough exam. I mean…this mystery doctor seems to have gone to extensive trouble to get you."

Luna's attention shifted to Sawyer and Flynn. "Before the exam…do you want me to give you some memories?"

Longing flashed on Flynn's face. Maddox could see the emotion so clearly.

But Flynn shook his head. "Get yourself checked out first." His voice was gruff. "I've been waiting this long. I can wait longer."

Sawyer nodded. "Let Elizabeth do her tests." He caught Elizabeth's hand. Brought her fingers to his mouth and pressed a kiss to her knuckles. "I want my past fucking back, but at least I've got my present. And it's a damn good present."

Maddox's gaze slid down to Luna. He had his past. He had his present. And he wanted his future—a future with Luna. A future where they weren't hunted. Where they were free. Where they could be happy.

And that future was close. So fucking close.

His fingers skimmed down Luna's silken cheek.

So close that he could touch it.

***

"Before we begin the tests…" Elizabeth cleared her throat. "I need to ask…because there will be things we can't do. Like, um X-rays. We can't do them if you're…"

Luna frowned at her. They'd gone into an exam room. Just the two of them but she knew Maddox would be in soon, too. He'd promised to come right in. He'd just stayed behind to speak with Sawyer for a moment.

"Is there any chance that you're pregnant?" Elizabeth asked.

Luna felt her cheeks ice. "I'm a dead woman. A dead woman walking. How the hell could I give birth to a child?"

"You *were* dead," Elizabeth corrected her quickly. "But your heart beats now. You breathe. Luna, you are quite alive. And you can have kids. You can have any life that you want."

Her chest burned. Any life?

A life with Maddox?

"Is there any chance you're pregnant?" Elizabeth asked again, her voice so very careful.

Luna's hand slid to her stomach. "It would be very, very early." Far too early to tell, surely? But… "We didn't use anything."

Elizabeth nodded briskly. "Just in case, I will take every precaution."

Luna's hand was still on her stomach.

"*Every* precaution," Elizabeth promised.

***

He needed to be in the exam room with Luna. And he *would* be in there, but first...

Maddox stared at Sawyer. "You knew Adam — or freaking Four. Whatever you want to call him."

Sawyer nodded. "He was part of my team. I...didn't realize how dangerous he was." His jaw hardened. "But this isn't the first time I've been misled."

"He got a job as a guard at our facility." Jett's hands had fisted at his sides. "How the hell did he even find the place? How would he have known about it?"

Sawyer glanced over at Jay.

Jay rubbed his nose. "Maybe Adam stole some intel from the Arizona lab before it blew. Or maybe...hell, maybe this mystery doctor that we keep hearing about? Maybe she's the one who told him. We assumed that all of the people in the Arizona lab died when it blew to hell and back."

"Wyman didn't die," Flynn cut in, coming closer. "If that bastard faked his death, others could have done the same."

Sawyer nodded. "So maybe Four — Adam — found out from a doctor there. Someone who has been helping him." But he still hesitated. "Emotional connections cause memory triggers for some of us. If Adam...if he had some kind of connection —"

Now Maddox was the one to explain, "Luna told me…Adam said he could find other Lazarus subjects. He could home in on them, like they were flashing beacons at him." He rolled one shoulder in a shrug. "That explains how he found a *partner* to help him and how he found our facility." *How he found Luna.* But how the hell had that Sam bastard found him and Luna on that godforsaken road? Maddox felt as if he was missing something.

Sawyer seemed to hesitate. "We're absolutely sure he's dead? Because with a talent like that, he could be very, very dangerous…to us all."

Flynn nodded. "And Four—I mean, Adam— he was always a damn good tracker."

Jett's thumb jerked toward Maddox. "No one is better at tracking and hunting than Maddox."

"No?" Sawyer raised his eyebrows. "That what your special talent is? Hunting?"

He wasn't ready to play the sharing game on exactly what he could do, not yet. "You'll know my talent when you see it." He turned away.

"Fire."

Maddox stilled.

"I remember…" Sawyer's voice had turned musing. "Adam could manipulate fire."

Maddox glanced over his shoulder, a very bad feeling spreading in his gut.

"Saw him do it once, when we were in the field. A vehicle had exploded after taking some bullets." Sawyer's lips thinned. "The line of flames was coming straight for us, but he, hell, it's hard to explain, but it was like he pulled back his hands and he could push the fire back. Like send a surge of wind at it. Thought it was damn impressive at the time, but he told me it would only have been really impressive if he'd been able to make the fire. He couldn't do that. He could only control it once the flames started."

"That's why the sonofabitch set our labs to blow," Maddox realized. "Once he started the fire, he could get it to do anything he wanted."

Sawyer looked as worried as Maddox felt. "Did you *see* him die?"

Maddox's gaze flew to Jett. "No." He swallowed. "Jett was trapped downstairs. I went to get him out."

"And I'm going to fucking be forever grateful for that fact," Jett muttered.

"You don't leave a friend behind." His gaze swung back to Sawyer, and the guy was watching him with a glint of respect in his eyes. Maddox's jaw tightened. "Luna saw him die. Luna fired the shot that ended him."

"Maybe we need to make *extra* sure of that. Ask your lady again, get full details." Sawyer shoved back his shoulders. "I'd like to know all of the enemies we've got coming for us. Easier to stop them that way."

Maddox turned from him, heading for Luna. The last thing he wanted to do was grill Luna about her ex. The guy was dead. Time for Adam to stop haunting them.

He marched down the corridor. Rapped lightly at the door to the exam room. Luna's voice—nervous and a little shaky—called out, and he pushed open the door.

She was alone in the room. Sitting on the exam table, wearing a hospital gown. Her feet were bare, and her toes were curling nervously under. She gave him a weak smile before speaking. "Elizabeth…she, um, she had to set up some different tests." Her gaze wouldn't meet his, and he could hear the frantic racing of her heartbeat. "Little change of plans."

He shut the door behind him. Stalked toward her. His hand curled under her chin as he tipped her head back, forcing her to look at him. "What's happened?"

Light spots of color stained her cheeks. And her eyes gleamed. "I…I just didn't think. I was *feeling* with you. And I was—I wanted you. I was happy, and I didn't think…"

Her words were tumbling out in rapid-fire succession.

"Baby, slow down."

She eased out a slow breath. "Pregnancy."

Her heart was racing. His absolutely stopped.

"You and me," she continued quickly. "I mean, I know the sex just happened recently, so it's too soon to tell, but I didn't stop to think that we weren't using protection."

She thought he'd made her pregnant. He damn well wished. "It can't happen."

The gleam in her eyes died away.

"Henry told me—back in the early days at the lab. He said the Lazarus subjects couldn't have kids. We died, Luna. We're dead men and women. Life can't come from death."

Her lips trembled. "But...but Elizabeth said..."

A knock sounded at the door. He caught Elizabeth's scent, drifting to him, and she called out, "Luna? Is it okay if I come back inside?"

The spots of color weren't on Luna's cheeks any longer. If fact, she seemed too pale. "Luna." He barely breathed her name. "Did you want to have my baby?"

"I did." A hoarse whisper. "I think a little boy who looked like you would have been quite spectacular." A smile came and went on her lips. "For some reason, after Elizabeth asked me if I might be pregnant, I just started picturing him. And us playing together on a beach, making sand castles." Tears filled her eyes, but she blinked them away. "But it was all just a mistake. Elizabeth didn't understand."

The knock came again. "Luna?" Elizabeth called. "Everything okay?"

No, everything was not okay. Luna was crying. A tear had slid down her cheek.

But Luna replied, voice husky, "Yes, it's fine. You can come in."

Maddox stayed planted right in front of Luna, shielding her. He didn't want anyone else to see her pain. His hand moved to her cheek, and he brushed away the tear. Anger coursed through him as he stared into Luna's eyes, and when he spoke, that anger burned in each word, "Dr. Parker, if you want our cooperation, you shouldn't lie to Luna."

Elizabeth's footsteps stopped. "I haven't lied to her."

"You told Luna that she could get pregnant." He finally turned to look at the doctor. "But Henry Danwith explained to me and Jett that Lazarus soldiers couldn't have kids. Hell, the bastard acted like we should be pleased. Said when we were on missions, we should always take some time to enjoy ourselves since the risk was gone."

Her eyes widened. "OhmyGod."

Not the response he'd expected.

She bounded toward him. "He was encouraging you to have unprotected sex?"

"Henry said our bodies would heal from any diseases we got. Sure, we don't heal as fast as

Luna, but he told me our genetics were different. He —"

"He *lied*," Elizabeth exclaimed. "Didn't you notice? Wasn't he giving off any signs? Elevated heartbeat? Sweating? Pupil dilation? I know you can pick up things like that. Lazarus subjects are nearly human lie detectors."

Maddox's shoulders stiffened. "Henry was good at lying."

"Probably because the guy sounds like a psychopath. And to think, I knew him and didn't even realize this shit." She rocked forward onto the balls of her feet. "He lied, though, he did because…oh, man, it sounds like he *wanted* you and the others to get women pregnant. Probably another experiment."

"What?" Maddox didn't like where this was going. *Henry loved his freaking experiments.*

"Listen to me." Elizabeth's whole body was tense. "There is no reason why you can't have children. I mean, unless there's something I don't know about you, specifically, and I can certainly test you both to make certain but…as far as the other Lazarus subjects are concerned…the subjects I've examined before…you *can* have kids. Your bodies are functioning normally so there isn't any reason to suspect a problem."

Maddox felt rooted to the spot. "But Henry said…" He stopped because he realized the truth—*another fucking lie.* "He wanted the kids. That bastard *wanted* us to get someone pregnant."

Elizabeth nodded. "As far as I know, we haven't had a Lazarus birth. We don't know if the enhancements the test subjects have will or will not be passed to future offspring." She bit her lower lip. "I suspect they would be."

And Henry had wanted to see for certain. Sonofabitch.

"If you've had unprotected sex with other women out there, women who *might* be pregnant, we'd need to find them." Elizabeth's voice held an urgency. "It's possible that Henry could have been tracking them, watching for the development of the pregnancy—"

"I told you already," Maddox gritted out, "Henry is *dead.*"

"But other scientists from your facility aren't. And a Lazarus child would be something they'd be very interested in seeing. So I'm sorry, but we need the names of those women. We need to check them for their own safety, and if any of them are about to have a Lazarus baby, a baby with genetic enhancements, don't you think that is something the mothers should be told about?"

Maddox looked back at Luna. "There was no one for me...no one but Luna."

She stared into his eyes.

He bent forward, his forehead resting against hers. "If I'd known, I would have used protection, Luna. I would never take a choice like that away from you."

Elizabeth cleared her throat. "Do you happen to know about Jett—"

"You'll have to talk to him." And Andreas— wherever the hell he was—he'd been told the same lie, too.

So many lies. Would they ever stop?

He backed away from Luna, but she caught his hand in hers. "I can't imagine having a child…"

Pain knifed through his chest.

"With anyone but you," Luna finished softly.

Sweet hell. "Luna?"

"Maybe when we're safe. Maybe when the madness is past us…maybe then we can have a real life." Her gaze didn't waver from his. "Because I'd really like to have that, with you."

She wasn't saying she loved him. Wasn't swearing eternal devotion. But what she was saying was one huge step in the right direction. He brought their linked hands to his mouth. Pressed a kiss to her knuckles. "Sweetheart, one day you'll realize, I'll always give you everything you want."

Everything.

CHAPTER EIGHTEEN

"We have a problem." Elizabeth shoved her hands into the pockets of her lab coat as she faced the occupants of the exam room.

As soon as she heard the one word, *problem,* Luna felt her heart squeeze in her chest. They'd finished the exams — so many exams that her head had been spinning. But the tests had finally ended. Luna had dressed in jeans and a loose top, put sneakers on her feet, and she'd started to feel normal.

Until Elizabeth had just made her little announcement.

Luna immediately rose from the couch. Maddox was right with her, rising, too, his shoulder brushing against hers. Sawyer stood to the left, his intense gaze on the doctor.

But Elizabeth's stare was on Luna. "I think we should talk alone, first."

Luna shook her head. "No." She'd been alone plenty. "Whatever you've got, I want Maddox to hear it." What was wrong? *What is wrong with me?*

Sawyer stepped toward the door. "I'll give you privacy —"

"No," Luna said again. No more secrets. No more lies. If they were all going to work together, then... "Is this something that will influence us all?"

Her expression grave, Elizabeth said, "Yes, I'm afraid it is. And we need to act *now*."

"What in the hell is it?" Maddox's hand wrapped around Luna's. Tightened. "Is she sick? Is something wrong?"

"There is a tracker inside of Luna."

Luna shook her head. Her hand automatically moved to her side. "No." She smiled, realizing that Elizabeth was wrong. "I cut it out already. There was one under my scar before, but —"

"It's inside your heart, Luna."

What? Luna laughed because... "No." She pulled her hand from Maddox. Touched her chest. "That's just not possible. I mean...I don't have any scars or anything at all. If something was put in my heart —"

"You don't scar any longer, baby," Maddox said, his voice halting. "You heal too fast. Look at your neck in a mirror. The skin is still pink, but you don't have a scar."

She shook her head, and her gaze stayed on Elizabeth. "I can't have something in my heart."

"You do. And I almost missed it since we weren't doing all of the exams and scans because…" Elizabeth exhaled, then gave a brisk shake of her head.

Luna knew what the other woman had been about to say. *Because of the possible pregnancy.*

"It's there," Elizabeth told her. "A small tracking device was implanted in your heart. Whoever did it probably suspected you would never find it there. Normally, it would cause death to the person it was implanted in but because of your healing strengths, your body is constantly adjusting to it."

"I'll be damned." Sawyer's rough exclamation. "Someone wanted to *always* be able to find Luna."

"Get it out of me," Luna snapped.

All eyes turned to her.

"Get it out," she said again. Fear and fury pulsed within her. As long as that tracker was inside of her, none of them would be safe. Whoever was tracking her could find them all. Her tracker would lead to Maddox, to Jett, to Sawyer, to Flynn, to—

"I can't," Elizabeth said quietly. "Not without killing you."

"Fucking hell." Maddox's face was lined with fury.

"No." Luna was definite on this. "There has to be a way. I mean…heart surgeries are done all the time. People are sedated or whatever, and surgeries are done."

Elizabeth's expression remained grave. "I'm not a heart surgeon. I don't have the skills to remove the tracker."

"Then we find a surgeon who *can* do it!" Maddox immediately fired. "We get it out of her."

"We'd have to get a heart surgeon we could trust." Sawyer crossed his arms over his chest. "He'd want to know how the tracker got in her. Why it was there. How the hell she could heal so fast because there would be anomalies occurring during the surgery itself."

Her heart was racing in her chest. "That's what happened to me in that shithole hospital." Her hand pressed to her heart. "I was strapped to the table, and our mystery doctor put the tracker in my heart."

"Someone went to one hell of a lot of trouble…" Sawyer added darkly.

She turned to face Maddox. "That someone knows where I am right now. We can't stay here." She motioned toward Sawyer and Elizabeth. "And they aren't safe with us. If I can be found — they can all be found."

Run. That's what they had to do. Run and get the hell away from there.

"We need to all just take a moment and think," Sawyer said. He was obviously trying to sound calm. A tactic that didn't work because when Luna focused, she could hear his frantically pounding heart. He was just as worried as she was. "Look, we don't know what kind of range that tracker has on it. We don't know if it's even transmitting. We—"

"First order of business." Maddox pulled Luna's hand from her heart. "Find the best heart surgeon in the world."

"Jay can do that." Elizabeth nodded. "He'll throw money at the doctor, enough cash to buy his or her silence."

"Step two," Maddox added, "is we separate. Right the hell now. Because we don't know who could be tracking Luna, and until we do…" His gaze swept the room. "It isn't safe for us to be together. We get burner phones, we keep in contact that way. Once you've got the surgeon, you call Luna. We work out step freaking three then." Maddox shook his head. "The people tracking her could be closing in on us right now. Oh, shit…" He seemed to come to a realization. "That's how the asshole in the big rig knew where we were. He was waiting there to ambush us because he was monitoring Luna. I wondered how he'd gotten to us, and that's it."

I'm putting them all in danger. That big rig crash…Maddox had been hurt so badly. And if she hadn't gotten him out of the flames…*he wouldn't have come back to me.*

She was a danger to everyone until the tracker came out of her chest.

"Getting us away from that scene by using your chopper bought us time." Maddox was obviously considering all angles. "We moved fast and far, so whoever is out there got left behind. And the fact that the super soldier they were using is dead — that's another road block in their path."

But road blocks wouldn't be there forever. Luna straightened her shoulders. "We have another option."

Their stares slid back to her. "Cut it out," she said, nodding briskly, "and let me heal."

"I told you," Elizabeth argued, voice strained, "I could kill you —"

"It's not a bullet to the brain." She tried to sound confident. "I'll come back."

Maddox spun her to face him. "And you'll lose *everything*."

Didn't he understand? "I almost lost *you* in that crash. I led that bastard to *you*. You are everything to me, and I can't lose you. So if I have to get strapped to a table and get this *thing* cut out of me in order for you to survive, I'll do it."

"No." His eyes blazed. "Not an option. Not ever a fucking option."

"Maddox —"

"No." A guttural growl. "Not. An. Option."

For his survival, it was.

"We have vehicles waiting downstairs." Sawyer's voice held no emotion. "And we've already got plenty of burner phones and cash set to go."

Luna turned to him in surprise.

A faint smile curled his lips. "Definitely *not* my first ball game." The smile faded. "And before we start cutting into you, before we risk you losing your memories—let's explore the other options. I'm betting Jay can have us the best heart surgeon in the country on stand-by within hours. We get to a different facility—we regroup in case someone has tracked us to this location—and we keep going forward."

She could only shake her head. "You're all risking your lives for me."

"You're one of us," Sawyer replied simply. "It's what we do." He glanced down at his watch. "Now we need to get moving. We don't know if we've got time to spare, or if the enemy is about to be at our door, and I'm not the kind of man who takes chances."

Luna hurried toward him. He was a stranger, but he was doing so much to help her. It seemed only fair that she try to pay him back. "Thank you." Her hands pressed to his chest. She felt the tingle in her fingertips. Saw the flare of his pupils. She lifted her right hand. Touched his temple.

"Luna..." Maddox touched her shoulder.

She didn't stop, not yet. She had to give something back.

Sawyer's breath rushed out. His hand lifted and his fingers curled around her wrist. "Thank you." His voice was gruff. "But you need to go now. Take the blue SUV downstairs. There are plenty of vehicles down there, but the SUV has a burner phone *and* a gun in the glove box." He dug a pair of keys from his pocket. Pushed them into her hand. "I'll call you as soon as Jay has a doctor ready for you. I have the burner's number. I can make contact with you. In order for this to all work, you have to *go*."

Right. Time for the separation.

And she would need to separate from everyone.

"You need to get the hell out of here, too," Maddox advised Sawyer. "All of you."

"We will," Sawyer assured him. "I'll get a chopper to land on the roof. We'll be gone in moments."

Luna and Maddox hurried away. The ride down in the elevator was conducted in silence. She tried to get her breathing under control. Tried to fight back the fear. And tried to find the right words to say to Maddox.

Because there was no way she was leaving that place with him. She wouldn't put him at risk. There were plenty of vehicles in the garage, that was what Sawyer had said. So Maddox would take one of those other rides, and she'd take the blue SUV.

"*Jett.*" Maddox's voice slipped through her mind. She knew he was pulling her and Jett into a psychic web. "*Meet us in the garage. We've got trouble.*"

Yes, they did have trouble.

She was the trouble.

And she would not bring Jett and Maddox down with her.

***

Sawyer exhaled on a long sigh.

"We need to go," Elizabeth murmured. She stood by the door, but her beautiful gaze was on him. "The sooner we all clear this place, the better. The *last* thing I want is for any of the Lazarus bastards to ever get their hands on you again."

He strode toward her, lifted his hands, and cupped her cheeks. "The first time I saw you…I thought you were the sexiest thing I'd ever seen."

Her eyes widened. "Sawyer?"

"Way out of my league, though." And he smiled. "Didn't think I would have a shot in hell with you."

"You…remember? The first time we met?"

"Your hair was in one of those twists you like to wear, and a few locks had come loose. You walked into the exam room, nibbling your lower lip, your gaze on the chart in your hands. I stared at you and knew I'd never want anything more in my whole life."

Her lower lip trembled.

"Then you looked up at me. And you smiled."

Shit. He'd been a goner before she'd even spoken.

And he had that memory now. He could remember every detail, even the shoes that Elizabeth had worn. The way she'd laughed nervously when she'd caught him staring at her. The way her grin had come and gone when she'd straightened her shoulders and tried to be all business-like and professional.

The way her eyes had sparkled when she looked back at him.

"It works. Luna's power can bring back memories." And the joy was there, wanting to break free. The promise of getting back the life he'd lost. So close...

We just have to make sure Luna stays safe.

"It works," he said again.

"That's why someone tagged her, permanently." Worry shone in Elizabeth's eyes. "Someone else wants what she can do. That someone wants to be able to control Luna. We have to get that tracker out. We have to help her."

If they helped Luna, she could help all of the other subjects. "We will." A vow. *Absolutely will.*

***

"There's a tracker inside of you?" Jett demanded. "Shit, let's cut the bitch out!"

"*Not* that easy." Maddox didn't want the guy whipping out a knife. "They put the thing in her heart. Elizabeth said she didn't have the skill to get it out, not without possibly killing Luna."

Jett backed up a step. "Hell."

"Exactly," Luna mumbled, rubbing a hand over the back of her neck. "And that's why we're separating. Now. You need to get out of here."

Maddox glanced around. There were plenty of cars in that garage, just as Sawyer had said. "Hot-wire one," Maddox ordered him because he knew that Jett could easily do that. "Get a car, and *go.*"

"Luna, Maddox, shit, this isn't the way things are going to work." Jett shook his head.

But Luna's expression didn't alter. "It's the way things have to work. Go," she urged him. "I can be found, wherever I go, but it doesn't mean you need to be caught, too."

She wasn't going to be found, wasn't going to be caught. Maddox would make sure of it.

"And take Maddox with you." Luna's spine was ramrod straight. She didn't look him in the eyes when she made that little announcement. "After things are…safe, I'll get in contact with you both. Sawyer said he'd call when a doctor was lined up. Once my surgery is complete, I'm sure that I will be able to find—"

"Oh, hell, no." Maddox bit back his rage.

Luna glared at him. "Oh, hell, yes. You're not going down with this sinking ship."

"You're not a fucking ship, and there is no way I'm leaving you." He jerked his head toward Jett. "Go."

Jett hesitated. "I don't want to leave you two."

"Elizabeth talked to you, didn't she? About the fact that we can have kids?" A hard edge cut into Maddox's voice. "Dammit, man, what if they've been watching Savannah?" He hadn't wanted to say anything to Elizabeth because it had been Jett's story to share, but…

Jett had rescued Savannah Jacobs from a kidnapper, a domestic job that their team had been sent on a while back. Only Jett and Savannah had gotten very close, very fast.

Then Jett had been forced to vanish from her life.

"Get to Savannah," Maddox ordered him. "Make sure…"

"How the hell will I explain all of this to her?" Pain flashed on Jett's face. "She'll hate me even more."

"She needs protection. And if she's pregnant…" Something Maddox knew was a definite possibility given the fierce connection the two had seemed to share. "The baby will need you, too."

Jett stared hard at him. "If this shit goes south, if you and Luna need me…you call, got me? And I'm not talking about on a freaking phone. You know I can hear you, wherever we are."

Because that was Jett's talent. He was an amplifier. He could pick up psychic communication from Maddox and make it stronger, send it farther. That was how their group had been able to communicate over such long distances during their missions.

Jett pulled Luna into a big hug. "You stay safe, you understand me? Safe and alive."

She squeezed him back. "I'm absolutely working on that."

Jett was gone moments later, a Jeep's growl filling the parking garage. He'd hot-wired that ride in seconds. Luna watched him leave, then she squared her delicate shoulders and turned toward Maddox. "You should have gone with him."

"Screw that." He headed for the blue SUV.

"If you take that vehicle, I'll take another—"

He whirled around, grabbed her wrist. "Screw *that*."

"Maddox…"

"*Luna.*"

She glared. The woman was so sexy when she was angry.

"Don't do this," Luna snapped at him. "Don't put your life at risk for me."

"Sweetheart, time for you to wake up and see the truth."

She blinked at him.

"You *are* my life. And if you think I'd just turn my back and leave you to face a nightmare on your own, you need to think again."

Her expression softened. "I want you safe."

"And if I'm not with you, then I'll be going absolutely insane. If anyone comes after you, they'll have to go through me first. That's just the way it's always going to be. I'll always stand between you and any threat."

She swallowed. "You did that before. You stood between me and Adam. And you remember how that worked out? Both of us dying?"

"Won't happen again."

She leaned onto her toes and her lips brushed his. "Damn right it won't. I won't let it happen."

His eyes narrowed. "Don't even think it."

She didn't respond.

"You aren't ditching me. We're in this together. All the way to the end."

Luna glanced away from him. "Were you always this hard to deal with? Or is it a new Lazarus thing?"

"You used to say I could drive you crazier than anyone else. And I always took that as a compliment." They'd wasted too much time. "Get into the SUV, Luna. Or I'll put you in there."

"Don't play the domineering asshole with me." She yanked her hand free. "You and I both know you'd never do anything I didn't want."

That was where Luna was dead wrong. When it came to her safety, her life, he'd do absolutely anything necessary.

But she headed around the SUV. She jumped into the passenger seat. He followed, and he slammed the door behind her. Moments later, he'd cranked the engine, and they were driving out of that hospital's garage. And even as he left, he heard the whoop-whoop-whoop of a helicopter overhead.

Everyone was clearing out. Because they all feared they were being hunted.

CHAPTER NINETEEN

"Tell me what happened to Adam."

Luna stiffened. They'd just pulled into a little motel. A place where they could crash for a few hours. The door had barely shut behind them—

"Walk me through everything, Luna."

She turned to face Maddox. "He's dead. I told you that already." She wrapped her arms around her stomach. She'd been trying to shove those particular moments *out* of her head, not relive them.

He leaned his broad shoulders against the door. "I learned something new about him today." He tossed the burner phone onto a nearby chair. "Turns out that Sawyer remembered Adam's psychic bonus."

Did she want to hear this?

"The guy could manipulate fire."

For an instant, she was back in the lab, she could feel the burn of flames as she ran down the hallway, desperate to get to Maddox.

"He couldn't create fire, but once it was there, burning from say…oh, I don't know, freaking bombs that the jerk had set off, he could control it."

The flames had been so hot all around her.

"So I'd thought...even if a bullet to the brain hadn't killed Adam back at the Lazarus facility, then the flames would've taken him." His jaw was locked tight as he gritted, "But that doesn't seem to be the case."

Her heart was beating so—

"Why are you scared right now, Luna?"

She couldn't look him in the eyes.

"Why is your heart racing so fast? Why is your breath catching?"

"I-I need a shower."

Maddox stepped toward her. "Luna—"

"I need a shower. Give me a few minutes, okay? Then I'll tell you everything." And then he could look at her not with that bright, shining love in his eyes.

But with hate.

***

She was holding back on him. Maddox stared at the closed bathroom door, every muscle in his body tight. He wanted to go in there, pull Luna in his arms and *make* her tell him the truth but...

But his gaze slid around the cheap motel room. A motel room that reminded him far too much of the damn place where they'd once died.

So he didn't bust in the bathroom. He stalked to the edge of the bed. Stripped off his shirt. Tossed it. Then he sat on the sagging mattress with his elbows propped on his knees. His head tipped forward.

And he waited for Luna.

***

She didn't feel better after the shower. Didn't feel stronger or more prepared. When she came out of the bathroom, a thin robe wrapped around her body, Luna just felt more vulnerable.

Maddox sat on the edge of the bed. His head had been bent forward, but when the bathroom door creaked open, he immediately snapped to attention.

Always the good soldier.

While she…wasn't.

She didn't go to him. Instead, she paced away, moving toward the lone window in the room. *Another motel.* She didn't know why she wanted to put space between them. Like space was going to make anything easier.

"Luna…"

"It's, um, it will be better if I just get it all out." As fast as she could.

He waited.

Right. *Deep breath.* "You ran down to get Jett. You told me to leave. But…Adam came back. I heard him, and I ran back into the lab." She pulled in another deep breath. Exhaled. "He said he'd set the most explosives down below. That's where you'd just gone. *Down below.*" Her fingers fisted. "I had picked up the gun from the floor. The same gun he'd put to my head. It felt comfortable in my hand. Like I'd held a gun so many times. Too many."

"Baby…"

She gave a short, negative shake of her head. "He kept saying you were dead. 'Fucking dead.' But I couldn't let that happen. I couldn't let you die." The idea of being in a world without Maddox? *No.* "I shot him. The first shot was to his upper body, to make him let me go. He fell back, hit the floor, and he…Adam said he could get me out. Begged me not to shoot him because he said he'd get me to safety. That he could make sure I got out all right."

A muscle jerked in Maddox's jaw.

"But he only wanted me out. Just *me.* Not you." She turned away from him. Stared out the window. Just saw a small parking lot. A dumpster. "Adam said you were already dead, that you wouldn't come back from the fire. So I…shot him again." Her lips pressed together. "God, you think I don't know how this makes me sound? I shot him in the leg the second time. I said I'd keep shooting until he told me how to find you. How to get us both out of there. And

I…did." She'd shot him several times, all in locations designed to cause pain, but not to kill. Not yet. Because she'd needed the information that Adam had.

She'd asked for the chance to speak, to say everything fast, but the silence from Maddox seemed deafening.

He knows I'm a monster.

"Adam was saying that he loved me. That he knew he'd screwed up, but that everything he'd done had been designed to get me back. That he didn't want to live without me. That if I just gave him the chance, we'd leave and he'd make me happy again. That he was sure he could do it." And she'd known exactly how he planned to do that. He'd planned to kill her. To let her wake with no memory. Maddox would be dead then, and Adam would be the only lover she knew.

Her heart was beating so fast, but her words were getting softer and softer as she said, "So I put the gun to his forehead. I said if he didn't tell me how to get you and me out of that building, I would pull the trigger." Her eyes closed. "He told me. Told me how to get out. And then Adam thought I'd let him get away. He said I didn't have it in me to kill him. Not with our past." Her breath heaved out. "And…maybe…maybe if I had remembered him more, then I wouldn't have been able to pull the trigger. Because maybe then I would have been able to remember something good about him. He was bleeding so much by then. I had turned for the door, because I wanted to get to you. I just wanted *you*. Adam was saying that he knew I couldn't kill him…and then he lunged for me." She swallowed. Her eyes opened as she turned back to face Maddox. "I fired. I aimed for his head, and I fired."

Maddox's face could have been carved from stone.

"I closed my eyes when I pulled the trigger." A hushed confession. "Because I just couldn't see that bullet going into his brain. I was killing a man who said I'd loved him, and I couldn't see it happen. When I opened my eyes, there was blood sliding down his temple. His body was on the floor. I ran out, and I locked the door behind me, just in case…" Her words trailed off.

Maddox tilted his head to the side as he rose from the bed. "Just in case of what?"

Say it all. "I'd aimed to hit him in the forehead. But when I closed my eyes, he must have dodged — you know how fast Lazarus subjects are. There was blood streaming down his temple, but I didn't see a place where the bullet had gone *into* his head." Her stomach knotted. "The gun was out of bullets. So I locked the door behind me, thinking the fire…" *God, say it.* "Thinking the fire would finish him off."

"Fuck."

She flinched. He hated her. She'd tortured a man. She'd left him to burn.

"The fire wouldn't have killed that sonofabitch," Maddox's voice was thick with fury. Fury directed at her? "And if the bullet didn't go straight into his brain, then the bastard could still be out there."

"Maddox…"

"If he's out there, then he's coming for us."

***

"I'm not going to ask you again, Dr. Paul." He let the tip of his knife cut into her pale, white throat. The blood dripped down, such a stark crimson. "Where is Luna Ashton?"

He'd tied her hands to the arms of the chair. Roped her ankles together. Getting to her had been ridiculously easy. Mostly because she still thought that he was working on her team. She'd opened her office door for him, a smile on her face.

The smile had now been replaced by tears. "Sam knows! He said that he was closing in on her!" Regina Paul sobbed as she craned back her neck, trying to avoid his knife.

Sam seemed to have fallen off the face of the earth. Adam lifted the knife away from her neck.

Regina Paul sucked in a deep, relieved breath. How cute. She thought he was going to stop using the knife. No...

He drove the knife into her right hand.

She screamed. *"Adam! Please!"*

Was he supposed to stop because she begged? Luna hadn't stopped when she had him in that lab. And he wasn't about to stop now. *Luna and I were always so much alike.* "Not going to be able to do those surgeries any longer, are you, doc? Not with the damage I'm doing." And he twisted the blade.

Tears leaked down her cheeks. "Stop! Stop! *Stop!*"

"I want to know Luna's location. Now!"

"Sam had government clearance. He is the one in charge. You don't have clearance—"

"Don't spout bullshit to me about clearance. You're not working for the US government."

Shock flashed in her eyes.

Adam laughed. "What? Did you seriously think you were? No, you were hired to *steal* government tech. That's what Luna is, you see, a piece of government property. Only someone else wanted her—wanted that beautiful tech. That's why you were hired to tag her. To put that wonderful device right in her heart." He tilted his head. "My former boss hired you, by the way. On *my* recommendation. Not Sam's. Sam was never a leader on this. I was. I might have lost my past when I first died. But I'm a fucking bulldog when it comes to digging. After I got out of that hell in Arizona, I took some intel with me. Intel about me, about my connections, about how the fuck I'd wound up as a caged lab rat." He yanked the knife out of her. "So at the first shot I had, I went back to my former boss. Showed him what a super soldier could do, and he was only too happy to start financing me."

"L-let me go…"

"Like I said, you weren't working for the good old U.S. of A. Try a different government." He positioned the knife over her left hand.

"*No!*" Her desperate shriek. "Please, *no!*"

"What good is a surgeon without her hands, Regina?"

"Please…" Now it was a whisper.

Did he look like the kind of man to be swayed by begging?

"I-I thought you could find her." Tears slid down Regina's cheeks. "Can't you…find them all? Thought that was…your g-gift…"

"It takes fucking *time* to feel the pull and to zero in on a target. If I had a few weeks, yeah, I could track her. But I don't have weeks. I need Luna *now!* Why the hell do you think I came up with the idea of putting that device in her heart? So I would *always* know exactly where she was! So I could always control her!"

Regina was shaking. And bleeding. And crying. And he was losing time that he didn't have to waste. "I want the codes to access and control Luna's implant. I want to know exactly where she is. *Now.*"

"Okay…okay, just…*stop.* I'll give you — you the codes!"

He put the knife down. Smiled at her. "Got your laptop handy?"

Less than five minutes later, he had her laptop up and running. He had access to Luna's implant. He could see Luna. She didn't know it, but he now damn well owned her. He just had to get closer…Luckily, she was only a few hours away. *Luna, you're mine.*

The sweet lover who'd shot him over and over again. The woman who'd left him to burn.

The woman who was his perfect match. He was gonna have to kill her. Payback, after all, was a bitch. But then when Luna woke up again…

It will be fun fucking her.

He could fuck her, kill her, and repeat. Over and over again. So easily. The touch of a button. And each time she woke up, he could pretend to be her hero. Just like he'd done all those years ago, when they'd just been kids. Pretended to be normal, like all the others. Pretended to fit in. Pretended that he didn't hate most of the world around him.

Only Luna had mattered.

Only Luna ever would.

He'd realized that truth when he'd had her strapped to the exam table in the abandoned hospital. When he'd forced Luna to give him back his memories — right before he killed her.

"You have what you want..." Regina's weak voice. "Please...untie m-me. I need to...to get to a h-hospital—"

He picked up the knife that he'd put down on her desk. Whirled toward her. And drove that knife right into her heart. Her eyes widened. Her mouth opened.

"Why? Why the hell would you need a hospital?" He yanked the knife out. "Hospitals can't help the dead."

CHAPTER TWENTY

Maddox opened the bathroom door. Paced into the little motel room. Luna was in the bed, her back turned to him. The covers concealed her body. He paused a minute, a towel wrapped around his hips. He listened to the pattern of her breathing—erratic. He heard the mad drumbeat of her heart.

No way was Luna sleeping. But if she wanted to pretend, he wouldn't stop her.

He took a step toward the bed.

"You think I'm a monster." Her voice was low and husky.

Maddox stilled. "I'd never think that."

Her shoulders stiffened beneath the covers. "Are you sure? Because there have been times when I saw suspicion in your eyes…a flicker of doubt."

Shit. "Baby…" He exhaled. "Adam told me you were working with him, okay? That you were selling government secrets. That was part of the memories you gave back to me."

She turned toward him. "He…said that?"

Grimly, Maddox nodded.

"Was I? I mean, did I?" Horror flared her eyes.

"No."

"How do you know? Did you…did you remember some kind of proof—"

He advanced toward the bed. Sat on the edge and put his hands on either side of her body. "I know you."

She stared up at him.

"You wouldn't do that. It's not who you are—"

Luna gave a broken laugh. "Don't be too sure. I'm the woman who just tortured the guy who was once her fiancé. I shot him, over and over again." Her eyes squeezed closed. "The worst part is—I'd do it again. If it meant I could get you out alive, I'd do it again in an instant."

His hand lifted. His fingers trailed over her cheek as he tucked a heavy lock of hair behind her ear.

"How can you stand to touch me?"

Because I love you. "I trust you, Luna. Adam is a lying bastard. I didn't realize how good he was at lying, not until too late."

"I was going to marry him," she whispered as her eyes opened and locked on him. "Why him? Why did I fall for him and not—" But she stopped, pressing her lips together.

Maddox reached for her left hand, lifted it up. Stared at her slender fingers. "You'd broken up with him a month before…" He cleared his throat. "A month before we died. You didn't tell me why. Just said that you'd given the ring back and that you'd realized some things."

Her eyes widened. "You think I knew what he was doing?"

"I didn't tell you I was investigating him, not until the very end. But you didn't act shocked. You said justice finds everyone." And he'd realized that she had suspected Adam of wrongdoing.

"He seems so evil to me," she whispered.

"It wasn't so apparent before Lazarus."

A furrow appeared between her brows. "The formula made him worse?"

"If it amplifies the darkness in us, then, hell yes, that's what I think it did to him. And that's why he is so dangerous now. If there is no moral compass at all holding him back—"

"It's why he *was* so dangerous." She sat up, holding the covers to her chest with her right hand. "He's dead."

He knew that was what she hoped.

"You think I'm a monster because of what I did to him. Because I…tortured him." Her gaze fell.

"You were trying to find a way out of the fire. Trying to figure out how to save me and Jett." He shook his head, but she wasn't looking at him. "And, no, baby, I don't think you're a monster. I couldn't ever think that about you."

Now her gaze lifted once more. "I think I am." Soft. Sad. "I think the formula made me worse, too, and I don't think you should be around me. We should have gone our separate ways. You should stay safe. You should get a life away from me."

He stared into her eyes. Saw his whole damn world. "That's the last thing I want."

Her lips trembled. "What if I can't give you what you need?"

He didn't know what she meant. "Luna..."

"I want to love you."

His muscles stiffened.

"When I'm with you, I *feel* so much. I'm warm, inside and out. And I'm happy. I feel safe. I feel..." She pulled in a deep breath. "It's so hard to understand. I want you to touch me. I want to dance with you. I want to walk on a beach. I just—" A nervous laugh. "I get all of these ideas. Things that could be. Should be. And I think...it would be so easy to just love him."

Maddox's chest ached.

Her lashes flickered. "But then I think, he deserves better. I tortured my ex-fiancé. I have darkness inside, weighing me down. What if that darkness gets stronger? What if I'm too dangerous? What if I...lose you? Because being near me puts you at risk. And I want to love you…" Tears filled her eyes, but she blinked them away. "I want to love you so much." A painful swallow. "But if I love you and I lose you, what will I do then? I don't think I'd get over that. I don't think I'd get over you."

"You won't lose me." Not ever.

"I want to love you," she whispered again. "But I'm too scared."

And he realized what she'd really been saying all along. *I want to love you.* No, she was protecting herself with those words. Hiding the real truth. The real truth was in her eyes. But fear held her back. What Luna was saying —

I love you.

"If I lost you…" His voice was gruff. "I wouldn't get over it."

Her breath caught.

"If I lost you," Maddox continued. "I'd lose my mind."

She shook her head. "No, don't talk like that. Don't every say — "

"The world is better for me when you're in it."

A tear slipped down her cheek.

"And, yes, I'm fucking afraid of what might happen to me without you." He pressed a soft kiss to her lips. Lingered a moment. Then eased back enough to say, "But I lived a lifetime already, afraid of telling you how I felt. Holding back because I didn't want to lose what I already had with you." She'd been his best friend for so long. "I'll never hold back again, and I don't care what the risk is. I'll love you with every breath that I have. And as for the future, as for what might happen…" His shoulders lifted, fell. "I'll have you now, and I'll love you."

"Maddox…"

The phone rang. The burner cell.

Dammit.

He slid from the bed and grabbed the phone. Answering it, Maddox said, "You'd better have good news."

"I do." Sawyer's low voice. "We've got a doctor lined up."

"The best in the country?" Wasn't that what he'd been promised?

"Couldn't get her. Dr. Regina Paul is out of touch."

Maddox frowned. "Then who—"

"Jay has someone else on a plane en route right now. He says the guy is damn good. And we don't want to waste more time, do we?"

No, they didn't. But he wasn't sure if "damn good" was good enough. Not when it came to Luna.

"I need you to meet me in three hours. Can you do that?" Sawyer wanted to know.

Yes, he could.

Sawyer rattled off the address. "Be there, okay?"

"Count on it." But he hesitated. "*You* shouldn't be there. Just send the doctor, got it? The last thing we need is to all be in one place."

Silence.

"Sawyer," Maddox growled.

"Hell, look, I won't be in the building, okay? But I'll be watching. I'll be keeping close tabs on everything, and if anything happens, I'm coming in."

Fair enough. "You need to know that Adam Brock could be alive."

The bed covers rustled. Luna crept toward him. About two feet away, she stopped. Stood there, wearing Maddox's shirt. He hadn't even realized she'd put it on.

"He could be alive," Maddox said again. "I got the full story from Luna. I don't think the bullet went into his brain. Sounds like it might have just grazed his temple. Head wounds can bleed like a bitch. She'd shot him several times, and she locked him in the lab, thinking he'd die in the blaze. But considering what he can do, the fire wouldn't have taken him out."

"This changes things," Sawyer replied curtly.

Yeah, it did. "If he survived, he's closing in."

"If he's part of the group that held Luna in that hospital, then he'd know about her tracker.

And he could be finding her right the hell now."
Frustration boiled in Sawyer's voice.

"Can we move up the timeline? Does it have
to be three hours?"

"The guy won't land until then. Dammit,
watch her. Keep her close."

Always.

They talked for a few more moments, and
Maddox was far too aware of Luna watching
him. When he ended the call, he knew she'd
heard every single word.

Beautiful Luna. His shirt fell to mid-thigh on
her. Her thick hair slid over her shoulders. Her
eyes were wide and dark. Her delicate shoulders
were stiff with determination.

"If he comes for me, I won't hesitate again."
She gave a nod. "I won't close my eyes. I won't
hold back. I will end him."

Not if I see the bastard first. Because if Maddox
had his way, Luna would never need to lay eyes
on Adam Brock again. "We have three hours."

Her gaze flickered. Her stare drifted over his
body, down to his chest. "Your heart is racing."

"Because I'm afraid."

She hurried toward him, reaching out her
hands. "Maddox—"

"The surgery scares the shit out of me. That's
why I am going to be there, every single second.
I'm not going to leave you alone."

Her hands pressed to his chest. "If I die…"

"No." Guttural. "You *won't*."

"But Maddox, if…if something happens, if—"

"I'll be there," he said again. "No matter what, I'll be there." If she woke up and didn't know him…if she woke up and stared at him as if he were a stranger, then he'd take that pain.

He lifted her into his arms. Carried her back to the bed. The need he felt for Luna was so fierce and wild, burning him from the inside. But he held back that need. This time, he wanted to show her more. This time, he wanted to give her tenderness.

Love.

He pulled off the shirt she wore and tossed it to the side of the bed. He kissed her, savoring her taste. Then his mouth trailed over her neck. Her moans and sighs filled his ears as he moved down her body. Kissing, licking, stroking everywhere. Her breasts were perfect. Dusky nipples. Round and firm. And when he licked them, her hips shot off the bed.

He'd dreamed of making love to her for so long. And if he had his way, he'd spend the rest of his life with her.

He pushed her legs apart. Put his mouth on her.

"Maddox!"

He was addicted to her taste. She was so incredible. Perfect. *His.* He stroked her with his mouth, savored her, pushing her to orgasm with his tongue and lips. When she called his name — oh, hell, yes. He loved the pleasure in her voice. Loved that she could go wild with him. Loved that he could send her over the edge.

He worked her with his tongue and his mouth. Fucking worshipping her. He could get drunk off her taste. Go mad with the pleasure he got from her body. Luna. His Luna.

Forever.

He eased back, started to thrust into her.

But her hands pushed against his chest. "Not yet."

What?

She pushed him back, and he let her. She crawled over his body, and her sweet mouth…oh, fuck…

He fisted the bed covers.

She started at his neck. She licked and kissed, and guttural growls escaped from him. She worked her way down. Her little pink tongue slid over his nipple. She had desire spiraling through him. One nipple, then the other got her sensual attention. His dick was hard and thick, shoving straight into the air. He had no clue where the freaking towel was, and he didn't care. He wanted to grab hold of her hips. Drive deep into her —

But she kept kissing him. Caressing him. Soft, tender movements.

Her hair slid over his abdomen as she lowered her head. Her fingers brushed over his cock.

"Luna!"

She took him into her mouth. That hot, wet heaven. He nearly lost his mind. She was licking and sucking, and he tried to hold back. The bed covers ripped in his hands, and his control shredded at the same instant.

He grabbed her. Lifted her up. Drove into her.

Her knees were on either side of his hips. Her hands pressed to his chest. He thrust into her, she lifted up, pushed back down. Again and again in a frantic rhythm that had the headboard pounding into the wall.

She came, tipping back her head. Gasping out her pleasure. The most beautiful sight in the world.

He erupted within her, his grip on her hips far too tight, but he didn't want to let her go. He wanted to hold her, forever. Wanted to just stay right there.

Luna collapsed on top of him. He pulled her against his body, rolling them and hauling up the covers. He kept his arms around her, holding her carefully. Maddox pressed a kiss to her temple.

She shivered in his arms. "I want to love…" Her words trailed away. Such a soft whisper.

He swallowed.

She turned toward him. Stared at him. Seemed to gather herself. "I *do* love you."

Hell, yes. Hell, *yes*.

"I do," Luna whispered again. "I do love you."

***

The building was small, one story, square and hidden behind a high, wooden privacy fence. It didn't look like a doctor's office. Definitely not a hospital, and Luna got a real bad feeling in the pit of her stomach when she climbed out of the blue SUV. "You're sure this is the place?" There was no hiding the doubt in her voice.

Maddox walked to her side. His gaze swept the perimeter. "Yeah, this is it. Exact address." He nodded. "Good location."

Were they looking at the same place?

"Sawyer is out there, watching." Once more, his stare swept the scene. "Because it's so remote, he'll be able to see anyone coming from a distance. He can keep a good watch on the place. See what's happening. No one in or out except for the folks he wants to get here."

True. But…

Maddox linked his fingers with hers. "I'll stay with you. Every minute. Just like I said." His head turned, and he held her stare. "But you don't *have* to do this. There's risk, it's your *heart*.

We can just run freaking far away. Get out of the country. Go someplace where the signal won't transmit. If we go far enough, fast enough, we'll get away."

"I don't want to spend the rest of my life being afraid. Worrying that someone will find me." And she wanted that thing out of her. "We can do this."

She hoped.

There was a code lock on the door. But Maddox knew the code, she'd heard Sawyer give it to him. A few moments later, they were inside, and while the outside of the building had looked rundown and almost abandoned, the inside was in perfect condition.

The inside was…an operating room.

And Elizabeth was there, wearing green scrubs and offering a reassuring smile.

"What are you doing here?" Maddox asked her, frowning. "I told Sawyer to keep everyone at a distance."

"And I wanted to make sure Luna was okay." Elizabeth's shoulders straightened. "I'll be assisting today." She motioned to the man in green behind her. "I want to introduce you both to Dr. Jeremiah Brennan. He's an amazing cardiac surgeon. You are in good hands, Luna."

Jeremiah came forward. Tall, handsome, with deep caramel skin. His dark eyes slid over Luna. "This is…very irregular." He licked his lips.

Nervous energy seemed to roll from him. "I've been briefed on your case, and there is a great amount of risk involved here."

Yes, she was trying not to focus on the risk part.

"I've never worked on someone with...um, with your condition." His head tilted. "Can you truly heal as fast as I've been told?"

She didn't know what, exactly, he'd been told, but she felt safe in just saying, "Yes."

"Fascinating." He looked fascinated. And scared.

Luna swallowed. "How about we get this show on the road, okay?" Lingering didn't seem like a good option. The longer they waited, the more afraid she'd become.

But Jeremiah didn't move. "It's not a fast procedure. I won't rush. And if there is any sign of danger, if I do not think I can remove the device safely, then I will stop the surgery."

She nodded. "Fair enough."

He pointed to the right. "There's a hospital gown in there for you to use."

Okay. Great. She headed into the small room, and Maddox came with her.

He closed the door, then turned toward her, frowning. "Baby, are you sure about this?"

No. But... She released a fast breath. "There's something you should know. Just in case — well, in case things don't go quite as planned."

"Luna—"

"I, um, I got my period today. Right before we left the motel, actually," she blurted those words. But they mattered. She needed him to know this. "It's light right now, but, I'm not pregnant. I needed you to know that. My body had been giving me signs, Elizabeth had checked my hormone levels and did all kinds of other tests that I didn't really even understand. She told me that my period was close, that I probably wasn't pregnant, and now I know. I mean..." God, she was rambling. "In case something goes wrong, it's just me. There isn't a baby, there—"

"*Nothing* is going wrong." He stared into her eyes. "And there's not a baby *yet*. But there will be. Because we are going to have all the time in the world. We're going to have a long future, and we can have as many kids as you want."

She tried to smile for him. "Let's start with one."

His hand slid over her cheek.

A knock sounded at the door.

Maddox immediately spun around, tensing.

"It's okay," Elizabeth called. "I wanted to let you know that the anesthesiologist just arrived. We need him on hand for this operation. I'll let him inside."

Maddox narrowed his eyes.

"Go check him out," Luna whispered because she knew that was exactly what Maddox wanted to do. "I'll get changed."

He brushed a kiss over her lips. "It's going to be okay."

She made herself smile. "Of course." And she stared hard at his face, wanting to memorize every single detail. Wanting to imprint him in her mind.

Wanting to never, ever forget.

***

Luna was waiting for him. About two miles away.

He'd moved heaven and earth to get to her. He'd finally tracked her to what seemed like an old, abandoned storage building. But he knew things were hardly ever as they seemed. He didn't go down that long, narrow road that led to the building. He'd pulled up maps online, looked at the place from all angles. If he went down that road, he was sure he'd be spotted. Maddox was too smart not to have taken precautions. When he'd been working as a guard at the Lazarus facility, he'd made a point of learning everything he could about his former friend. A leader until the end, Maddox would be on guard, especially since he didn't want to lose his prize.

Luna.

Getting that two miles to her wouldn't be possible. At least, not without really seeing what—or who—else might be in play.

It was a good thing he didn't have to get closer in order to do his worst damage.

He parked his vehicle. Took out the laptop he'd taken from the helpful Regina. And he typed in the code to access Luna's implant.

"See you soon, sweetheart." He tapped on the keys.

***

Luna eased herself onto the exam table. Maddox stood to her right. He reached for her hand. "I'll be here when you wake up."

Her lips started to curve…

But her chest burned.

Luna's breath choked out as the burn grew worse. Her heart was racing far too fast.

"Luna?" Maddox's fingers tightened on hers. "It's okay. Don't be scared."

"H-hurts…" It wasn't just a burn now. It was a blinding pain. She cried out, her hand ripping from his as she shoved her palms against her chest. "S-something…*wrong!*"

"Luna?" Elizabeth's voice. Elizabeth was suddenly near her, frowning.

She couldn't talk. The pain was too intense. It had stolen her breath. Her heart was *blazing.* And she wanted to claw through her chest in order to make the pain stop.

"Her heart is racing too fast," Maddox's voice was thick with fear.

"Move her hands," Jeremiah ordered. "She's cutting her skin. Do it, *now*."

"Baby…" Maddox pried her hands back. Pinned them on either side of her head.

She twisted in his grip. The pain was getting worse. She struggled to speak.

Jeremiah put a stethoscope against her chest. His eyes widened as he listened. "Oh, my God."

"M-make…" So hard to get that word out. "*S-stop…*" Her chest hurt. Hurt. Hurt. Hurt! Hurt so much.

"What in the hell did you do to her?" Maddox shouted. Was he talking to Jeremiah? Or the anesthesiologist who'd arrived? The anesthesiologist hadn't even touched her yet. He'd just been prepping his supplies. Elizabeth had said different drugs and dosages would be needed in the surgery because Luna was Lazarus.

All of her pain was coming from inside her body. And it was just getting worse. So much worse.

"It's her heart. Something is happening to her heart," Jeremiah fired back.

"Obvious-fucking-ly!" Maddox roared. "Fix her!"

"It…could be the device inside of her. Maybe it has shifted position or maybe—"

Luna screamed because the pain was so consuming.

Maddox's eyes widened as he stared at her in sudden realization. "Maybe someone fucking triggered it."

She couldn't take the agony. Her heart was going too fast. She could feel it. Too much. *Too much.* Her heart was going to explode.

She reached out to Maddox, unable to talk, but needing him so badly. *"Maddox, help me!"*

"I will, baby, I swear!"

But the pain hit her, even harder, and her body twisted in torment.

She heard a distant ringing. A phone? She didn't know, she didn't—

Luna screamed again.

"It's Sawyer!" Elizabeth cried. Luna opened her eyes and saw Elizabeth clutching a phone. "He says—"

Luna could hear what he was saying. She knew Maddox could hear, too.

"There's a car parked two miles away. Tinted windows. The driver didn't get out. Suspicious as all hell. I'm moving in."

"So the fuck am I!" Maddox snapped.

Her breath heaved in and out. The pain kept coming. It wouldn't stop. It wouldn't *stop.*

"She's having a heart attack." Jeremiah's voice. "Everyone, clear back. Let me help her. *Now*."

Maddox stared down at Luna. "Adam is doing this to you."

She couldn't quite follow what he was saying.

"He's here. I know that's the sonofabitch out there, and, somehow, he's doing this."

"Maybe it's not just a tracker," Elizabeth's words were rushed. She'd backed away from the table so Jeremiah could work on Luna. "Maybe...maybe it's some kind of weapon in her. Something to control her. To keep Luna in line."

"It's not about control." Maddox brushed away a tear from Luna's cheek. "It's about killing her." He pressed a kiss to her lips. "I'm killing *him*. I love you, Luna."

Then he was gone. Luna tried to call him back. She wanted him at her side. She wanted him. Maddox had said that he'd stay with her. But the pain wouldn't stop.

It wouldn't stop.

"Hold on, Luna," Jeremiah told her. "I can help you." His breath rushed from his lungs. "Or at least, I sure as hell hope I can."

***

Maddox saw the damn car. Parked on the edge of the road. Parked near the trees. Maddox rushed toward it even as Sawyer burst from the cover of nearby woods. Sawyer was armed and ready, just like Maddox was. Elizabeth had given him a gun before he'd raced out of that little building.

But as they bounded toward the vehicle, the door opened. "Stay back!" A man's voice shouted. "Or I kill her!"

It was a voice Maddox knew.

Adam Brock.

Adam slid from the car, and Maddox took aim. He'd hit the SOB in the brain and be done with him.

"Don't!" Adam's sharp warning. "You can hit me, but not before my finger hits this button and sweet Luna's heart *stops*."

Maddox froze. He could see the laptop in Adam's hands.

"And don't even think about pulling that psychic knock-out bullshit of yours." Adam shook his head. "Yeah, I know all about what you can do. I was a guard at your facility — I made it a point of learning everything I could. You see how close my finger is? One tap, just a tap, and it's her end. I bet I can hit the button *before* your power makes me hit the ground."

Maybe. Maybe not…

Can I risk Luna on a maybe? No, he couldn't risk her at all.

"That's right. You can't chance it. Not when it's *her* life on the line." Adam smiled at him. "Got a perfect signal out here. How lucky is that? Just had to get close enough to activate."

"What in the hell are you doing to her?" Sawyer barked.

Adam turned his head toward him. "Number One." Disgust was thick in his voice. "Still the arrogant prick, I see." Adam eased away from the car. Kept the laptop cradled close. One hand held the laptop, and the fingers of his other hand brushed the keyboard.

"He's not armed," Sawyer called to Maddox. "We can take the bastard."

"No, you can't. Not before I kill Luna." Adam's gaze slid back to Maddox. "And it's really all about her staying alive, isn't it? Because this once—this one damn time—you finally got lucky. She loved you. You, instead of me. But if I kill her, and she comes back all fresh and shiny…*poof*. Luna doesn't love you anymore. Your one shot is over. Maybe she loves someone else. Maybe she loves *me* again."

Maddox took one hard step forward. "Not gonna happen. It's impossible to love a dead man." He kept his focus completely on Adam. "And that's what you'll be if Luna dies. I will put a bullet into your brain, and you will end."

Adam just shook his head. "She gave you all of your memories back, didn't she? Does that make you feel special?" he mocked. "Because guess what? As usual, when it comes to Luna, I got there fucking first." A taunting smile curved his lips. "Before you found her in that hospital, Luna worked her magic on *me*. I made her do it. I'd heard Henry Danwith talking, he suspected that she could recover memories because of what she'd done with Andreas, and if anyone was going to get all of his memories, it was gonna be *me*." Spittle flew from his mouth. "She gave me the memories back because I didn't give her a choice. Want to hear about how I hurt her? How I used my knife on her to *make* her heal me? She called for you. Screamed for you." A muscle flexed in his jaw. "That made me just cut her more. Good thing her body heals so well, huh?"

Rage was a living, breathing monster inside of Maddox. All he wanted was to destroy Adam.

"After she restored my memories, I knew I could *never* let her go. She's a gold mine, right? So I got a doc to put that sweet little tracking device in Luna's heart. Don't worry, I used the best cardio surgeon I could find. Slid it into Luna only…well, Luna woke up just as the procedure was ending. She attacked the doc. I had to get Regina out of there. Figured I might could use her again."

"You left Luna there alone?" Sawyer's hard stare never faltered.

"No, that was where my *partner* came in." A sneer. "Luna had given Sam just a few memories, too. Enough for him to want more. He was supposed to be guarding the hospital, but the dumbass got desperate to see his old lover. Luna had put images of her in Sam's mind. Fool said he only left for a bit, but when he came back, Luna was gone."

"I took her away." Maddox could imagine firing the weapon. Killing the bastard in front of him. It would be so freaking easy.

But I can't risk Luna.

"The whole time all of this shit was happening," Adam just seemed to love bragging, "I came and went, sliding back from that hospital and heading to the Lazarus facility. No one suspected me. Why would they? I'm fucking amazing at putting on a perfect front."

"You don't look perfect to me." Maddox didn't lower his gun. "You look like a traitorous bastard."

Adam took a few steps away from the car. Sawyer and Maddox advanced.

"Know what happened to your buddy, Sam?" Maddox challenged. "He's dead."

"Then that's just one less person who I have to split my money with." Adam laughed. "It's funny. We're back where we fucking started. I'm selling secrets again—only this time, my secret *is* Luna. Luna and the whole super soldier program. My old boss is willing to pay *billions*. That's what happens when the future is at stake."

"You're not getting Luna." Maddox's vow was guttural. Adam was selling US secrets again—and Maddox would *not* let him sell out Luna.

Adam's mouth twisted into a smirk. "I'm not afraid of you two assholes." His gaze slid to Sawyer. "The *leader* who left me..." Then he glanced at Maddox. "And the friend who stabbed me. Who *killed* me."

"You were selling out your country, just like you're freaking trying to do now! And since you have your memories back, then you must *remember* that you were going to take a shot at me first. I knocked the gun out of your hand. I was going to take you in alive, but you kept fighting. I had to use my knife to stop you."

Rage burned in Adam's eyes. "There was no way I was going to let you walk out of that motel with Luna. I knew what would happen. You'd *take* her. You were always so lost in Luna." He laughed. "Since Luna gave you all of your memories, you know how long you've loved her. I can tell. I can damn well see it in your eyes."

"I've got them." Maddox moved closer. Sawyer was now standing right next to the open driver's door of the car.

"It's for the best." Adam nodded. "With those memories, I know you'll do *anything* to keep her safe, won't you?"

"Yes," Maddox gritted. Sawyer was silent.

"Good. Because this is how it will work. You're going to get in that car, right there, you're going to drive back to that little shack, and you're going to put *my* Luna in the car. You'll bring her to me, and then Luna and I will drive away."

"That isn't going to happen." Maddox never lowered his gun.

"No?" Adam raised his brows. "Then you want me to kill her? Because I will. If you don't do exactly what I say, I will kill her now."

"He'll kill her anyway," Sawyer shouted back. "We both know it. If we follow his orders and he drives off with her, she'll be dead in minutes."

"Maybe." Adam shrugged. "Maybe not. Maybe deep inside, I do love her. In my own way. I remember caring when she fucking fell in that motel room and her blood was all around me." His expression turned shuttered. "I remember hating that I'd done that to her. And who do you think put the freaking hospital ID bracelet on her? I did that. I wanted her to have her damn name, even if she had nothing else."

"You took everything from her!"

"I can love her!" Adam almost sounded as if he meant those words. But then, Maddox now understood just how good the man was at pretending.

"I'm not staying in the open much longer," Adam warned him. "I figure if Number One is here," his head jerked toward Sawyer, "well, then his bastard buddy Two will be hiding close by —"

"His name is Flynn," Sawyer cut in. "We all have names, not just numbers any longer, *Adam*. And, yes, Flynn is close by. He has a rifle pointed at your head right now."

Maddox heard the quick rush of Adam's heart as it accelerated. Then Adam screamed, "Get in the fucking car, Maddox, or she is *dead!*"

He wanted them in the car too badly. And Adam had deliberately retreated from the vehicle. Maddox's gaze cut to the car door. Sawyer was right beside it.

Is Adam keeping his fingers poised over the laptop because he's about to hurt Luna more…or because he's about to trigger something else? Every time he'd been attacked in the last few days, there had been one constant…*fire.* And Maddox knew just why fire kept being used against him…Shit. Shit! "Move!" Maddox roared at Sawyer, but he also heard…

Tap.

Adam had just clicked a button on that laptop. Maddox grabbed Sawyer even as the vehicle exploded. A great ball of fire erupted from beneath the hood. Adam's laughter echoed with the flames, and the impact sent Sawyer and Maddox hurtling through the air.

When Maddox hit the ground, he landed face down. He shoved up to see that Sawyer was several feet away, not moving. And the flames from the car...

They are coming right at me. Because Adam was controlling them. He'd set the bomb so he could get his fire *and* the upper hand.

"Nowhere to run!" Adam's voice boomed. "I've got you now."

The sonofabitch was sending the flames right at Maddox. Adam was controlling the fire. The whole scene had been a trap. Maddox leapt to his feet even as the fire surged toward him.

"She's dead!" Adam cried, and he was smiling. *Smiling.* "She was dead from the first flicker of pain! I didn't have to trigger anything else, you dumb bastard. Her pain will just keep getting worse and worse until the heart attack kills her. That's the only time it will stop! When her heart does. And it should have stopped by now! She's dead, dead—"

The fire had wrapped around Maddox, forming a circle. He had the gun in his hand. *Luna, I love you.* He leapt forward, surging through the flames, feeling the burn all along his arms and body. But he didn't care.

When he came through the fire, he still had his gun. He aimed it at Adam. At the man who'd been his friend. At the guy who was his worst enemy.

He fired.

One shot. Straight to the head.

Adam's eyes flared wide.

And he fell.

Maddox kept rushing forward, and the flames stayed behind him. He stood over Adam's body, and he fired again, needing to be sure. Absolutely sure. *You won't hurt her ever again. You won't hurt anyone.*

But Adam wasn't moving. He couldn't move. The guy was gone, and there was no smile on his face any longer. He was dead. There would be no rising for him.

"Hey, buddy! I'm Adam. Great to meet another kid around here, you know? Hate being the new guy. Always feel so lost in a new place." The voice slid through Maddox's mind. Vanished into darkness.

"Fucking hell!" Maddox bellowed.

Then he whirled. He raced back toward the small building only to see Flynn running toward him. Flynn held a rifle in his hands.

"Didn't have a shot," Flynn gasped out. "When the fire started, it was blocking everything, and shit, man, you've got burns all over your body!"

He didn't feel them. Didn't care. "Check Sawyer." That was all he said as he flew past

Flynn. He was desperate to get back to that little building. So desperate to get to Luna.

Be alive. Be alive.

She had to still be alive.

"Luna!" He screamed her name in his mind.

But there was no answer. There was nothing.

CHAPTER TWENTY-ONE

Maddox kicked in the door to that building. Smelled the blood. Saw it.

Luna was on the exam table. Her eyes were closed. Jeremiah was right beside her. His blood-covered hands were—

Oh, sweet Christ. His hands are in her chest!

"I got it out!" Jeremiah yelled. Sweat covered his forehead. "I need her to heal. You said she'd heal! You said she was something special, Elizabeth! Why the hell isn't she healing?"

Elizabeth was staring down at Luna, shaking her head even as tears rimmed her eyes.

Jeremiah kept pushing inside Luna's chest.

"What in the hell are you doing to her?" Maddox reached for the guy—

"No!" Elizabeth shoved Maddox's hands away. "Jeremiah is pumping her heart. Her heart hasn't stopped, not the whole time. Do you understand? He got the device out—he made her heart keep pumping. It hasn't stopped. *She* hasn't died. She just has to heal. She has to come back." Her frantic stare landed on him. "*Make her come back, Maddox*. Make her come back right the hell now."

He dropped the gun. Reached for Luna's hand.

She was so pale. Absolutely chalk-white. And there was so much blood. Her poor chest…

"There was no time for anesthesia…" The hoarse whisper came from the doctor in the corner. The anesthesiologist? He'd pressed his back to the wall, and he stared at them in horror. "He…he just cut into her chest while she was awake. It was horrible. Oh, God, the pain that poor woman must have felt!"

Jeremiah didn't stop his work. Maddox glanced at him and saw the torment on his face. "I got it out," Jeremiah whispered.

Maddox bent, moving even closer to Luna. "Baby, I need you to fight for me."

Nothing.

"I need you to use that beautiful power inside — the power that is *you* — your strength, your determination, *you, baby* — and wake up."

Nothing.

"Luna, you aren't gone. I can feel you. You're still right here. And I'm here. And this is always where I'll be. With you. When you open your eyes, you're gonna see me."

"She's dead!" The other doctor called out. That anesthesiologist was pissing Maddox the hell off. "There's no way she can be alive! You didn't see what he did, you didn't see —"

"Jeremiah did what had to be done!" Elizabeth blasted. "Now shut the hell up!'

Maddox ignored them. Only Luna mattered.

"You'll open your eyes," Maddox told her, tenderly stroking her cheek. "And you'll be okay. You'll see me. You'll remember me. And I'll tell you that I love you, and you'll say that you love me. We're safe now. No one will ever track you again. No one will hurt you. Because I'm going to be at your side. Fucking always, do you understand? Fucking *always*." Carefully, tenderly, he brought her hand to his lips. He kissed her fingers and then…

Then he put Luna's hand on her chest.

"What in the hell are you doing?" Jeremiah barked, not stopping his work. Not hesitating.

"Her fingers are warm," Maddox rasped. He had to blink because things had just gotten a little blurry for him.

"What?" Jeremiah kept working. "What does that —" But he broke off, jerking his hands out of Luna's chest. Her poor, savaged chest. "Oh, my God."

"*Keep fighting, Luna.*" Maddox pushed the thought at her, and he could feel Luna's response. No words, but a surge of warmth that came back to him.

Warmth like he'd felt in her fingertips.

"Heal yourself, baby. Do it, please fucking do it. Because I need you back. I need you."

The warmth strengthened. The magic that was pure Luna. Not dead. Just weak.

But growing more powerful every single second.

"I love you."

A wild smile curved his lips because her heart...her heart was beating on its own once more.

***

She opened her eyes. Found a white ceiling above her. Heard the beep of nearby machines. She twisted her head and realized she was in a bed.

A hospital bed.

"No," she gasped out the one word.

She lifted her hand—

"Easy, sweetheart. Your body has been working overtime on healing itself. Jeremiah stitched you back up, and then your healing power took over. I could see you getting stronger every single minute that passed." He smiled at her, a broad grin making his green eyes shine. "I knew you were going to be okay. I just had to wait for you to open your eyes." But he held his breath. She could tell...she could...could see the fear on his face.

"How…long?" she managed.

"Days, but I would have waited forever, if that's what it took." Then he swallowed. He leaned close. "I love you."

He was waiting. Staring at her as if she were his whole world. That look…

Her hand lifted. She touched his cheek.

His gaze searched hers. So much hope there. So much fear.

She didn't want him to be afraid. "I love you."

His eyes went wide. She heard the quick rush of his breath.

"We're safe now," she said, speaking the words that had seemed to play endlessly in her head. "No one will track us. No one will hurt us. Because we're going to be together, always."

"You…you remember me?"

Her chest ached. "I remember everything." Some of the horror she almost wished she could forget. The frantic apologies from the surgeon as he'd grabbed the scalpel, the first cut into her…

Luna swallowed. "I remember."

"You didn't die. You didn't…you didn't lose yourself, baby. You fought. Fought harder than anyone I've ever seen. You didn't die, and you kept your memories!"

"I was fighting for us." Because she hadn't wanted to lose herself again, but…she also hadn't wanted to lose him.

Her lover.

Her partner.

Her best friend.

"I love you, Maddox."

"Luna, baby, you fucking *own* me, body, heart, and soul." Carefully he eased into the bed and pulled her against him. His mouth brushed over hers. "Always have, always will."

Her hand slid to his cheek. Then up, up to the line of his temple. She touched him, and, voice husky and low, she said, "I watched you on the beach."

A furrow appeared between his brows. "Luna?"

"You weren't paying attention to anyone around you, not at first. You were walking and your head was down, and I thought…that has to be the cutest boy I've ever seen."

His eyes widened.

"My hands were shaking when we met. You could always do that. Make me nervous. Make me *feel*. But I didn't think you liked me the same way, and there was no chance I could tell you how I felt. No chance."

"Baby…"

"I was content to be your friend. I hoped for more. Didn't think it would happen. Then you went away, you joined the army, and I felt like you'd taken my heart with you."

Shock was plain to see on his face.

And the memories — the memories poured through her. "Adam was there. Every single day. Promising that he'd never leave me. Telling me stories about girls that you'd met. And the next thing I knew, he asked me out. And I thought...maybe I should try to be happy. If I can't be with Maddox, then I should be happy with someone else..." Her voice trailed away. "But I couldn't love Adam the right way. I couldn't love him fully, and we both always knew why."

"You didn't say. You *never* said..."

"Neither did you. It's funny, isn't it? I wasn't afraid when I was pulling Gs at the Air Force Academy. I wasn't afraid when I went on my first mission. But I was terrified that I'd lose you."

His eyes gleamed. "You will *never* lose me."

"I got tired of being afraid. I got tired of trying to make a life for myself, a life I didn't really want. I broke up with Adam. I gave the ring back to him. And before that motel..." Her breath sighed out. "Before the gunfire and the pain, I wanted to tell you. I *planned* to tell you..." *Don't be afraid. Not ever again.* "Maddox, I don't want to just be your friend."

His gaze burned her.

"I want to be so much more. I want to be your lover. I want to be your partner. I want to be the person you wake up with in the morning. I want to be the person in bed with you at night.

When you laugh, I want to be there. And when you hurt, I want to be there. I want *you.*"

He kissed her. Not frantically. Not with wild need. A tender kiss. Passionate. And her hands lifted to sink into his dark hair. She held him even as tears stung her eyes.

"You remember," he whispered against her lips.

She did. Not everything, but the pieces that mattered most.

Maddox. He'd been the biggest piece of her life since she was fourteen years old.

He'd been at her side when she buried her mother and father, after they'd been taken in a terrible car crash right before her eighteenth birthday. He'd held her tight while she cried. He'd promised her that he'd always be there for her. Always.

He'd been the one sitting proudly in the front row at her high school graduation. He'd gotten leave from the army, and he'd been in the audience, sitting beside her grandmother. When she'd been announced as the valedictorian, he'd let out a whistle that had been so high, it cut right through the applause. She'd laughed as she'd gone to the microphone to deliver her speech.

He'd been there…silent, his face hard and controlled…when she told him that she was engaged to Adam. He'd stared down at her and only asked one question. "*Is he what you want?*"

She'd lied then. Lied because she thought she'd never have what she wanted.

"I want you," Luna said softly. "I love *you*."

"You have me," he promised her. "Always. Fucking forever."

And she believed him. He kissed her again, and Luna let go of her fear. The fear that had held her back for so long. The fear that had stopped her from loving, from living. Maddox wasn't going away. Neither was she. They were going to stay together. They'd fight for their life together. They'd *live*. They'd win.

"He's gone," Maddox told her. He'd eased back just a little. Just enough to stare into her eyes. "Adam is dead." A pause. "I killed him. He *won't* be coming back."

"Will anyone else come after us?"

He hesitated.

Oh, no. "Maddox?"

"Adam was working for his old boss. Selling government secrets. Sawyer and Jay are looking for him. Until he's brought down, there will be a risk to *all* of the super soldiers. Our secret is out, and that's something we all have to face. Maybe it's time to stop being in the shadows. Maybe the whole world needs to know what's happening."

So it wasn't completely over, not yet. Maybe it was just beginning.

"The tracker is out of you, baby. No one will be able to use it to hurt you again. You're free. You can go anywhere you want."

She didn't want to run. Not yet. "I want to help the others." To do what she could for them.

"Figured you'd say that."

"And then…" She smiled at him. Smiled even though her chest still ached. "Then I want to be with you. I want a life. A home. A child." Everything. The whole package. With him.

"I'll give you anything you want." His gaze seemed to see into her very soul. "I swear it. All you ever have to do is ask."

In that case… "Maddox, will you marry me?"

"Hell, yes." He kissed her. "Hell, *yes*."

***

"You remember?" Elizabeth's brows rose. "You have your memories back?" Even as she asked the question, she shined a bright light into Luna's eyes.

Luna tried not to blink. Maddox was beside her, holding her hand tightly. "Yes."

Elizabeth dropped the light. "The damage to you was extensive." She tilted her head. "I wasn't sure you'd be able to recover. It took days…and sometimes, when I'd come in here, you'd be as still as death. I wasn't even sure that you were breathing."

"She was," Maddox growled.

Elizabeth's gaze swung to him. "You were here with her every second."

"There's no other place I'd want to be."

Elizabeth smiled, but the curve of her lips only lasted for a moment. "The damage was extensive," she murmured, as if puzzling over something in her mind. "So the healing was extensive, too. You were as close to death as anyone I've ever seen, Luna. Your healing power kicked in because you *had* to use it on yourself to survive. And I wonder…because you were so very close to dying…is that what led you to be able to retrieve your memories again? Because the healing process in your body was so intense and prolonged? Once you started healing, once you let yourself go…maybe there was no holding back any longer."

"You thought I was…holding back on getting my own memories?" Why on earth would she do something like that?

"Sometimes our past can hurt us." Elizabeth gnawed on her lower lip. "Sometimes, we don't want to face it. Sometimes, we're afraid," Elizabeth added. "And we try to protect ourselves without even realizing it."

"I'm not afraid," Luna said. *I'm not afraid of Adam. I'm not afraid to tell Maddox how I feel. I'm not afraid of living or loving.*

There wasn't room for fear. Not anymore.

Maddox's hold tightened on her.

"I'm going to help the others," Luna promised. She wouldn't leave with Maddox before she did her part. None of the Lazarus subjects deserved to lose their pasts. Their lives.

"I'd like to perform brain scans before and after you attempt any memory restoration on the others." Elizabeth's gaze had turned distant. "Maybe I can see what areas of the brain light up after your treatment. The more we understand about what has happened to those in Lazarus, the better it is for us all."

Yes. "Count on me for anything you need."

Elizabeth came closer to the bed. "Thank you, Luna." Her lashes covered her eyes as she glanced down. Her shoulders slumped a bit. "I'm...I'm so sorry for everything that happened to you. I created Lazarus. I swear, what's happened was never my intent, but that doesn't make it right. I tried to play God because I didn't want to lose anyone else in my life. I thought I could stop death. I didn't realize how many people would be hurt. Destroyed." Her lashes lifted. "Again, I am so sorry."

"We can't change the past." Luna cleared her throat. "But we can go forward. We can make things better. I figure with you and I working together, there's not much that we *can't* do."

Elizabeth licked her lower lip. "Thank you, Luna. Thank you." Then she backed away from the bed. A moment later, the door shut softly behind her.

Luna was left alone with Maddox. Her head turned. She met his watchful stare. "What?"

"I love you."

She'd never get tired of hearing those words.

"I loved you yesterday, I love you today, and I'll love you for all the tomorrows that we have coming."

Very, very nice. She offered her hand to him. When his fingers curled around hers, Luna pulled him closer.

"Baby, your chest...I know it's still tender...I don't want to hurt—"

"You've never hurt me, and you never will." Something she knew with absolute certainty. "Now kiss me and then tell me what we're going to do...*after.*"

One brow lifted. "After?"

"After everyone has their memories back. After you and I start a life together. After we have a house..."

He pulled her close. "What kind of house do you have in mind?"

She considered his question for a moment. Maybe one on a beach? "I've always liked the sound of the ocean."

His laughter warmed her very soul. "Me, too, Luna, me, too." He cleared his throat. "*After*...we're going to get a house on the beach.

And a sailboat. And we'll take that boat out, and we'll have our little girl with us."

Her breath slid in and out.

Her heart beat in a steady rhythm.

"Before the little girl comes, though, we're going to get married. Maybe married *on* the beach. And *after* that..."

Her head tilted toward him. Their mouths were so close.

"We'll do any damn thing you want."

"I like that."

"Good. Because there's not going to be any more pain. Just good memories. Memories that *we* make."

"How about we start making them right now?"

And he kissed her. The start of a new life. Their life. Not trapped in some lab. Not hunted prey that was being stalked. They were free. They were together.

And nothing was going to stop them from having their happily ever *after*.

The End

A NOTE FROM THE AUTHOR

Thank you for reading LIE CLOSE TO ME.

This was the first Lazarus book to feature both a hero and heroine who were test subjects. I loved getting to change up the dynamics of the story, and I wanted Luna to be the one who could help the others to uncover their pasts. I hope that you enjoyed reading about Luna and Maddox (and seeing some of the characters from other books).

If you'd like to stay updated on my releases and sales, please join my newsletter list.

http://www.cynthiaeden.com/newsletter/

Again, thank you for reading LIE CLOSE TO ME.

Best,
Cynthia Eden
www.cynthiaeden.com

ABOUT THE AUTHOR

Award-winning author Cynthia Eden writes dark tales of paranormal romance and romantic suspense. She is a New York Times, USA Today, Digital Book World, and IndieReader best-seller. Cynthia is also a three-time finalist for the RITA® award. Since she began writing full-time in 2005, Cynthia has written over eighty novels and novellas.

For More Information

- *www.cynthiaeden.com*
- *http://www.facebook.com/cynthiaedenfanpage*
- *http://www.twitter.com/cynthiaeden*

HER OTHER WORKS

Romantic Suspense
Lazarus Rising

- Never Let Go (Book One, Lazarus Rising)
- Keep Me Close (Book Two, Lazarus Rising)
- Stay With Me (Book Three, Lazarus Rising)
- Run To Me (Book Four, Lazarus Rising)
- Lie Close To Me (Book Five, Lazarus Rising)

Dark Obsession Series

- Watch Me (Dark Obsession, Book 1)
- Want Me (Dark Obsession, Book 2)
- Need Me (Dark Obsession, Book 3)
- Beware Of Me (Dark Obsession, Book 4)
- Only For Me (Dark Obsession, Books 1 to 4)

Mine Series

- Mine To Take (Mine, Book 1)
- Mine To Keep (Mine, Book 2)
- Mine To Hold (Mine, Book 3)
- Mine To Crave (Mine, Book 4)
- Mine To Have (Mine, Book 5)
- Mine To Protect (Mine, Book 6)
- Mine Series Box Set Volume 1 (Mine, Books 1-3)
- Mine Series Box Set Volume 2 (Mine, Books 4-6)

Other Romantic Suspense

- First Taste of Darkness
- Sinful Secrets
- Until Death
- Christmas With A Spy

Paranormal Romance
Bad Things

- The Devil In Disguise (Bad Things, Book 1)
- On The Prowl (Bad Things, Book 2)
- Undead Or Alive (Bad Things, Book 3)
- Broken Angel (Bad Things, Book 4)
- Heart Of Stone (Bad Things, Book 5)
- Tempted By Fate (Bad Things, Book 6)
- Bad Things Volume One (Books 1 to 3)
- Bad Things Volume Two (Books 4 to 6)

- Bad Things Deluxe Box Set (Books 1 to 6)
- Wicked And Wild (Bad Things, Book 7)

Bite Series

- Forbidden Bite (Bite Book 1)
- Mating Bite (Bite Book 2)

Blood and Moonlight Series

- Bite The Dust (Blood and Moonlight, Book 1)
- Better Off Undead (Blood and Moonlight, Book 2)
- Bitter Blood (Blood and Moonlight, Book 3)
- Blood and Moonlight (The Complete Series)

Purgatory Series

- The Wolf Within (Purgatory, Book 1)
- Marked By The Vampire (Purgatory, Book 2)
- Charming The Beast (Purgatory, Book 3)
- Deal with the Devil (Purgatory, Book 4)
- The Beasts Inside (Purgatory, Books 1 to 4)

Bound Series

- Bound By Blood (Bound Book 1)
- Bound In Darkness (Bound Book 2)
- Bound In Sin (Bound Book 3)
- Bound By The Night (Bound Book 4)
- Forever Bound (Bound, Books 1 to 4)
- Bound in Death (Bound Book 5)